D1593328

Edge of a Dream

Edge of a Dream

Lee Fishman

TransMedia Publishing Group
Philadelphia, PA

Cover design Gayle Slurzberg

Library of Congress Cataloging-Publication Data on file.

ISBN 978-0-9820255-1-2
ebook **ISBN** 978-0-9820255-4-3

http://www.leefishman.net

TransMedia Publishing Group
Philadelphia, PA

For M.B.H.

"Remember, remember always, that all of us...are descended from immigrants and revolutionists."

Franklin D. Roosevelt

Chapter 1

Soaring fifty stories above city streets, the building's glass exterior shimmered with the sun's reflection. On the pavement below, Rija shielded her eyes against the glare, checking the address one last time before she ducked through the revolving door. Inside she paused, her gaze drawn from white marble walls to an American flag unfurled above brass letters that proclaimed One Liberty Place.

It's not too late. You don't have to do this. But she knew it wasn't true. Though part of her wanted to run, she knew she had to stay. This was her chance to start over, and now was the time to take it. Today was the day.

Rija inhaled deeply, allowing the city heat and noise to recede into the air-conditioned stillness. The lobby felt empty until she spied a guard dozing at the desk. Setting him in her sights, she pulled her shoulders back, uncurled the knot in her stomach and forged ahead.

At the sound of her heels striking the granite floor, the man stirred. Rija cleared her throat and waited while he shook himself awake, crooking his head from side to side before he seemed to remember what he was there for. Bleary-eyed, he looked up. "Help you, miss?"

"I'm here to see Mr. Fowler, I have an appointment."

"Gotcha."

Squirming a little as he gave her the once-over, Rija looked away and the guard pressed the intercom button. "Someone to see you at the front desk." He turned back to Rija. "Says to tell you he'll be right there."

Rija nodded and moved aside to wait. She smoothed nonexistent wrinkles from her dress until further inspection revealed a gaping hole in her stocking, but there was no time to worry over it. A gray-haired man in a white shirt and black tie walked toward her with his hand out.

"Jerry Fowler. Glad to meet you." His eyes, behind steel-rimmed glasses, were difficult to read. "Let's go to my office," he said. He steered her toward a bank of gleaming elevators and pushed the down button.

Before the mirrored elevator doors parted, Rija caught a glimpse of her own reflection. The hazel eyes staring back looked worried, and she reminded herself to smile. She drew herself to her full height, tucked a few unruly wisps of auburn hair behind her ears, and moistened her lips as the car opened into a fluorescent-lit corridor.

A whiff of ammonia made Rija's nose twitch. Down the hall, vacuum cleaners, lined up like soldiers, stood next to an open door. Leading the way, Fowler stepped through the door and into a small office. He took a chair behind a large metal desk and motioned for Rija to take a seat in a guest chair facing the desk. He glanced down at a clipboard for a moment and then came to the point. "So, you got any cleaning experience, Miss? Miss Mal..." He looked to her for help.

"It's Malacovik. Rija Malacovik," she told him.

"Okay, like I said, done any cleaning before?"

"Before I came to America, I have cleaned offices in Sarajevo."

She lowered her eyes so he wouldn't see she was lying. It would do her no good to tell Mr. Fowler that she had studied languages for two years at university in Bosnia. He didn't seem to care where she came from.

Fowler leaned forward in the chair and gave her an appraising look. "You have your green card and Social Security number, right?" He watched her pull the documents from her bag and place them on the desk. "Okay, Miss Ma...,"

"Malacovik," she said again.

"Right." He pushed back in his chair and let his gaze stray past her shoulder. "I'm gonna give you a try. Someone just called out sick, so can you start tonight?"

"Oh yes. Thank you. I can start right now."

Rija tried to look excited, but a wave of anxiety clutched at her as she thought of Lili, her six-year-old, waiting alone in the schoolyard. Her mind raced ahead. She must call her mother and tell her to pick up Lili at 3:30. But for now, Fowler was talking to her. She dug her fingernails into her palm and tried to listen to what he was saying.

"You'll be an independent contractor. Know what that means?"

"No."

"That means we pay you a flat rate. You come to work, you get paid. No benefits and you pay your own taxes. The pay is $350 a week and we pay twice a month. You do four floors a night, and we supply the cleaning products and the vacuum. Understand?"

Rija could feel the flush creeping over her cheeks. "Yes, thank you. I understand." She patted her bangs back in place to cover the small scar on her forehead.

Fowler pawed through a pile of papers at the edge of his desk, frowning until he found what he was looking for. His annoyance faded a little as he pushed an application across the desk toward her. "Fill this out now and be sure to sign down here at the bottom." He pointed, then sat back to wait, drumming pudgy fingers on the desktop while she filled in the blanks.

When Rija was finished he scooped up the paperwork and swiveled toward the photocopier behind him. They watched the green light move back and forth over the glass. When it was finished, Mr. Fowler stapled the copies together. "Your shift starts at 5:30 when the building clears. Report back then and we'll get you started."

Rija thanked him and made her way to the elevator. She looked at her watch. It was almost three o'clock. She asked the guard to let her use the lobby phone, thanking him before he turned away to take a delivery. She dialed, counted five rings and whispered a prayer into the receiver. "Pick up the phone."

After the sixth ring, her mother, Elena, picked up, and Rija heard her mother's familiar, "Hallo."

"*Idi brzo*, Mama! Go quickly," Rija said. She urged her mother to run to the schoolyard where her daughter, Lili, would be waiting.

Back on the street, bus exhaust added to the late summer haze. With two hours to wait, Rija wandered aimlessly until a glimpse of greenery in the distance suggested a destination. She turned, drawn forward as though by a magnet. When she found the deep shade of full-grown trees and a fountain set back from the street, it felt like a gift.

An empty park bench beckoned, and Rija sank down with a sigh. On the grass nearby, two sparrows squawked over a morsel of bread until the loser flew off in defeat. Peace restored, Rija allowed her eyes to close. Cooler air soothed her brow, calming her worry. The job wasn't what she'd hoped for, and she wondered what it would be like to work for Mr. Fowler. His eyes made her nervous, but she told herself it didn't matter. As her social worker said, it was a start. Behind on their rent and with their welfare checks ending, a job was what she needed. Any job.

A breeze rustled the branches overhead. In the distance, a siren blared, and her eyes blinked open to see a young man in jeans and a white shirt, his brown hair streaked with blond. Something in his walk, his easy confidence, conjured up an image of her husband, Josef, as he was the last time she'd seen him, nearly two years ago.

3

She remembered Josef checking his watch several times as she sat on the bed folding his clean laundry into the canvas bag. He was dressed that day, as always, in jeans and his favorite leather jacket. Anxious to be on his way, he'd nibbled her ear, tweaked her nose, and promised to call her that night. Abruptly, he kissed their daughter, gave Rija a second hug, grabbed his satchel, and was gone.

A tear burned the corner of her eye until her pride overcame the anger that scorched her. If only there was a way, she wanted him to know of her new life, the life she was creating on her own, without him.

Fowler looked up at the clock, smiling approval as Rija returned. It was a little after five. "Welcome aboard," he said. "Let's get you started."

He walked her down the hall, and when his hand rested a little too long on her shoulder, Rija ducked behind him, staying out of reach. Fowler stopped next to a yellow utility cart and bent down to check the wheels. As he moved the cart back and forth, Rija noticed the gap in his tight shirt from a missing button, saw a pasty slice of his mid-section. She looked away until he finally pushed the cart toward her, satisfied that it moved well enough. "This one will be yours. Carlene will take you up to your floors as soon as she gets back."

"Carlene?"

"My assistant."

The elevator door opened and a tall, dark-skinned woman in a pink T-shirt emerged. Her shirt read, "Keep it Clean with Carlene."

"Hi, you the new girl?"

Rija held out her hand. "Pleased to meet you. My name is Rija."

Carlene's eyes flickered over her. "You don't intend to work in those clothes do you?"

Rija winced. "It's all I have with me. I didn't plan to start work today."

Carlene touched Rija's elbow. "Come with me. I can give you something to cover up your dress."

Rija followed Carlene to a locker room and watched as she rummaged in a metal locker. With an air of satisfaction, her new co-worker extracted a sleeveless green smock. It was well worn but looked clean. "Here, put this on," Carlene said. "Do you have shoes?"

4

Rija shook her head. A blister had already begun forming on her heel, and she was worried about getting through the night in her shoes.

"What size you wear, honey?" Carlene asked.

"In American sizes, I think size 8."

Carlene pulled a pair of old clogs out of the locker. "These are an eight and a half, okay?" She put the shoes on the bench between the lockers. "Maybe a little big, but they're a hell of a lot better than working in heels. Try them on."

Rija slipped on the shoes, walked back and forth to make sure they would work even with the blister. "They fit. Thank you, Mrs. Carlene."

The other woman laughed. "It's not Mrs., it's just Carlene. Come on, let's go."

They left the locker room, and Carlene moved the cart to the freight elevator. "We've got to get moving now because I'm meeting someone, and I want to get out of here before midnight."

On Floor 19, Carlene headed to the women's restroom, motioning for Rija to follow. Inside she asked, "Done any cleaning before?"

Rija said, "Only at home."

Carlene pushed up her sleeves and pulled out yellow latex gloves. "Okay, Miss New Girl, welcome to Bathroom 101."

Carlene grabbed a bottle of toilet bowl cleaner from her cart, flipped the toilet seat up, and squirted blue liquid around the inside of the white porcelain rim. "So, you have no commercial cleaning experience?"

"Maybe just a little. My father was in charge of our apartment building. Sometimes I would help him clean the hallways. But that was before."

"Before what?"

"The war."

"War?" Carlene frowned. "Which war?"

"In Bosnia. Our city, Sarajevo, was under siege for months. We were trapped."

"Oh."

The puzzled look on the face of her co-worker didn't surprise Rija. Most Americans seemed never to have heard of the city where she was born or the war that destroyed it.

"Our country fell apart, and the leaders and politicians did nothing to stop it," Rija explained. "There were soldiers up in the hills firing shells down on us for months."

"Why would they let them do that?"

"Why do the politicians do anything? For their own greed and power."

Carlene pressed her lips together and shook her head. "I do remember something on the news, but I didn't understand it. I'm trying to picture where Bosnia is."

She handed Rija a long-handled brush and watched as Rija scrubbed and flushed to rinse the toilet, repeating the process in all of the stalls. "So how'd you get out?"

"My husband, Josef, always had a dream to come to America. We escaped with my daughter and my mother."

They moved to the sinks next, spraying and wiping to remove spots from faucets and countertops.

"And now you're here."

"Yes, we're here. We live near the river in the Port Richmond neighborhood." Rija looked away. "Since my husband left."

"Oh, I'm so sorry."

Rija felt her face burn.

"Where's he now?"

She looked back at Carlene. "I don't know."

"That no-good skunk! He brings you here and then he splits?" Carlene patted her shoulder. "They say the Lord doesn't give us more than we can bear, but sometimes I wonder."

In the corridor, Carlene punched the button to call the freight elevator. "I'd love to talk more, but we really better get started on our cleaning. You ready?"

Rija nodded.

"You know what to do in the bathrooms. Just remember, empty the wastebaskets, vacuum the floors, and give the corner offices a little extra. Got it?"

"Yes."

"Good. I'll check up on you later, but you'll be all right. I can see you're a quick learner. Some people Fowler hires can hardly walk and chew gum, if you know what I mean."

Rija looked puzzled and Carlene laughed.

"No, I guess you don't."

Four floors and several hours later, Rija stopped for a moment and removed the shoe from her blistered foot. The blister had been rubbed raw and was bleeding. Better to work in bare feet, she thought, and took off the other shoe. She stretched her back, but the ache there had taken hold long before she would finish emptying the last wastebasket. Despite the pain in her foot and back, she knew she had lived through much worse. She knew she could do this job for as long as she needed to do it. If things worked out right, it wouldn't be more than a year.

The building was quiet when Rija finally finished her shift and returned to the basement on the freight elevator. Quickly, Rija returned the shoes and smock to her locker. She was starving and exhausted. It was past midnight when a different guard waved her through the revolving doors, out into the Philadelphia streets, dark and wet after a late rain. Rija avoided the puddles as she trudged down concrete steps to the subway platform. She didn't like the idea of waiting on the gritty platform at this time of night and was gratified when the familiar sudden wind, bright lights, and engine's roar announced the arrival of her train.

She boarded a nearly empty car and gratefully collapsed into a seat. She stared unseeing as blurred platform lights split the darkness of the subway tunnel. The train rumbled and shook, finally emerged above ground. One more stop to go. Elena and Lili would be asleep now, and Rija couldn't wait to get home, back to her life, the life she'd made for herself and her daughter since Josef disappeared into America.

Chapter 2

What were the odds? Josef told himself he should have known better. How did it happen? Right on schedule he and Sergei collected the money, no problem. That was the easy part. The Japanese businessman, hands shaking, met them in the lobby of the hotel to pay off his marker like he promised. Josef insisted on holding the cash while Sergei made a stop, and the two men made a plan to reconnect at midnight. After that they would find Nick, give him his twelve thousand dollars and get paid for their trouble.

Josef checked his watch. Almost eleven o'clock. He had an hour to kill. Maybe he should grab a sandwich. Was it really twenty-four hours since he'd stopped to eat or sleep? On a whim, he cut through the hotel's second-rate casino. Across the floor he saw her at the craps table. Her hair was long and auburn, her dress, his favorite, a leopard print. The seats on either side of her were empty. It looked like she was alone.

He turned and spotted the cage in the corner. He'd get a couple of good-sized stacks of chips, maybe go a couple of rolls, but that was it. All he wanted was to get her attention. His own wallet held less than twenty bucks, but he felt confident as he peeled five thousand from the envelope that held Nick's payoff.

At the table, he signaled the waitress and ordered a double whiskey. The drink warmed his belly as he won on a first roll, then a second. Josef's heart was pounding a little faster, and his hands tingled. When he looked over, she returned his glance and smiled.

By the time it was Josef's turn to roll, he noticed she'd cashed out yet she stayed close, watching. When their eyes met and held, Josef tried to read her expression.

Energized, he pulled the chair back to stand. He was still puzzling over her expression when he felt perfumed breath on the nape of his neck. The fleeting touch on his thigh set his mind reeling. Before she moved back, he caught her fragrance for a second time, musky attar of roses. For several rolls, he'd bet with the crowd. Now, the time felt right. Josef pushed all of his chips to the center. If he won, the odds were three to one. He could walk away with thousands, restore Nick's cash to the envelope and no one would ever know. He looked around at his silent companion. She smiled again, her wide-set eyes smoky, dark, and promising.

His stack of chips grew. He was on fire. Feeling the heat, the rest of the table fell silent as he rolled. The dice hit and the stickperson called it.

"Seven".

Josef's heart lurched. In a stroke, his chips disappeared from the box, and the woman vanished just as quickly. He staggered from the table, unable to think. From nowhere, Sergei appeared, grabbing him just as the enormity of what he'd done hit him between the eyes. He let the burly Russian drag him off the casino floor.

"Okay, Mr. Fucking Big Shot, I saw you at the table."

"I just stopped for a minute."

In his mind Josef worked to concoct a story but Sergei was having none of it.

"What have you done, asshole? I told you to stay away from the dice. I know you gonna give me some bullshit. Let's hear it."

People were starting to stare. Sergei pushed Josef out the door just as hotel security showed up. On the sidewalk, Josef twisted in his jacket but Sergei's grip held firm. "Where's the money?" He jerked Josef around to face him. "Answer me, what did you do with it?"

In a panic, Josef managed to free himself momentarily, running ahead until Sergei trapped him again. Inside the parking garage, the Russian pushed him against a wall. "You'll get us both killed. We have to meet Nick in an hour, and you blew how much of it at the table?"

Josef fished out the envelope, handing it over.

Sergei thumbed through what was left. "How much did you lose?"

"Maybe a couple thousand," he lied, knowing only seven of the twelve thousand remained.

"Remember what happened when Alexei took Nick's money?"

Josef remembered.

Sergei struck Josef with the back of his hand. "Yes, and where is Alexei? You don't know, do you? Well, I do! And that could be us!"

"Wait. I have an idea," Josef said.

Even as he spoke the words, Josef knew his idea was too simple really to do them any good. Still, he looked to see if Sergei was listening. "We'll find a couple of convenience stores. They're open all night, no?"

He felt encouraged by Sergei's silence until the Russian came at him again. "Are you crazy? Did you ever rob a store?"

Josef ducked out of range. "No." He tried to catch his breath in case there was another swing.

The sound of Sergei's voice rang in his ears. "No, I didn't think so. Sometimes they keep shotguns under the counter. Did you think about that, genius?"

"Do you have another idea?" Josef asked.

"Fuck you, you know I don't. Nothing we can do at this time of night." The veins stood out on either side of Sergei's neck. "If you get your head blown off, don't blame me."

Josef straightened his clothing without taking his eyes off the Russian's face. "Then we'll take turns, okay? First I do one, then you."

At a traffic light, Sergei pulled the vial of white powder from his shirt. He inserted his little finger into the container and scooped some up with a nail. He bent down and inhaled deeply into one nostril, then the other. A few crystals hung on the end of his nose as he rubbed a finger over his gums. He held the coke out in a silent offer that Josef refused with a shake of his head.

They worked it out as they went. One would drive, the other would get the cash. Sergei claimed the first store, and they drove down Decatur looking for the 24-hour MaxiMart. Calmly, the Russian tucked the Glock into his waistband and pulled a baseball cap low over his eyes. Only a line of sweat on his upper lip betrayed nerves as they sat in the parking lot, waiting as the single customer came out holding a box of Pampers. When the taillights disappeared, Sergei took a breath, let it out slowly, and opened the car door.

For someone as big as Sergei, Josef thought, his speed was impressive. Within sixty seconds, he'd already moved behind the counter, holding his gun against the young clerk's head with one hand while he cleaned out the cash register with the other.

From where he sat, Josef could see Sergei jerk the young man to his feet. He could imagine the loud stream of Russian curses if his friend was not satisfied with the take. He watched Sergei and the clerk march in lockstep toward the rear of the store. Time seemed to stop. His mouth dry, his heart pounding, Josef checked his watch over and over.

Finally, Sergei reappeared and got in the car. "Go!" he roared.

Josef hit the gas and they were back on the street. Less than ten minutes had passed. "Well?" He asked.

"The safe was empty, the fucking safe was empty."

Now it was Josef's turn. They drove until the neon Golden Farms logo beckoned across an intersection. Blowing the stop sign, they pulled in and parked in a corner of the lot away from the lights. Sergei passed the gun across as Josef pulled a pair of sunglasses from his pocket and exited the car.

Cold air rushed out as the automatic doors slid open. Inside, Josef cursed himself silently at the sight of a stocky gray-haired woman, Golden Farms embroidered on her cap, her shirt boldly striped in red and white. At the sight of the gun, the clerk blanched and began inching backward.

"Stop!" Josef commanded.

She froze.

"Give me your cash."

Now when he wanted her to, the stupid bitch didn't move. His panic growing, Josef aimed the gun at her head. "Give me your money or I'll kill you."

Josef was momentarily distracted as he spotted a video camera above but it was too late to worry about. He turned back to focus on the clerk at the register.

She hit a key and stepped back as the cash door shot open. She was trembling and avoiding his eyes.

Josef reached around to scoop wrinkled bills into a bag. Out of the corner of his eye, he saw her hand inch toward a red button on the counter. As he pulled back to strike her, Sergei hit the horn. Josef shoved her away from the button and grabbed the cash as the clerk fell to the floor. After a second blast from the horn, he was out the door, brushing past two teenagers with skateboards out late.

They repeated the exercise at two other locations. The total take was less than fourteen hundred dollars, nowhere close to had the five thousand Josef lost at the table. They wouldn't be meeting Nick tonight. Now there was only time to run. They'd take the seven thousand that was left and maybe head west to Los Angeles or Tahoe.

Reality in the form of a white police car cruised past. Josef stared straight ahead, willing himself to look casual.

"Get off the Strip!" Sergei hissed.

As Josef pondered the quickest way out of town, he saw a black BMW M5 a few car lengths in front of them, heading the opposite way. There were two men in the front. "Oh, fuck me!"

As the car passed, Josef saw Nick's driver spot them. Moments later, he heard brakes squeal, heard Sergei screaming frantically in his ear. Josef gunned the accelerator, narrowly missing an SUV. He heard more brakes screeching, followed by a chorus of car horns, but he kept going. He glanced at the rearview mirror and saw the BMW close behind.

Josef turned right as soon as he could and floored the accelerator. He ran a couple of amber lights and one red and kept going. He hung another right, and the car careened into an alley. A dog howled, and a second barked in response. A sliver of moon hung in the clear night sky above coils of razor wire. The Strip glowed in the distance, but they were far from the glitter. This was east of Fremont, gang turf. Not the part of town that attracted tourists.

Josef fought for control as the car skidded on sand and swerved. He hit the brakes hard, and the car spun through one hundred eighty degrees to face the BMW bearing down on them. He yanked open the door and jumped out, heard Sergei grunt and jump out from the passenger side. They tore down the narrow passage on foot. Behind them, two shots rang out.

Josef scrambled up a chain link fence into a dumpster next to a shed. He prayed the pile of debris next to it might shield him from view. Before the lid banged shut, Josef heard more shots, heard Sergei groan and stumble. Not far away, a siren wailed. Seconds later the BMW's motor roared and faded.

For what felt like forever, Josef shared the dumpster with oil-soaked rags, a dead rat, and a bad smell. The wail of sirens grew louder. When he could no longer hold his breath, Josef inched the dumpster's cover up so he could see back into the alley. The BMW was gone, but an overhead light revealed Sergei's body, unmoving, in a dark pool of blood. He scrambled out of the dumpster seconds before two patrol cars arrived to block the end of the alleyway. There was only one way out. He scaled the fence and dropped into the adjacent junkyard. Inside, a dog strained toward him, but a chain held it back. Josef ran toward sounds of traffic and vaulted over the gate. He emerged street-side as another police car screamed toward the alley. Josef breathed in the desert air, smoothed his hair, pulled down his jacket and crossed the street. He flashed on the envelope of cash. It was still in Sergei's pocket.

Out on the highway, traffic was sparse. A gray streak of dawn appeared above mountains at the edge of the horizon. Josef made a mental inventory of what he'd left behind. There was nothing worth risking his life for, but he could have used a shower. He popped a mint in his mouth, sniffed his jacket, and hoped he didn't smell too bad.

Shivering with cold, he rubbed his arms while he paced at the side of the road. He didn't know if he could get a ride but he'd try, first on one side of the highway, then on the other. At this point, east or west, the direction didn't matter.

It was almost fully light when he finally got lucky. Heading east, a white SUV with Ohio plates pulled over. Josef shot his most brilliant smile through the window toward the driver.

Behind the wheel, a heavyset blond woman eyed him up and down. Finally she unlocked the door. "Get in," she said jerking her head with a half-smile.

Before she could change her mind, Josef jumped inside and slammed the door. He cinched the seat belt in place.

"Leaving Vegas empty-handed?"

Josef chuckled. "Yes, a few unforeseen financial problems."

"Honey, I been there." She tossed her hair out of her eyes. "Name's Dolores."

Josef watched the speedometer climb to eighty-five.

With two hours of daylight left, they were making good time. Dolores took a drag of her cigarette and blew smoke out the window. "You said you're heading east, but you didn't say where exactly."

This was a conversation Josef didn't want to have. "My cousin lives in New York. I plan to stay with him."

Dolores glanced at her watch. "Just so you know, we should hit Oklahoma City by midnight. That's where I usually turn north. You might want to bail out then."

Josef thought bailing out was the last thing he wanted to do, but he nodded silently and turned to stare at the rush hour traffic blowing by. Long-haul trucks swapped lanes with pickups and SUVs like the one Dolores was driving. Ahead of them, Route 40 sliced through Albuquerque. Every quarter mile or so, billboards appeared on either side of the expressway, advertising motorcycles, car dealerships, and a lawyer who promised justice for the wrongfully harmed.

"They call New Mexico the Land of Enchantment," Dolores said. She chuckled to herself. "I sound like a God-damned tourist brochure, don't I?"

Josef smiled weakly.

"I could have gone north through Colorado but I like the southern route better. Winters in Cleveland are long and dark. So whenever I get the chance, I go with the sun for as long as I can."

Josef took in the red rocks, the swirling dust. "It's dry here, like Vegas."

Dolores jerked the wheel left, dodging a tumbleweed in their lane. "You're right, they're a lot alike. I have an aunt who lives here. Pretty much the only family I have left. She has a sweet little place near the mountain. I stopped by on my way out."

"Staying in touch can be difficult," Josef said. He closed his eyes. Unbidden, his wife, Rija, appeared before him with Lili in her arms. The image faded.

They changed lanes, cutting off a panel truck. Dolores didn't seem to notice what she'd done until the driver came up behind her, blasting his horn. Unfazed, she looked in the rearview, "Up yours, asshole."

Minutes later, she swerved again and they exited the highway at San Mateo Boulevard. At the bottom of the ramp, Dolores turned south, past a Super 8 Motel that promised HBO in every room. When a Village Waffle House beckoned, Dolores pulled in and found a parking space. She shut off the motor. "I'm starved."

Josef was past the point of hunger, but his mouth felt rough and dry. His tongue was thick from the day's dust and the six-pack of Pepsi he and Dolores had shared through Arizona. He patted his jeans in a search for the few dollars that remained after he'd handed the cash over to Sergei. "Sure, whatever you say."

Dolores led the way into the brightly lit restaurant. The hostess supplied menus and told them to sit anywhere. A pony-tailed waitress brought water. "What can I get for y'all?"

Dolores was ready. "I'll have the waffles and a side of bacon."

Josef chose a burger and fries and wondered if he'd be able to eat it. He gulped the glass of water, watching Dolores's sweat-shirted back retreat as she went to find the restroom.

At the counter, older men in Levis and cowboy boots slouched silently over their coffee cups, hats still on. Josef remembered seeing men like that in Vegas, their deeply tanned faces concentrating intently as they fed quarters into poker machines that rarely paid off. Poor losers. Josef felt pity for them, never once believing that he might one day become what they were-old, tired, and alone.

Dolores smiled as she sat back down. She raised her empty cup toward their waitress, who was making the rounds with a coffee pot. Josef noticed she drank it black with two sugars.

"One thing I love about traveling is eating in restaurants," Dolores said. "When I was a kid, my mom and I went out to eat all the time. I didn't mind. She hated to cook and it was just the two of us, her and me. So we did what we wanted, whenever we wanted." Dolores fixed Josef with an inquiring eye. "How about you? Any family? You know, brothers, sisters?"

"No brothers, two sisters, both younger. Katja was sixteen when I saw her last, and Dina was twelve. They're living with relatives."

"Here?"

"No, in Europe. I couldn't take care of them after my mother died."

"Father?"

"He died many years ago."

Dolores looked away. "That's rough."

He felt her sympathy, and a wave of longing hit him. "It's been years since I saw them, since they went to live with my aunt and uncle."

"They must be all grown up by now."

It was a long time since he'd talked about his family, but as he continued, Dolores seemed to regard him in a new way.

"How'd you get here?"

"Long story. There was fighting in my country, Bosnia. Have you heard of it?"

Dolores seemed to give it some thought. "I knew your accent sounded familiar. My neighbor was born near there, Croatia. She sent some things home during the fighting. They couldn't get any food, for God's sake."

"During the war, I worked as a translator. Can you believe it? I was even on CNN. The journalists and foreign news people who covered the war, they were my friends. When you saw them driving around the war zone with a camera, I was the one in the back seat telling them where to go. Sometimes they paid me in dollars, sometimes in cigarettes."

Dolores rolled her eyes. "Cigarettes?"

"In those days, our money was useless. Except for American dollars or German deutsche marks, we worked on the barter system, and cigarettes were what we had to trade."

When their order arrived Dolores fell silent, her focus shifting to the plate in front of her. She grabbed the syrup cup, decorated her waffles with puddles of syrup, and dug in.

Josef eyed his order but kept talking. "There was a man, an engraver. In better times, he worked at the mint in Sarajevo. His wife had cancer. She needed a special drug, but the hospitals were shut down. I found a way to get the medicine for her, and in return he made me travel documents so I could get special conduct to the border."

Editing the story, as he often did, Josef failed to mention his wife, his child, and his mother-in-law.

"So how'd you end up in Vegas?"

"I arrived in New York. When I heard about Las Vegas, it seemed like the place for me. So I headed west, and there you have it."

Dolores's eyes met his and she smiled. Josef absorbed her new interest like water. He felt his appetite return, and he picked up a couple of fries. Relaxing in the moment, he chewed slowly and wiped his lips with the paper napkin.

Dolores finished half her waffle and took a sip of coffee. "I'm kind of tired. Would you mind driving for a while?"

Josef smiled. "Sure, no problem."

Chapter 3

Lili jumped up and down on her mother's bed. Rija groaned and peered at her alarm clock-it was 6 a.m. She pulled the pillow over her head. Lili kept jumping.

"Go watch cartoons. Let Mama sleep. I'm so tired."

"But Mama, I want you to get up. Baba wants me to eat sausage. I hate sausage. Please get up."

"If I give you cereal, will you get yourself dressed and get ready for school?"

"Yes, Mama!"

Satisfied, the child sank down to put her head on the pillow next to her mother's. Rija gazed into daughter's eyes, wide-set and gray like her father's.

"Mama, where were you? Why weren't you home last night?"

Rija kissed Lili's cheek. "Here's why. Mama's got her first American job. Isn't that great? It's a real job, not like the one before, washing dishes at Jimmy's Coca Cola."

The six-year-old looked unconvinced.

"You'll see. Soon our lives will be better."

"Will you pick me up from school today?"

"No, love. Mama must work. Baba will pick you up, and you two will have dinner together while I'm at my job. Won't that be fun?"

Lili's eyes filled with tears. "But Mama, where will you eat?"

Rija brushed a wisp of hair from the child's forehead. "Don't worry. I'll bring something with me. Mama makes money so that one day we can have our own house. Do you understand?"

Lili tugged her mother's gown. "Now get up. I'm hungry."

Mother and daughter walked into the tiny kitchen. Elena stood by the stove. Sausages sputtered and popped in the frying pan.

"Baba, Lili doesn't want sausages. I'll get her some cereal."

Elena pressed her lips together. She turned off the stove with an angry flick of her wrist and threw the spatula in the sink.

"She eat too much sweets, and she don't finish her dinner last night. If she don't eat tonight, no dessert."

Rija made a face at her daughter. Then she took a bowl from the counter, filled it with Sugar Pops, and poured on the milk.

"Lili can eat cereal today, and tomorrow she'll eat a good breakfast, won't you Lili?"

The little girl stuck her spoon into the bowl and ignored the

17

question.

By way of a peace offering, Rija leaned over to pat her mother's shoulder. For the moment, Elena seemed to forget her anger. "How was your job?"

"The job is not good, is not bad. I will do it. We need the money. I'm just so tired right now. It was almost one o'clock by the time I got off the train."

Elena's face softened. She kissed her daughter's forehead. "You work hard. Go back to bed. I will walk Lili to school."

Rija hugged her mother. She bent next to her daughter's chair. They rubbed noses, laughing, until Lili squirmed away to reach for the box of Sugar Pops on the counter. Rija took the opportunity to disappear back into the bedroom.

Later that morning the phone rang. After four rings, Rija listened as someone from the gas company left a number for her to call. They seemed to call every day. The welfare check, though never enough to pay all the bills, still kept them alive. The happy thought that she would be paid soon made Rija feel a little better.

She threw on her robe and walked into the kitchen. The red linoleum tiles felt cool under her feet. Rija ran her hand over the stainless steel of the counter, its surface shiny clean and free of crumbs. She smiled. Her mother never left until everything in their four rooms was spotless. And once she'd cleaned their apartment, Elena didn't stop there. Beyond the confines of their small space, Elena made sure the second-floor landing outside their door was always vacuumed and dust-free.

From the window, Rija caught a glimpse of her mother at the corner of Mercer Street, her brown hair pulled up on her head. Despite a warm September sun, Elena still wore her sweater and scarf. How small her mother looked, Rija thought, older than her fifty-two years. Since leaving Bosnia, Elena, once outgoing and sociable, seemed to withdraw. Still, as the light turned green, Elena adjusted her kerchief and stepped briskly off the curb, pulling a shopping cart down the street toward the food bank in the church basement.

Above her on the third floor, Mr. Gracek was talking with their neighbor Tess. Rija could hear Tess apologizing to the landlord for the banister her five-year-old Timmy had damaged.

"Oh, I know how boys are," Gracek said.

"I'll be happy to pay for the repairs," Tess said.

"Fair enough, I'll send the carpenter around tomorrow."

He's a decent man, Rija thought. And smart, too. On their block alone, the thrifty Gracek owned four properties, two- and three-story brick houses with sturdy wooden doors perched atop marble steps. When they first looked at the apartment, Gracek described Port Richmond's history as he walked them past still-solid structures built a century ago. Then, he said, workers, many of them immigrants, clustered around the river, eager for jobs the port provided. Those jobs were long gone. The factories, warehouses, and piers that once drew people to the neighborhood stood empty. Yet he was proud of his neighborhood. The streets were still alive with "mom and pop" shops, corner bars, and people who were attracted by affordable rents and the hope of a safer place to live.

He'd been kind to them, and now the shame of how she had acted made her cringe. She threw on some clothes and waited for him to come down the stairs. At the sound of his footsteps, she opened the door. "Good morning, Mr. Gracek. May I talk to you?"

Gracek turned to her, his fisherman's cap covering a bald head. She thought his round face, usually creased in a smile, turned a little sour.

"What is it?"

"I have good news to tell you. Soon I hope to make up the back rent we owe. I have a job now, and my first pay will be in a couple weeks."

Gracek paused on the landing. "Good to know. Like I told you before, I'm willing to work with you on the rent, but you have to let me know if you're going to be late. I have obligations myself, you know."

"Yes, I know. I'm sorry."

"Winter's coming, and they're predicting a cold one. So I'm trying to put something away to get ready for the heat bills."

Rija tried not to frown as she thought of her own pink envelope from the utility company, the one with the words "Final Notice" she'd slipped behind the flowerpot. "I'll be sure to let you know the next time I have a problem."

Gracek, still annoyed, moved toward the stairs. "Okay, good. Now, I've got to get going."

"Please, wait. May I ask you one more thing? We, that is my mother and I, wondered if we could do some work for you. To help pay down part of what we owe."

While Gracek was angry with her, she knew he admired her mother's Old World ways. He would tease Elena whenever he found her outside, sweater over her apron, scrub brush in hand, washing down the marble steps unasked. Pleased, he would bow and thank her in his native Polish, "*Dziekiya bardzo.*"

Gracek thought a few minutes. "Well, I could use some help across the street at 3318. That couple on the first floor moved out, and the place is a mess."

Rija felt some of the weight lift from her chest.

"Ask your mother if she wants to help me clean it out. Before I go in to paint, I was going to have to pay someone anyway. So, yes, if she can do it in the next day or two, I'll be happy to take a hundred and twenty off of what you owe."

"That is so kind."

Rija closed the apartment door and let out a big sigh. Suddenly energized, she thought to empty the hamper. There should still be time to do a load of laundry before getting ready for work. Perhaps she could even pick Lili up at school and walk her home before she caught the train to Market Street.

Rija emerged from the subway. Her eyes took a few seconds to adjust to the glare bouncing up from the sidewalk. She pushed through the revolving door, and the security guard waved. She smiled and waved back.

She took the elevator to the basement to get her supplies and begin her shift. Fowler called to her from his office. "How'd it go last night?"

"Good, very good. Carlene was very kind and helpful."

"Okay, good deal. So you're all set for tonight?"

Rija nodded.

"Let me know if you got any questions," Fowler called out.

"Yes, I will. Thank you."

"My door is always open."

Rija was relieved when Fowler turned away to answer the phone on his desk. She'd covered yesterday's blister with a bandage and was ready to work. She hung up her things and pulled her long auburn hair into a ponytail. Carlene appeared, followed by a short, round woman with dark hair and freckles sprinkled across her copper complexion.

"Rija, say hello to Luz."

Carlene turned to Luz.

"Rija's the new 19th to 22nd floor."

"Hello, Luz." Rija held out her hand.

Rija extracted a picture of Lili from her purse to decorate the inside of the locker door.

Luz nudged Carlene in the ribs. "Did you tell her?"

"No. It slipped my mind. Rija, there's something I forgot to tell you to watch out for. Stay out of the stairwells when he's around."

"Who?"

"Fowler."

Luz nodded. "He likes to get friendly with the new girls. And with the way you look, with that hair and the body you got on you, you're just his type."

Carlene chimed in. "Yeah, he'll bump up against you, too, like it's an accident, except that it's not. And be careful in the elevators. Understand?"

Rija nodded. "I'll be careful. Thank you for telling me."

Fowler rapped twice on the locker room door. "Ladies, five-thirty. Time to make these offices sparkle."

Inside, Carlene made a face and Luz puffed out her cheeks. Rija, nearest to the door, had no choice but to push it open. She walked out, leading the way as the women marched past Fowler to where the vacuum cleaners were lined up in the hall. One by one, they pushed their carts and sweepers into the waiting elevator.

In a corner office on the 21st floor, Rija perched on the edge of a glass-topped desk and gazed out at the city's night skyline. Looking west between the buildings, the lights of the Parkway cut a diagonal path up to the Art Museum. She allowed herself to fall into the comfort of the cushioned leather chair and tried to imagine the person who worked in such luxurious surroundings.

A stack of documents caught her eye, and she selected the closest one before spinning to face her reflection in the plate glass window. In her best "practicing English" voice, she read aloud, "In the case of Stedler vs. Rosen, the final deposition is scheduled for November 9th."

The word deposition sounded familiar. She remembered hearing it in Mr. Doyle's lecture. It was on his list of many things he told them they would cover in class. And now she understood, the desk she was cleaning belonged to a lawyer. This was a law office. Rija smiled to herself as she replaced the letter on the desk, exactly as she had found it.

Chapter 4

Dolores told Josef not to call her at work and never stop by before six, which was when her boss finished his shift. Since she started working security, Dolores wanted to be serious on the job. But now, at half past seven, he figured it was safe for him to look in on her. When he stuck his head through the control room doorway, she swiveled away from the bank of monitors that spied on Eastgate Mall's customers.

"Hey, babe. What are you doing here?"

He ignored the tone of her voice and planted a kiss on the top of her head. "I just came to say hi."

"Okay, hi. You said it. Now what do you want?"

"I just need to borrow your car for a couple of hours."

Josef hit her with his most charming smile.

A frown creased her forehead. "Oh, babe, I don't think that's a good idea."

He pulled a stool next to her chair and looked deep into Dolores's warm hazel eyes. "But it's about a job."

"Babe, who's hiring at this time of night?"

"I heard they need guys for the morning shift unloading trucks at the Safeway on North Euclid. If I get hired tonight, I can start tomorrow." Josef massaged the solid flesh of her shoulders until he felt the muscles relax under his fingers. When her head lolled back a little he bent to nibble her ear.

She tried to pull away. "I don't know."

Feeling her determination start to melt, he held her gaze. "Who knows? If I do a good job and they like me, maybe I get hired full-time."

Dolores shot him a skeptical glance and turned back to the video console.

"Then I can pay rent, buy groceries, get a car. All those things."

"You always make it sound so easy."

He spun her chair back around and leaned in with a grin. "It is easy."

She pushed him away, sighed, and reached for her handbag. "Okay, you can borrow it, but just this once. The car is in section G."

As Josef made a swipe for the keys, she closed her hand over them. "Pick me up at the employee's entrance at ten o'clock, and I don't mean ten-thirty."

Josef blew her a kiss from the door and was gone. He found the car under the light in section G. Silently thanking Dolores for filling the tank on her way to work, he drove past the Safeway on Euclid, just for luck, and kept on going. It was going on November, and the sky was dark, but he didn't mind driving at night. He turned left off Euclid on his way back to the apartment, mulling over the limited options Cleveland offered a young man with ambition, an expired green card, and no money.

Inside, Josef threw his few belongings into a backpack. He opened and closed the empty refrigerator, gazed at the sagging furniture and overflowing ashtrays and wondered how he'd spent a whole month here. True, he needed a rest, a chance to slow down after Vegas, and so he let Dolores talk him into staying. But he was bored with Dolores, bored with Cleveland, and bored with doing nothing.

Her place wasn't much better than the apartment Rija had found for them in Philadelphia, and it certainly wasn't as clean. How could he even think of Dolores and his wife at the same time? He would not compare the two. An image of Rija flashed through his brain. Rija was smart and beautiful, and when he thought about her, he felt a twinge that reminded him how much he missed her and Lili. He wondered sometimes why he had left. It wasn't that his wife expected so much of him. That wasn't it. No, when he was with her, he expected too much from himself. It was too much pressure.

Working every day, doing the same things over and over, taking orders, being told what to do. That life was not for him. He could find a way for himself to survive, to get by, but having to worry about three other people proved to be too much. Josef shook his head and decided not to think about it.

In the bedroom, he came across a T-shirt, the one they bought on his second Sunday in Cleveland, the Sunday Dolores insisted on riding the roller coaster at Adventureland. The ride nauseated him, and to make it up to him, Dolores offered to buy him something, almost like he was a child. He picked out the green shirt with white lettering that read "Happiness is Cleveland in your rear view mirror." She didn't appreciate the sentiment, but she bought it for him anyway.

On a whim, he shook the shirt to get out the wrinkles and pulled it over his head. Stepping back, he checked himself out in the mirror. He found a few dollars in the dresser drawer and slid them into his jeans. Josef gave Dolores's photo a silent salute and tossed the front door key onto the bed. It was only seven fifty-five, and if he moved fast, he could be almost across the state line before Dolores thought to call the police. If he drove all night, he could be in Brooklyn before morning.

Chapter 5

Rija watched the instructor, Mr. Doyle, pace back and forth. The slide flickered on the screen behind him, and a few people in the front row laughed at something he said. Perched at the edge of her seat in the back row, she leaned forward trying to hear what they were saying, then refocused her attention on the presentation. She scribbled notes on a yellow pad, recording legal vocabulary words to look up later.

It was Saturday morning, barely seven hours since her head touched the pillow the night before. But she didn't care about lost sleep. She could hardly believe that she was here in a classroom. Today she would not push a vacuum cleaner down carpeted corridors or swab dozens of toilets. Today, textbooks would be her tools, and classrooms would be the setting. The two classes on her schedule-law office administration and real estate law-would be her focus.

"This is your basic law firm organization chart," the instructor was saying.

His laser pointer described a red circle red around the tip of the graphic's pyramid. "Here, you have your managing partner. He's your first among equals."

The pointer's squiggles moved further down the chart.

"Then you have your executive committee, they're your senior partners." He made another circle. "Here you have your partners, then your associates. After that you have your office administrator, then, if you will, your paraprofessionals, your paralegals."

He gestured expansively in their direction. "That's where you all come in. Most times, you'll be working with the associates, sometimes even with partners. But whatever you do, remember, as paralegals, you'll have an important role to play, a role that is not always acknowledged, but an important role nevertheless."

Rija liked when he said that. This is what she wanted, an important role. When she was young, Rija dreamed of becoming a teacher. Most summers, she and her best friend, Mira, played school by the hour, recruiting the younger children in the neighborhood, luring them into the courtyard of her family's building, arranging them according to their ages on the stone stairs in endless games of "step school."

25

Now she was studying law, and in a way it surprised her. It was Doni, her brother, who was to become a lawyer. Before the shelling started, he'd studied law for two years, and Rija remembered feeling pangs of jealousy whenever she heard her mother boasting to whoever would listen. "My son will be a lawyer, a professional man."

But that day never came. That dream died when Sarajevo's legal system, once housed in the crumbling Palace of Justice, was replaced by the rule of the gun. She shook her head to clear those thoughts away as the lecture continued.

On Monday afternoon, the sound of Carlene's voice reached Rija's ears almost before she stepped off the elevator. Her co-worker was holding forth on her favorite topic of conversation, and Rija smiled as she imagined Luz listening wide-eyed and nodding silently.

"It's official now. I got it registered. Someday soon you'll see trucks with my logo on the side, **Keep it Clean with Carlene,** because, you know, that's my trade name."

Carlene held a framed certificate and was showing it to Luz. "These papers just came in the mail from Harrisburg. My business is on file now."

Rija waved a silent greeting and opened her locker.

"You know, ladies, some day you might be working for me," Carlene said.

"I'd love to work for you, Carlene, but I have other plans," Rija replied. "I'll be working in a law office."

"You already work in law offices. You're cleaning them."

Rija straightened her shoulders. "I know, but it won't always be like that. I have a plan."

"Let's hear it."

"I'm studying to become a paralegal."

Carlene put down her certificate and put up her hand. "High five!"

Luz, too, held up a palm. Rija grinned shyly, and the three smacked hands in congratulations.

"Why didn't you tell me? Now if I need legal work, I'll know who to call on," Carlene said with a big smile.

Sorry now that she'd spoken, Rija could feel the heat rising in her cheeks, and she turned to her locker.

Luz pointed to the clock. "Okay, big shots. Time to go upstairs."

On the 21st floor, a hum of conversation echoed down the hall. Rija left her cart at the end of the corridor and padded silently toward light spilling into the hallway. An angry shout stopped her at the edge of the conference room's glass wall. Inside, two men in shirtsleeves and a woman in a suit were gesturing back and forth around a black lacquered table. A second woman pounded at a laptop.

"God damn it!" A young man stood, snapped a pencil in two, and threw the pieces onto the floor. "I didn't go to law school to be an ambulance chaser."

He kicked the wastebasket halfway across the room, scattering its contents. Rija pursed her lips in disgust as coffee sloshed out of a Styrofoam cup and a brown stain bloomed on the beige carpet.

The young lawyer's face reddened, and he ran a hand through his ginger hair. Rija looked on as his co-worker tried to cool his fire.

"Jesus, calm down. Neither did I, but if we want our numbers to match last year's, we have to compromise on some of these cases."

The first lawyer's face grew slack. "Yeah, I hear you, but it's hard to take."

The young woman at the computer looked up from the keyboard. "I don't think we can back down on this. Our unit billings are low."

The other male lawyer turned to look at Mr. Broken Pencil. "You heard what they said at the partners' meeting. We have three months to turn it around before year-end. So let's get real, or we'll be the ones crying at bonus time."

The voices rose and fell as the debate continued, but Rija's fascination gave way to reality. She decided the room would keep until she came back to finish it. She dragged her cart down the hall. She needed to keep going if she wanted to get home before one o'clock.

When she returned to the conference room, she was relieved to see that it was dark and silent. She wiped streaks from the top of the conference table, emptied the trash-which someone had picked up from the floor and deposited back into the wastebasket-and blotted the still-wet coffee stain.

When she exited the room, she saw a light at the far end of the corridor. "Lazy creatures," she muttered. "They could at least turn the light off."

But instead of an empty office, Rija found a dark-haired young woman around her own age drowsing in a chair, her feet propped up on a desk. Crumpled sheets of yellow paper lay on the floor near the wastebasket. Half a pizza congealed on top of the filing cabinet.

Rija stepped back. "I'm sorry. I didn't realize ..."

The young woman opened her eyes and jumped to her feet. "Wait, stop. Don't go. Please, I'm almost done here." She moved to where Rija stood at the door. "Please, this office can so use some work. I've made a real mess."

Yes, Rija thought.

"I've been here pretty solid for the last three days. First-year lawyers like me get all the grunt work."

Rija wasn't sure how to respond.

"My name's Marti." She made a gesture that encompassed her desk and the filing cabinet nearby. "Welcome to my world."

Rija wiped her palm before taking the hand Marti offered. "I'm Rija."

"Rija. That's an interesting name."

"It means hope. I was named for my father's sister. She died just before I was born."

"Where are you from?"

"From Bosnia."

"I know where that is. I've been to Dubrovnik. Your country is very beautiful."

"Dubrovnik is very close, but it's in Croatia." Rija said.

"Oh, sorry."

Marti stood and pulled on her jacket. "Your English is very good."

Now it was Rija's turn to smile. "We all learn English since we're children."

Marti looked surprised.

"Now I am studying to become a paralegal." Rija wasn't sure why she had shared the information-for the second time that evening-but although Marti was a stranger, she was also a lawyer.

Marti pushed back her chair. "That's excellent. I'm very impressed."

The young woman turned off her computer. "I guess it's time we finished our work so we can both go home."

She grabbed her briefcase. "I'm sure you'll see me here again. It's not much of a life, but I figure maybe if I work long enough and hard enough, someday it'll pay off. Good night, Rija."

"Good night to you, Miss."

Rija moved around the desk. She bent to retrieve candy wrappers from the floor before brushing crumbs from half-eaten crackers into the wastebasket.

By the time Rija dragged her cart back toward the elevator, the digital face on her watch read 10:57. Though one more floor waited for her attention, she hesitated for an instant, looking out at the night sky.

Across the corridor, beyond thick plate glass, the city's lights beckoned. Drawn to the window, Rija's eyes moved from the towering office buildings and high-rise apartment buildings down to the horizon of low-rise neighborhoods nestling at the edge of the river. While she gazed, hypnotized by the lights, her father's face appeared, as if bringing her a message. Surprised, she fell back, grabbing the wall for support. She closed her eyes, and when she looked again the face was gone. Tearfully, she berated herself for a missed opportunity. Unable to call him back, her thoughts turned to the last time she had seen her father alive.

It was freezing that night in Sarajevo, but somehow when they were together, the small kitchen felt cheerful. Elena was proud of herself. She had arrived home after dark, her cart filled with branches she'd gathered in Veliki Park, her coat pockets stuffed with a packet of rice, some dried beans, three eggs, and an onion. More times than Rija liked to remember, they'd gone to bed with only a cup of tea and a piece of bread to allay their hunger, but tonight's meal would feed them all. Her papa, Anton, beamed at his wife as she bustled about the kitchen preparing the meal.

Later, Elena heated water for tea while Rija cleared the table. Doni went down to the cellar in search of stray pieces of coal. Anton sat smoking at the table.

Four loud thumps shattered the quiet. The lights at the front of the house were dark, and Elena put a finger to her lips, signaling silence. Seconds later, three men carrying rifles barged through the rear door.

Anton jumped to his feet and looked around for a weapon to defend them. "How dare you?" he roared at the intruders.

The bearded leader, fur hat perched atop long greasy hair, grabbed Papa's arm.

Shaking himself loose, Anton spit through clenched teeth. "Javor Babic, you coward."

At the sound of the name, Rija looked up at the leader, only now recognizing the face of the man behind the beard as her father's former business partner, the man her father had taken to court for stealing his truck and selling it. The man her father called thief.

"Get out, scum!" Anton roared. "You use a war to settle your own grudges?"

Babic ignored the insult. "Anton Petric, you are ordered to come with us for questioning."

Papa snorted, "Questioning at whose order?"

An underling hit Papa with the barrel of his gun. Rija noticed her mother slowly backing up against the cellar door. Silently, she pushed the bolt shut, locking Doni in the cellar.

"The Serbian Central Committee."

Papa's mouth bled as he spat in the man's face.

"Filthy swine, this is not Serbia. Your committee has no power here."

Again, the rifle hit Papa. He slumped to the floor and Mama ran to his side. The others pushed her away and lifted Papa to his feet. As the three men dragged Anton, half conscious, down the alley, Mama ran after them. Her curses echoed the words of her husband on the nights when he came home drunk. "Death to all Serbs. You are murderers and sons of whores."

When Rija got home, she hung up her coat and slid the door chain into its slot, taking care not to make too much noise. As she reached out to turn off the lights, she heard a yawn. In the living room, a drowsy Elena looked up from her favorite chair.

Rija perched on the footstool at her mother's feet. "I'm so glad you're still awake.

"Why, little one?"

Rija chose her words. "Tonight was so strange."

"***Recite mi***, tell me."

"It was Papa. I saw Papa's face reflected in the window, at work in the building. And for a moment I felt like he was there with me. It felt like he wanted to tell me something, to tell me he was all right."

Elena picked up her empty cup and walked to the kitchen.

"Yes, I know. I see his face before me many days. I don't tell you, but he is with us. He watches over us. He is our guardian angel."

Rija laughed. "Anton, the angel. Papa would laugh to hear himself called that."

Elena patted her daughter's hand.

Rija hugged her mother. "I know Papa watches us, but you, Mama are our guardian angel. How would Lili and I live without you?"

Elena said, "Yes, and you are my guardian angel, too. We take care of each other."

Chapter 6

It was Josef's idea to meet at the track. He knew his cousin loved the horses. On the drive from Cleveland, he'd called ahead, hoping Milos would offer him a place to stay. When he didn't, Josef suggested they meet in Queens the next day. After he hung up, Josef cursed himself. He'd forgotten to ask for news of his own sisters. Traffic on the George Washington Bridge seemed unusually light, and Josef pulled into the Aqueduct lot sooner than he planned. He found a space and wondered how he would pay on the way out. Soon his pockets would match the car's empty gas tank.

A discarded racing form offered distraction while he waited in the clubhouse, and when the announcer's voice called the next race, Josef's eyes moved down the sheet accordingly. Circled in red, Number Six, Big Easy, looked promising. The odds were good and he took that as a sign. Out on the paddock, Number Six wore his lucky color, red. Suddenly optimistic, Josef walked toward the window but turned away just before he reached it, barely managing to stop himself before he bet his last ten-dollar bill.

Behind him, the crowd's roar turned silent as a race ended. Josef heard his name and looked up as Milos strode confidently across the clubhouse, his face familiar yet changed. The old Milos had been thin and wiry, with a haunted, hungry look in his eye. The dark curls were still unruly, but this new Milos looked prosperous, relaxed, and well fed.

Josef hurried to meet him, drawing closer as Milos stopped to stub out his cigarette. The two hugged, clapping each other on the back. When Milos turned to a man next to him, Josef realized his cousin wasn't alone.

"Tomas, this is Josef. He's been out in Vegas for a few years."

After a night spent in the car, Josef felt scruffy next to the well-dressed men. Determined not to show his displeasure at the intrusion, he grasped the stranger's hand and smiled a greeting before turning back to his cousin. "Milos, how's the family? How is your father? I must get in touch with him."

Milos smiled. "He's fine. The farm does well. He managed to get his hands on some of the reconstruction money. He bought new equipment with the Euros they spread around. Peace and prosperity agree with him."

"And my sisters? I've had no news of Katja or Dina in a very long while."

"But didn't you know? Katja got engaged! Did you not get the card I sent?"

How could he not know that? Josef felt a blush of shame as the faces of his sisters appeared before him. "No, I guess I didn't."

"Dina's at university. She wants to be a doctor, and Katja, she's all grown up now. Her fiancée is an engineering student. They are living near Mostar. They sent me a photo on the Internet. Remind me, I must show it to you. I can give you a telephone number, their e-mail, whatever you want."

Josef told himself he only wanted what was best for his younger sisters and he'd meant to stay in touch. He remembered how relieved he'd been when his sisters left Sarajevo. With their mother dead, it was better for them to stay with Milos's parents. It was safer in their village than in the streets of the city. He could rest easy knowing their aunt and uncle would take good care of them, and, most important, they would be able to finish their schooling.

"I will write Katja soon with my best wishes."

Milos raised an eyebrow. He peered into Josef's eyes. "And you? How are you?"

"I'm back, looking to get reconnected on the East Coast. Anything you have for me, I can get it done for you, top notch."

Milos laughed out loud. He grabbed Josef playfully around the neck. "That's my cousin, he's top notch."

"Let's find a place where we can talk," Tomas suggested.

They found seats in the bar, and after Milos ordered beers, he turned to Josef. "Tomas needs a delivery. You have a van right?"

Josef nodded. "It's an SUV, and it's big."

"Good. We have three crates coming in, and we need someone to bring them back here. Are you in?"

"I told you, I'm ready to make a move whenever you need me." He turned to Tomas, "What is the merchandise, my friend?"

Tomas looked away.

"What is it? I need to know what you send me for."

Only after Milo's nod of approval did Tomas answer. "Two crates of Zastava, M53s, and a crate of double action revolvers."

Josef's face fell. He wasn't looking to go to jail.

Milos jumped in. "No worries. No risk. He has a buyer, but for safety, he needs someone with a fresh face, someone who can slip in, get the merchandise out quick, and deliver it."

Josef sipped his beer and was silent.

"You know, the ATF is a pain in the ass with their surveillance and their agents," Milos added.

32

"They know me too well," Tomas said, attempting a chuckle.

Palms up, Milos shrugged. "Some you can pay off and some you can't."

Flat broke, tired of sleeping in the car, Josef allowed his cousin to convince him there was little risk in what they wanted him to do. "I'll need expense money first," Josef said, determined to get some cash in his pocket.

Milos raised his glass. "Done."

Glasses clinked and the deal was made. With some cash up front, Josef would make the pickup. On delivery, he'd get three thousand more. The money would be enough to keep him going for a while, but then what? His spirits lifted then fell. Walking back to his car, he wondered, how did this happen? After all this time in America, he was right back where he had started three years ago.

Josef was filled with anxiety, nearly overwhelmed by a rising sense of panic. Papers in hand, he hid his fear, chatting brightly as he kept Rija, Elena, and Lili together amidst the bustle of the Newark airport. They were part of the line of weary travelers shuffling forward in an endless queue.

Beneath the swagger, he felt Rija's distress as she looked down at her shabby dress and second-hand shoes. She'd done well on the airplane, but now she looked pale and exhausted, her shiny auburn hair mussed and disheveled. Still, she managed a smile, and he saw the light return to her eyes. Even in old clothes, his wife was beautiful.

Three-year-old Lili, oblivious to the family drama unfolding around her, alternately laughed and cried, while Elena, nauseated for most of the flight, worked to soothe the exhausted child. Despite her own weariness, Elena held firm to both the canvas bag that contained her few possessions and the child she loved.

Josef had found a cart, and they piled their meager luggage, which contained all their worldly possessions, onto it. As the line inched forward, he leaned over to give the cart another push, and the family edged ahead.

The sight of Milos and Valentina waiting for them near the exit erased Josef's anxiety and brought a welcome feeling of relief. Finally in the land of his dreams, Josef could only babble over and over, "You look like Americans!"

Despite his jeans and American-bought Nikes, Milos looked the same as Josef remembered him. But Josef would never have recognized the slim young woman standing before them in designer jeans and dangling gold hoops as the same skinny girl who grew up in the village where he spent summers as a child. This Valentina seemed so confident and contented that it was if she'd undergone a miraculous change. Josef could only hope that Rija would soon begin her own transformation.

Valentina even insisted on driving so Milos could catch up with his cousin and point out the sights to Josef and his family. In the rear, Rija, Lili, and Elena dozed until they reached the couple's Brooklyn apartment. They would stay there until the social services department of the International Refugee Committee could find something permanent.

After allowing the new arrivals a few moments to splash water on their faces, Milos ushered their Bosnian friends into the couple's small kitchen. Valentina made sure everyone's glass was full so that when Josef and Rija entered the room, drinks were raised in a toast. "Velk, welcome, welcome".

United by a shared past and a common language, well wishers gathered around the table murmuring words of encouragement both in English and Croatian. Looking around, Josef's heart pounded and he felt his face grow tight with emotion, choosing to believe the tears he saw in his wife's eyes were tears of joy. But that night as he waited for sleep, Josef felt Rija trembling beside him. He pulled her close and tried to distract her with a kiss and a laugh as he always did.

"Tell me, draga. Why are you so unhappy? What is wrong?"

"Why did you make us do this? Milos and Valentina are kind, to be sure, but we are strangers to these people. We could have gone to Austria or Germany like so many others and waited for the war to end. Then we could have gone back, gone home. How will we live here? We know no one, we have nothing, and we look just like what we are, poor refugees."

"Don't worry. Tomorrow or the next day, I will go to New York City. I will look for a job."

"What job?"

"I think I will work in the stock market. What do you say?" He kissed her eyelids and held her close, and they fell asleep in each other's arms.

Chapter 7

Rija slept until her daughter's frantic protests penetrated her consciousness.

"No, Baba, no! I won't go. My stomach hurts."

Despite the protests, Elena struggled to pull the school uniform over the child's head. "She cries when I go to pick her up yesterday." Elena said.

Lili raised a tear-stained face to her mother. "My stomach hurts, and I can't go to school."

"Some boys chased her and they call her names."

Lili jumped onto the bed and pulled a quilt over her head. Rija pulled the cover aside and held her daughter's chin in her hand. Gently, she wiped tears from the little girl's face. "Tell Mama what happened."

Lili's eyes flashed. "They called me illegal. They said Baba can't talk right. They said she was a witch."

Elena looked to Rija to translate. "Mama, they called her an *izbjeglica*, an outsider."

Elena shook her fist. "I will chase them and sit on them," she threatened with eyes flashing.

Rija laughed at her mother, but Lili cried harder.

"No Baba, you stay away."

Rija grabbed her daughter by the shoulders and shook her. "No, Lili, Baba must pick you up every day. Mama works so we can have our own home. You understand, don't you?"

Lili tried to squirm out of Rija's grasp. "No. I want to go to a better school. I hate this school. I won't go back!"

Lili stayed home that day. At the end of the school day, it was Rija who marched up the steps of St. Casmir's. She moved aside to avoid the streams of children running into the schoolyard where mothers and fathers waited to walk them home.

Ms. Gardner, the first grade teacher, stood by the office, right where Rija remembered seeing her on Lili's first day. Then, Lili had waved her mother away and walked fearlessly down the hall. Now it was Rija who followed the young blond teacher into the classroom. Pilgrim hats and turkey feathers decorated the windows and Rija noticed a large pumpkin in the corner. A whiff of chalk dust conjured up her own childhood dream of becoming a teacher.

Ms. Gardner pulled a chair next to her desk. "Mrs. Malacovik, I'm glad you're here. Please, tell me what happened."

Rija leaned forward. "Until today my daughter loved school, but this morning Lili was crying. Some boys chased her, grabbed her book bag, and called her names. They said she was an illegal immigrant, and they called her grandmother a witch."

The teacher's mouth set in an angry line. "I'm so sorry, Mrs. Malacovik, I didn't know. Sometimes the teacher's aides don't tell us everything that goes on in the schoolyard. If Lili can point the boys out for me, I'll make sure that it doesn't happen again."

"Yes, Lili will tell me who they are." Rija's relief at the teacher's willingness to help was tinged with wariness. The more she considered what the teacher was asking her to do, the less she liked the idea. "But if she tells and they get punished, the boys will only tease her more."

"We'll see what we can do. I promise to pay more attention when the children are in the playground, and I'll ask the aides to do the same. But I still want to know who they are. Can you find out for me?"

As Rija shook the teacher's hand, she couldn't help sneaking a look at her watch. If she walked quickly, there might be enough time to get home and ask Lili the names of the boys before she caught the subway to her job. A chill wind blew across the schoolyard, a reminder that winter was coming.

As she ran toward home, Rija told herself she would do anything to protect her daughter, but the child's father should have been there to defend her, to defend all of them. But he'd brought them here, cast them off like an outworn garment, and disappeared.

Chapter 8

In America, almost fifty percent of all marriages end in divorce." Ms. Spadafora paused for effect and looked around the classroom. "Divorce can be a very difficult time. That's why many law offices are devoted to the practice of family law. A good divorce lawyer is often a mix of pit bull and guidance counselor, with a little bit of financial analyst thrown in for good measure."

The class laughed at the appropriate spot. Rija listened intently as the instructor continued. "The role of the divorce lawyer is to make the most advantageous settlement for the client."

In the second row, a young woman raised her hand.

"Yes, question?" Ms. Spadafora asked.

"What if the husband or the wife disappears? What about a settlement or support then?"

"Years ago a man or woman could just disappear and assume a new identity. Now it's not that easy. Between drivers' licenses, tax records, and the Internet, it's hard to hide. In addition, there's something very useful called a skip trace. Anyone heard that term before?"

A hand shot up in the back. Rija noticed the young man on the other side of the room, who, like her, rarely spoke in class. The way he usually sat, dark hair hiding his eyes, she often suspected that he might be dozing.

Wide-awake now, he spoke confidently. "Lawyers use it to find people. We have an online subscription service at our law firm to trace missing people. You can search a lot of ways, by names, Social Security numbers, driver's license, credit cards."

Rija clicked open her ballpoint pen and turned to a fresh page in her notebook. On it she wrote the words "skip trace." Only after everyone else filed out did Rija find the courage to approach the instructor.

Ms. Spadafora gave Rija an encouraging smile. "You looked like you wanted to ask a question today. Why didn't you?"

"Sometimes, it's hard for me to raise my hand. But I wanted to ask you how to do the skip trace."

"Usually, it's done in a law office."

"Oh."

"Now that we've talked, I hope you'll decide to contribute to the class. Things work best when everyone takes part. Here's my card, you can call me or e-mail me if you have any questions."

Rija rolled her cart down the corridor toward the light radiating from Marti's office, and this time she knocked. The young lawyer broke into a smile as she turned from her computer.

"Hi there, Ms. Paralegal. How are you?"

"Fine, thank you. I'm sorry to bother you. May I interrupt?"

"Sure. It gets pretty lonely here some nights. I could probably use a little human interaction about now."

"I have a question. About my course work."

"What's up?"

Rija sat on the edge of a chair. "How can I do a skip trace?"

Marti laughed. "Are you sure this is for your class?"

Rija blushed and looked away. "We talked about it in class, but you're right. It's for me. I want to find my husband."

"Tell me more. What's going on?"

"Our teacher explained how you use it to find people. My husband disappeared, and I don't know where he is. I wondered if it would help me find him."

"I wish it was that simple. And like most things, a skip trace isn't free. It's something the firm charges for. Do you have any of his personal documents?"

"I have some papers we filed when we arrived. I think I have a Social Security number."

"Let me find out what we usually charge for that service. Maybe there's a way I could help you with it, but I'm just not sure." Her gaze strayed back to the computer screen. "For now I better get this brief ready to file so I can go home. I really have a home to go to, if you can believe it."

Chapter 9

Map in hand, Josef navigated Brooklyn's congested streets until he spotted the Café Warsaw tucked away at the end of Brighton Avenue. Not taking any chances, he circled the block until he found a legal parking space and made sure to drop more than enough coins in the meter before locking the car.

Josef pushed open the café door. He attracted the momentary interest of two young men in leather jackets sitting in the corner. He checked his watch before slumping down next to the window and tried to look nonchalant while they stared. They soon returned to their conversation. Josef checked his watch again. Tomas should have arrived by now. Josef was eager to make the delivery with as little stir as possible.

A waitress approached with a menu. "Can I get you something to drink, sir?"

Josef turned from the window and smiled at the waitress. Even his tenseness couldn't trump his natural impulse to charm a pretty woman. "Tea with lemon, please."

He liked the way her long dark hair fell across her eyes. Too bad they wouldn't have time to get to get to know each other. But he wanted to get this meeting and transaction completed. Even with clean plates, like Milos said, there was always a risk.

The waitress brought his tea. Josef looked at his watch for a third time. Despite a "No Smoking" sign, the air was thick with the pall of cigarette smoke. He added three sugars to the steaming mug of tea, stirred, and sipped. He lit a cigarette, blowing the smoke out through his nostrils. After another drag he stubbed it out and stood up. He threw five dollars on the table, and in two strides he was out the door. Across the street, Tomas was getting out of a maroon van. Josef stopped him at the curb and steered him to where Dolores's white SUV was parked.

The money felt good in his pocket. He appreciated the way his cousin had found some work for him to do, but he needed more than a little cash. The money would buy some time, but he needed to start over. His life had no center. He hoped Milos could hook him up with something more permanent, and, most of all, he needed a place to stay, a base of operations. He told himself aloud, "So far, your life as an American has not been a big success."

He followed a sign to Coney Island. Though summer was long gone, an urge to feel the ocean air on his face pulled him to the boardwalk. Watching an elderly jogger lean into the sharp November wind, Josef thought about the snow that would be covering the mountains around Sarajevo by now.

He thought of Rija and Lili and the brief life in America he had shared with them. He should have waited to see how that life would turn out. Instead, frustrated and impatient for excitement, he'd taken off.

As he re-counted the cash in his wallet, the treasured photo of his mother dropped to the ground. He picked it up and slid it back into the vinyl sleeve. On the other side was his picture of Rija, the one taken before they got married. He surprised himself by kissing it. Thankful for the few mementos he'd managed to hold on to, he rubbed his thumb against the plastic-enclosed photos. Had he ever mentioned Philadelphia to Nick? He wasn't sure, but he didn't think so.

The weak afternoon sun was fading. Only five o'clock but it would be dark soon. And then what? Josef let the wind push him down a concrete ramp toward the Coney Island streets. One block over, faint strains of music lured him on. "Club Oasis" flashed in neon red over violent green palm trees and a yellow pyramid. It was the only sign of life amid neighboring storefronts whose empty windows proclaimed, "Going Out of Business - Everything Must Go."

Music burst forth as the Club Oasis door swung open. A young man in a tight black T-shirt emerged.

Josef approached him. "Got a light?"

The young man produced a butane lighter, and Josef bent over the flame, nodding thanks as he moved toward the door. The young man blocked his way. "Cover charge is twenty dollars."

Josef peeled off a bill and handed it over. He felt lightheaded. The words "Live Adult Entertainment" flickered overhead. He walked inside and felt the music's throb, found an empty barstool. He just needed to relax a little. He knew what he would do afterwards. He had a plan.

Chapter 10

Rija pretended to listen to Luz as she reported on the recent trials and sacrifices of Celia, the long-suffering heroine of Pasion, her favorite telenovella. "And then she told him she was pregnant," Luz was saying as she changed into her work clothes. Rija nodded absentmindedly.

After struggling with her coursework all morning, Rija hoped for an easy night. She prayed there would be no big dirty surprises waiting for her upstairs. Her dreams of tranquility evaporated when Carlene burst through the door of the locker room.

"That fucker, I'll rip his fucking eyes out his head, if he talks to me like that again."

Rija's heart beat faster at the sound of her co-worker's anger. "Who?" She asked.

"Fowler!"

Luz rolled her eyes. "What'd he say this time?"

"He told me the management company is putting him in charge of all three of their buildings and if I treat him right, he'd see to it that I get his job. I would be the crew chief, and all the cleaners in the building would work for me."

"But that sounds good!" Luz said.

Carlene glared at her. "Didn't you hear what I said? He wants me to treat him right, girl. Like maybe give him head whenever he wants it. I thought I would vomit."

"Give him head?" Rija was puzzled.

Carlene's face twisted in anger. "Blow him, suck his dick. Understand?"

Rija nodded. She understood. Her stomach twisted with the memory of that day in Sarajevo, and she fought to push the soldier's face from her mind. Sometimes she thought it might be easier to put it out of her thoughts if she could tell someone else what had happened, but she could never find the words. And so she kept her secret.

"What you gonna do?" Luz asked.

"I'm gonna call Rollie."

Luz turned to Rija. "Her brother Rollie's a cop."

Carlene's posture straightened. "Rollie's not just a cop, he's a detective now."

Luz folded her street clothes and put them into the locker and closed the door. "Good. He'll find a way to take care of Mr. Fowler, won't he?"

"Yes," Carlene said. "Mr. Fowler will get some advice he won't soon forget."

"Where's Fowler now?"

Carlene slipped on her work shoes. "He went down to the boiler room."

"Do you want us to wait for you?" Luz asked. "You know, in case he comes back."

"No, you go on up. I'll be there right after I leave Rollie a message to call me."

Rija finished filling her cart. "You are lucky to have a brother like that. My brother would be like that, too."

Inside the freight elevator, Luz turned to her, "You have a brother?"

"I did, but we lost him in the fighting. His name was Doni."

Doni. It felt good to say his name. She wanted to say it again. A tear stung her eye. Except for her mother, and Josef, wherever he might be, there was no one now who would even know who Doni was. Rija always asked herself if she could have stopped him, if she could have stopped her tall, strong older brother the night he decided to go up the mountain and join the fighting.

Doni and Josef whispered together in the hallway, but from where she hid, Rija could hear Josef droning on as he worked to convince her brother to go along with his idea. "We can join him by Monday. Think of what that means-to join the Shadow. He and his men are leaving through the tunnel. In two days, he'll join his brigade up in the hills, and we can be with him."

As Rija listened, she realized why Papa's old gun had been hidden beneath the clothes in Doni's knapsack, where she had found it. Like everyone else, she knew of the Shadow, the mythical Croatian Army officer whose self-appointed militia of Croats and Bosnian Muslims fought against the Serbs. To join him in the fighting soon became a rite of passage for the boys and young men of Sarajevo. But for many it had proven fatal.

Drunk on his own words, Josef's excitement grew. "If we leave by tomorrow, we can be with him!"

Still Doni hesitated. "Yes, I want to fight the Serbs, and yes, I want to join the Shadow's men, but what of Mama, what of Rija? They'll be alone."

Josef continued. "It's what your father would want you to do.

42

Besides, Marko can look out for them."

How dare he? She and Mama could look out for themselves. She wished that her brother, the brother she looked up to, would decide for himself what was best. Yet once again, Josef, always looking for adventure, was able to convince Doni to do what Josef wanted.

Rija's hands balled into fists as she stepped from behind the door. "Josef, stop talking! You don't know what our father would want."

Josef looked surprised. "Who is our little eavesdropper hiding there?"

Rija ignored him. She put her hand on Doni's arm. "You shouldn't go to fight for Papa's sake," Rija told him. "It's not what he would have wanted you to do."

She turned to her brother's friend. "And Josef, what do you know of our family or life in our building?"

True, except for Marko, Doni was the only man still in the building. But Marko and Alia, his crippled Muslim wife, were more likely to come to them for help than the other way around.

Doni peered at the ceiling, then he looked back at his sister's face, but the sound of footsteps on the stairs silenced them all.

Elena's head appeared. She looked from Doni to Josef to Rija and back again. "What's happening? What are you talking about?" She searched Doni's face. "Where are you going?"

He grabbed his mother's bundles. "Nowhere."

Elena wasn't fooled. "I see your bag is packed. Answer me. I asked where you are going."

"Some students are going through the tunnel," Josef told her. "We're taking supplies to the Shadow, and then we'll be back."

"We'll only be gone for two days," Doni promised.

Elena's face seemed to crumble. "You say two days. How can you know how long?"

Despite her pleas, Doni and Josef slipped away in the middle of the night and met the others near the sports stadium. Once assembled, they walked single file, following the soldiers of the Shadow's ill-equipped brigade through the secret tunnel that led into the hills beyond the city. They reached the other side and stayed on the move while the Shadow's ragtag militia joined with the Army of Bosnia. They fought against the Serbs for the survival of Bosnia, struggling on with little food and less ammunition. They battled the Serbs wherever they found them, on a front that shifted and changed and split like an amoeba.

Doni came back through the tunnel only once. On a warm night in early June, he arrived unannounced carrying a precious packet of tea and sugar for Elena, chocolate for Rija. In the fading light, Elena's face reflected pride and pain as she listened to her son's stories of the fighting. At one point, she lifted up his sleeve, pointing to dried blood on a bandage underneath. "Doni, what is that?"

"A landmine exploded. I was carrying Alani, trying to get him to the medic. It was only after I put him down that I noticed shrapnel in my arm."

"Alani?" Rija asked.

A cloud crossed his eyes. "We met that first night, going through the tunnel. He was only sixteen years old. There wasn't enough air down there and he got dizzy. I helped him out, and after that he was always tagging along with us. Josef told me to duck him, and I begged him to go home. Then it was too late."

Just before Christmas, Josef came with news that Doni, too, was dead. Artillery fire had rained down on them as they rode a truck on the road to Banja Luka. Thirty-seven of the Shadow's men were wounded that day, and six soldiers died. Doni was buried in an unmarked grave at the side of the road. Josef tried to leave a stone marker, but they would never know exactly where.

Elena shrank inside herself that day, and hope drained from her eyes. Their only keepsakes were his soccer medals displayed in a frame on the mantel and the picture taken the day he marched in the Olympic parade.

Chapter 11

Mama, did you forget the cookies? Everyone is bringing food for our Day of Many Nations. I promised Ms. Gardner I would bring in cookies for our party."

Oh God, what day was it? How could she have forgotten the cookies? Her panic subsided as she thought how wonderful it was that Lili had regained her zest for school. She blessed Ms. Gardner for her help. The teacher had kept her word and found a way to help Lili feel safe from the boys who teased her. She wondered if the Day of Many Nations might be part of Ms. Gardner's plan to encourage the children to value each other more.

Lili planted herself directly in front of Rija's chair. "I said you would make cookies, the most beautiful cookies in the world. Can you make them now?"

Rija's head ached, and her brain was foggy. She had hoped to work on her class assignment this morning; instead, she dragged herself to the kitchen where a quick inspection confirmed her suspicions. There was flour and sugar, but no nuts, butter, or chocolate.

"What time is the party, draga?"

"Ms. Gardner said it's before lunch. Can you make the cookies, Mama?"

Rija nodded. "Yes, I promise."

Satisfied, Lili trotted happily into the bathroom.

Elena whispered to Rija, "You take her to school, I will make the cookies."

Rija kissed her mother's hand.

Rija stopped at a local market on her way home from Lili's school and bought butter, nuts, and raisins with what little money she had. When she got to the apartment, she found Elena in the kitchen, pans ready, and the oven casting off heat. An hour later, the cookies were wrapped and ready to go.

Rija handed Elena her coat and scarf. "Here, Mama, put these on. We're going to school for the Day of Many Nations."

"Oh, no. No." Elena shook her head. She looked down at what she was wearing. "I have nothing to wear to a party."

"We're going to school for the Day of Many Nations, and it doesn't matter what we wear. It will help Lili if we are there."

Elena nodded.

In Room 203, the Day of Many Nations was already under way as Rija and Elena arrived with their offering. Lili squealed with excitement as she watched her mother unwrap the tray. "Where were you, Mama? I was waiting for you."

Lili grabbed a cookie and presented it to Ms. Gardner, who nibbled a corner of the pastry with exaggerated relish. Wide-eyed, Lili searched the teacher's face for approval until Ms. Gardner declared, "Lili, this cookie is certainly one of the best I've ever eaten."

Lili pulled her mother and grandmother across the room toward parents and relatives hovering over a long table. Savory aromas of garlic and spices wafted up from an array of food offerings, reminding Rija she hadn't eaten since the night before.

Elena's eyes, bright with pride, watched silently as Lili pirouetted around the table. Lili stopped in front of a little girl with dark glossy braids and looked up at Elena. "Baba, this is Karen. She's my best friend in the whole world."

Karen's mother smiled hello as she dug into a red-sauced casserole. She welcomed Elena with a nod toward the food. "Come try my kielbasa."

Elena grabbed a paper plate in time to catch the sauce dripping from slices of sausage that Karen's mother was holding in a large wooden spoon. Nodding in appreciation, Elena chewed enthusiastically, pronouncing the dish, "*Wyborny*! Delicious!"

Karen's mother beamed at Elena's Polish compliment and filled another spoon for her new friend. Rija was thrilled to see Elena and Karen's mother engage in a friendly conversation that was half-Polish and half-English. Scooping a portion from a tray of arroz con pollo, Rija managed to savor a few bites before Ms. Gardner clapped her hands for silence.

"Children, I want to thank you for inviting your families today. Parents, thank you for coming and for sharing your food of many lands. Next Thursday, you'll be celebrating Thanksgiving with your families at home, but here today we can also be thankful for the many ways that people from all backgrounds live and work together. I'm proud to see the way all of us at St. Casmir's co-operate and enjoy our differences."

The adults nodded and smiled and returned to conversations with newfound friends. The children resumed their boisterous activity, and the food continued to disappear.

An hour later it was time to go. As Rija looked on, Elena retrieved the empty cookie tray and then approached Ms. Gardner. Nodding and smiling, she shook the teacher's hand.

Rija was proud of Elena's efforts at the party. Devastated by her own losses, Rija had not spared many thoughts for her once sociable mother, who must have felt even more isolated than she.

Outside, as they turned toward home, Rija brought up a subject they hadn't discussed in a while. "Mama, if you like, I can find out about the English class. Would you like to try that again?"

Before Elena could answer, a young man in baggy pants cruised past on a skateboard, jostling her arm. The metal tray clattered into the street.

Rija called after him. "Hey, you."

The young man, deaf to everything but what his headphones were blaring into his ears, sailed on, totally oblivious. The light turned red and traffic stopped. Elena stepped from the curb to retrieve the tray. As she bent low, a taxi hurtled around the corner.

"Mama!" Rija screamed. For one horrifying moment her eyes locked onto the eyes of the driver wrestling the wheel in an effort to steer clear of her mother. A metal scream of brakes hung in the air. Time stood still as a fender hurled Elena to the ground. The vehicle jumped the curb and came to rest with a crunch against the metal base of a parking meter.

Turban askew, the driver emerged from the taxi, his dark complexion ashen above a salt-and-pepper beard. He ran to where Elena lay. "So sorry, miss. Too late, I saw her too late. So sorry."

The sight of her mother's body on the gritty asphalt, her leg angled unnaturally, was a nightmare. Rija knelt, gently wiping a smudge of dirt from her mother's cheek. "Mama, can you hear me?"

Elena's eyelids fluttered open, and Rija tried to lift her head. Her mother's stare, alarmingly blank, lasted only seconds before her head fell back and her eyes closed.

Rija watched the cabbie punch in 9-1-1. Within minutes, sirens filled the air. A police car arrived, then another. At the sight of two officers bending over her, Elena cried out, struggling to rise before she fainted again.

"Stay where you are, ma'am," the officer cautioned. "An ambulance is on the way."

Traffic inched around a second officer who was waving the gawkers past. Pacing at the curb, the cabbie addressed no one and everyone, so distraught he could only stammer, "So sorry. I am so sorry."

Rija watched him follow a third officer back to his vehicle. With shaking hands he produced the insurance and registration documents from the visor above the steering wheel, finally handing over his license. "My record is clean, sir. I have never before had an accident."

"Well, you've got one now," the cop said.

An ambulance maneuvered into position, and two medical technicians jumped out. They opened the ambulance door wide and pulled out a litter. After checking Elena for injuries, they applied an inflatable splint to her left leg and lifted her from the pavement to the litter. They wheeled it to the ambulance and secured it inside. Rija clambered in behind. As sirens blasted, the policeman waved the vehicle into traffic with the flattened tray.

Their journey ended outside Northeastern Hospital's emergency room entrance. The ambulance crew wheeled Elena's litter through double doors and into the emergency room, where she was transferred to a hospital litter and put in "room 6," not a real room but a small area enclosed by curtains, part of a row of similar areas.

Rija retrieved the medical card from her mother's purse. After whispering a promise to return quickly, she took a deep breath and approached the registration desk.

In the waiting area, she passed a small slice of distressed humanity hunkered down to wait their turns at relief. A young man held a bloodied towel around his neck. Across the room, two children lay dozing next to a man who might be their father. Head back and eyes closed, he cradled his arm in a homemade sling. The woman next to him thumbed through a magazine.

At the registration desk, Rija cleared her throat loudly to attract the attention of the clerk on duty, who was talking on the telephone. "Please, my mother was in an accident. She was hit by a car."

The clerk ended her telephone conversation and looked up from her computer screen. Reluctantly, she made eye contact with Rija. "Name?"

"My mother's name is Elena Petric."

"Insurance?"

Rija handed over the precious card with its life-saving information. She watched nervously as the clerk's fingers flew over the keyboard.

"Address?"

"Thirty-three forty-three Mercer St. Apartment 2A."

Rija recited all the correct numbers and returned to where Elena lay on the litter. She eyed the clock intermittently as staff in matching blue walked back and forth across the floor. After an hour, Rija approached a woman in a white coat carrying a cup of coffee and talking on a cell phone. "I think my mother's leg is broken. Please, can you help her quickly? Please."

The woman, halted in mid-conversation, held up a finger as though requesting a momentary pause in the proceedings and moved toward the swinging door. "Let me try to find an orderly. I'll be right back." The doors swung behind her.

While Rija waited for the promised orderly to appear, the injured man and his family were called for treatment. Soon after, a woman in jeans and a sweatshirt helped an elderly man with a cane into a chair and then left. As the minutes moved by, Rija realized that school would be out soon.

In the corridor she found a telephone and called their neighbor Tess. "I'm at the hospital with my mother. She was in an accident." The lump of pain that rose in her throat made it hard to talk.

"Rija, are you still there?" Tess asked.

"Yes, I'm sorry, Tess. Can you pick Lili up?"

"Don't worry," Tess told her. "She can come home with Timmy. They'll have a good time playing Candyland."

She promised to give Lili supper. "Timmy loves Lili. He'll be thrilled to have her stay."

Twenty minutes later, a nurse called from the corridor. "Mrs. Petric?"

Rija, dozing in spite of herself, awoke with a jerk at the sound of her mother's name. "Over here," she said as she stood up and waved.

A nurse in blue scrubs approached. She removed the inflatable splint and gave a quick glance at Elena's leg. She looked at Rija. "Didn't you tell them this was an emergency? That leg needs an X-ray!"

An orderly wheeled Elena into the corridor where they waited again. Finally, another orderly wheeled Elena onto the elevator and took her to the second floor and the Radiology Department.

Rija waited in the front area of the Radiology Department. A young doctor eventually appeared and confirmed that Elena's leg was fractured. "We'll need to admit her," he told Rija. "It may well be that your mother will need surgery on that leg."

That night Rija slept next to her mother's bed in the hospital. When Elena's groans woke her after midnight, she pressed the call buzzer, waited, then pressed again. The nurse's station was empty, but Rija spied a nurse down the hall backing out of what appeared to be a supply closet. Rija approached her and got her attention. "My mother's in pain. Can you give her something?"

"What's her room number?" the nurse asked.

"We're in 317."

"I'll get the medication and bring it down to her," she promised over her shoulder.

Next morning before seven, Rija watched Elena disappear down the hall on her way to the operating room, where a Dr. John Randolph would insert a rod into her shattered leg.

Three hours later, a nurse in scrubs found Rija in the lounge. "Are you the daughter?" she asked.

Rija nodded. "How is she?"

"Your mother's doing well. She's in recovery now. You'll be able to go in to see her shortly. God bless her, she's a very strong woman."

Elena remained in the hospital five more days. Beginning with her second day, she never missed an opportunity to declare, "I want to go home."

The nurses and aides who came in to take her vital signs, bathe her, and serve her meals heard it several times a day. So did anyone else who came within earshot.

"Mama, I see you can speak English when you need to," Rija teased her.

"Rija, why I stay here? I want to go home."

"Soon, Mama, very soon. Your leg needs to heal."

Once she was able to stand with help, Elena was transferred to a rehabilitation facility for a week of physical therapy. There, Rija acted as her mother's translator, explaining the exercises the physical therapist wanted her to do. Little by little, the strength in Elena's arms grew, allowing her to pull herself up more easily, but any weight on the leg caused her to wince in pain.

Without her mother's help, Rija's days seemed to have no end. She was lucky to get four or five hours of sleep before it was time to get her daughter ready for school. Once Lili was safely deposited in the schoolyard, Rija walked the ten blocks to the rehab hospital.

In the afternoon she picked up Lili, and they ate a quick meal. Then it was time for Rija to lead a sulky Lili upstairs to Tess Gallagher's so she could go to work. Strangely, the job now felt like a haven. Quiet, dark, and free of humanity, the dimly lit offices with their wastebaskets to be emptied and floors to be vacuumed allowed Rija a sense of control.

By the end of Elena's week of rehab, it was obvious that her incision was not healing properly. The leg was red, swollen, and painful to the touch. Rija begged the nurses to check it, and the aide promised to call the doctor. The doctor came the next day, his first appearance of the week. After checking Elena's leg, he told Rija it was infected and her mother would have to be readmitted to the hospital to have it treated properly. He directed the nurse to call for an ambulance, and she was transferred that night.

Back in the hospital, a dazed Elena was too tired to even ask to go home. Rija kept a vigil in Elena's room, watching the IV slowly deliver antibiotics to kill the bacteria, praying for her mother's health, and fearing for their survival. Rija slept in a chair next to the bed and woke with a stiff neck.

Rija knew she wouldn't be able to work that night. She dreaded the call to Mr. Fowler, the one where she'd have to tell him that she would be missing more shifts, precious hours lost, time she wouldn't get paid for. There was a pay phone near the hospital cafeteria. Rija dialed Fowler's number. She held her breath, waited for him to answer, and then blurted out her situation.

"That's too bad, kid," he told her. "You were doin' pretty good. You've been a good worker, but the 19th to 22nd floors won't clean themselves, you know." He laughed at his own joke.

"I know," Rija said.

"I think there's a check here waiting for you. What with the holidays coming up, you can probably use it. I'll send what we owe, and you call me when you can come back."

Rija hung up. Fowler's comment about the holiday jolted her back to the here and now. How had she missed seeing the Christmas tree in the hospital lobby? What day was it? She didn't even know.

She walked to the woman at the information desk. "Excuse me, miss. What is today's date?"

The woman held up a calendar and pointed. "Today is Tuesday, December 15th."

Rija thanked her and turned away. Oh God, one more thing to

worry over. One more thing to plague her thoughts on the daily trips between the hospital, Lili's school, and home. How would she ever be able to find time to decorate a tree or even buy a gift for Lili?

She walked slowly, deep in thought, eyes on the ground, struggling against the bitterness of it all. She thought about the war, their broken lives, their coming to America. She wondered why it had to happen. How would it be if they were still in Sarajevo? Would her mother be her old self, with friends and neighbors to help her? At least she wouldn't need to struggle with the language, with the doctors, with any of it. But they weren't in Sarajevo, they were here.

Two days after Elena's return to the hospital, Rija felt a chill as she walked Lili to school. She had a sudden sensation that she was being watched. She looked around and noticed a white SUV at the corner of Madison Street. Outside the schoolyard, she saw it again. She put it out of her mind and squeezed Lili's hand as they walked up the steps to the school's front door.

On her way back to the apartment, she glanced over her shoulder as she turned onto Belgrade and saw the white SUV behind her. A familiar voice called her name.

She froze. She should have known it could be only one person, the same person who was responsible for all their troubles and struggles. The car pulled alongside. She set her jaw and turned to face it.

Josef was just as she remembered him. His sandy hair was thick and a little shaggy, his gray eyes wide and pleading. He had dark smudges under his eyes that made him look older than she remembered.

Rija turned and began to run. And then she stopped. Why should she run from him? She had done no wrong. She turned and glared at the car as it slowly approached her and slid into an open space. Josef got out. He wanted something, she could tell by the look on his face. Rija walked to where Josef stood on the sidewalk. He opened his arms with a shrug and a smile. She swung a fist at him but he caught her. She pulled free and swung her handbag, landed a blow on his cheek. The anger that had smoldered for three years had erupted into a blaze.

"If I had a gun, I would kill you."

Josef rubbed his cheek. "No you wouldn't."

"I curse you for a coward and a liar."

Josef looked surprised. "I deserve your anger, but I still love you all the same."

She felt her anger ebb slightly. She almost wanted to believe him. He put his arms around her, tentatively, and she didn't pull away. She let him hold her as she fought back tears. She felt a bewildering mix of resentment and relief.

Josef's eyes too were wet. He was exultant. "I found you! I found you at last."

"We weren't lost. You were the one who disappeared."

"I'm so sorry. What can I say? That was the biggest mistake of my life." Josef stared at the ground in a gesture designed to convey regret.

Rija's eyes flashed. "More than a mistake. You didn't say a word. You threw us to the wolves. You brought us to America and then you left us with nothing."

"Let me explain. I got fired. I was ashamed. And I thought my cousin would help you. I know what I did was wrong."

"It was worse than wrong. And how could your cousin help us? They had nothing themselves. They had their own troubles. We were on welfare. We were alone in a strange country. Do you know what that is like?"

Rija fought back tears. She felt the eyes of the neighborhood at their windows watching her life unfold. Let them watch.

"And now, after all this time, you come back. Your daughter doesn't even know you."

"She can get to know me now."

"Life for us was getting better," Rija continued. "Without you. I got a job. I started going to school. But a car hit mama. Her leg was broken, and it doesn't heal right. I have no one to watch Lili."

Josef spread his arms wide. "But dearest wife, this is why I am here." He reached for her hand. "The angels sent me. I'm here to help."

"Angels, angels?" Rija snorted. "You're here because it suits you. You're here until you decide to leave again."

Josef fixed her with a pleading look that she recognized. "I'm different now. You can trust me." He tried to catch her in another hug, but she dodged away from him.

"Trust you?" Her laugh sounded like a bark. "For how long? Until you decide to leave us again? Will you disappear and leave your daughter with no father for the second time?"

"No, I promise I will stay for as long as you want me to stay. I'll do whatever you ask."

Across the street, the mailman peered over his shoulder at them, then looked away quickly. Shame-faced, Rija grabbed the railing for support. As they went inside, she fought away the kiss he planted on the nape of her neck.

The heart she thought she'd buried deep within hammered boldly against her ribs. In the vestibule, Josef spun her toward him, catching her lower lip in his teeth, holding it in a gentle teasing bite. Rija felt dizzy. Her breasts ached. With a man's arms holding her close, her body grew heavy. They clung together in an embrace that for Rija was half anger, half passion.

Later, Rija would feel the weight of other eyes, the curious stares of the parents as she and Josef walked into the schoolyard. She often told Lili that with her wide gray eyes and high cheekbones, she looked like her father. How would she introduce Josef to his daughter? Would the child know him from the one blurred photo she kept in her drawer?

Children jostled each other as they ran down the stairs in their dash to the playground. And at the end of a wiggling stream of first graders, there was Lili racing toward her. Focused only on her mother's face, she stopped short at the sight of the stranger next to her.

Rija hoped her smile was reassuring. "Lili, this is your papa. Say hello."

Josef knelt in front of his daughter. "My darling Lili. I have missed you so much. I'm so glad to see you."

He held out his hand and the child hesitated before peeking up shyly,"Hello, Papa."

Back at the apartment, Rija sliced lemons, filled teacups, and carried them to the table. She was glad for something to do with her hands. She poured her daughter a glass of milk before filling a plate with animal crackers. Josef sipped his tea, oblivious to Lili's stares. Rija watched her daughter, wondered what she was thinking and feeling.

With the natural frankness of a six-year-old, Lili's questions were blunt. "Where did you come from, Papa? Why are you here?"

Josef cleared his throat. "When your Mama and I first came here, I was working, but I had an argument with my boss. I was ashamed to tell your mama what happened, so I left. I went away."

"But where did you go?"

"Papa left to find a new job. I traveled across the country, until one day I found a job far away from here. I always planned to have you and Mama come and live with me there, but it didn't turn out." He shrugged.

Wide-eyed, Lili nibbled a lion cracker and drank her milk, but her eyes never left Josef. She seemed to be waiting for more.

"But I missed you and Mama so much that I had to travel many, many miles to come back home to you. And now Mama needs my help to take care of you, and here I am. And I wanted to find a way to be with you for Christmas."

Lili cocked her head to one side as she concentrated on his words. "Can we have a tree?"

"Yes, I will get you the most beautiful Christmas tree ever. I promise."

Then, seemingly satisfied, Lili jumped down and ran to answer a knock on the door.

It was Timmy Gallagher, their five-year-old neighbor. "Lili, want to go the playground with me and my mom?"

Rija turned to the youngster. "I don't think so, Timmy. Lili's father is here."

Josef held out a hand. "Hello, Timmy."

The little boy shook it before he turned back to Lili. "Okay, I guess you can't go then."

"Can I, Mama?"

"Yes, if you're sure you want to. Just take off your uniform first."

Rija and Josef exchanged a look.

The day before Christmas was bright and cold. Josef smiled a greeting as Rija and the nurse wheeled Elena out to where the SUV idled at the hospital entrance. He opened the passenger door. "I hope you will be comfortable, Elena." He adjusted the seat. "Is it warm enough for you?"

Elena merely nodded wordlessly before she sank back against the leather headrest and closed her eyes.

Later, when she had time to consider, Rija wondered at her mother's unquestioning acceptance of Josef's reappearance in their lives. Was she so disoriented by her injuries that she'd forgotten the years of his absence? Or, after the loss of both Papa and Doni, was her mother simply glad to have a familiar male presence back in their lives?

Josef, too, surprised her with the way he reconnected with the family. Hovering over Elena during her first day back home, he brought her endless cups of tea and helped her to the toilet whenever she called out. He won Lili's heart with a glittering Christmas tree and the toys she found underneath it on Christmas morning.

Even though she mistrusted this new domesticity, Rija appreciated the growing relationship between the three of them for the measure of freedom it allowed her as she tried to resume her life of work and school. The first Saturday after New Year's, Rija prepared her class assignment, checked on Elena, gathered her books, and made for the door.

"Where to now?" Josef asked.

"I told you, I have class on Saturdays."

"Don't sound so angry, I just forgot what day it is."

When Lili looked up from her cartoons, Rija softened her tone. "Mama is still sleeping. Her breakfast is on the kitchen table. I'll be home by 1:30."

"Do you want me to drive you?"

"No, I'll take the trolley." Feeling both liberated and ashamed, she closed the door behind her.

Josef bonded with his mother-in-law, accepting her as an ally. When they were alone together in the apartment, Elena enticed her son-in-law into conversing with her in their native language, something Rija did less and less. Though happy to comply, Josef remembered learning English from movies and television, and he encouraged his mother-in-law to give it a try. Making a game of American TV commercials, he teased Elena into repeating the words to jingles. They laughed together as she mouthed the words to their favorites, "Can you hear me now?," "You can't beat the great taste of Bud," and "Leggo my Eggo."

The programs Elena watched became her English tutors. One of her favorites, The Price Is Right, was especially effective. Elena loved pricing and bargaining on the household goods contestants bid for. Rija was encouraged one morning to hear her mother's enthusiasm as she called out, in English, "Higher, go higher."

Josef also prodded Elena into sticking to her daily exercise routine. He could even inspire her to give the walker a try, but there was little room for an extended trial in their small space. The few times she needed to leave the apartment, Josef carried his mother-in-law down the stairs where they waited together on the sidewalk for the transport van that would take her to physical therapy. Once she was comfortably ensconced inside, he climbed into the seat beside her.

Initially, the physical therapist was pleased by her progress. "Elena, your leg is getting much stronger. What's your secret?"

Josef translated for Elena, who pointed at her son-in-law with a smile. "She says that I am her secret. I make her practice her exercises every day."

Then, mysteriously, the leg began again to swell. At the next visit, the therapist recommended taking Elena to the doctor.

Calls to Dr. Randolph at his Orthopedic Specialties Clinic yielded only a message-taking assistant who advised she would phone in a prescription. "The doctor says that should do the trick. Just make sure she finishes taking the whole thing."

Rija picked up the antibiotics before she went to work and made sure Josef and Elena understood the instructions. But as night fell, the leg became more swollen, and when Josef picked Rija up at the end of her shift, he was concerned. "I was almost afraid to leave. She can't walk on it, and I think she has a fever."

Rija's face turned ashen. "Take her back to the emergency room. She has to go tonight."

Elena was readmitted at 2 a.m. Two hours later the resident ordered an antibiotic drip. The nurse on duty informed Rija that her mother had another bacterial infection.

Rija dozed at her mother's bedside, waking as the aide entered to take the first vital signs of the day. Through the morning and afternoon she prayed for the swelling in her mother's leg to go down. Rija beckoned a nurse into the room. "When will I speak with her doctor?"

The woman checked Elena's chart. "Dr. Randolph is listed as your mother's surgeon, but he's on vacation. I'll remind the resident to check on her this afternoon. He can request an examination when they do rounds."

Rija tried to coax her mother with a few spoonfuls of soup, but Elena refused it and could not even be tempted with a sweet roll. The door opened, and Rija looked up as a tall, dark-haired doctor breezed in trailing two white-jacketed students. As he moved closer to the bedside, Rija spied his name, Dr. A. Singh, embroidered on his jacket pocket.

Dr. Singh took Elena's pulse and checked her chart. "Looks like the fever is subsiding. The antibiotics are doing their job," he said to the two students before turning to Rija. "We'll give this one more day."

Rija was gratified to see the color returning to her mother's cheeks, but her mind was far from being at ease. There were so many unanswered questions. As the doctor turned to leave the room, Rija grabbed his arm. "But why does this infection continue?"

Dr. Singh shrugged. "It's more common than we like to see, but according to the rehab report, you mother was doing well enough after she was released."

Rija remembered what a nurse at the therapy center had told her. "But the infection was, I think the word is, dormant in her body. It could come back, even after she leaves."

"There are many reasons why, but poor overall health, not taking medication properly, these are all factors," Dr. Singh said.

That night, Elena's temperature shot up again. For fear of kidney failure, Elena was put on oxygen and then transferred to Intensive Care. Rija waited at the ICU doorway until the young resident on night duty materialized.

"Excuse me, please come."

He followed her to Elena's bedside, scanned her charts, and peered at her electronic monitors. Finally he turned to Rija. "We have one more antibiotic to try. I'm going to try a different drip, but if that doesn't work, dialysis might be her last chance."

Rija moved aside as the nursing staff responded to this new treatment plan. Blinking back tears, she tried to focus beyond the walls of the hospital room. She pressed her forehead against the coolness of the double-paned window. The only movement in the inky darkness was a red-lit river tanker gliding into port.

Later, Rija watched the pale liquid slowly enter Elena's system. She bent down close and sang a favorite folksong in her mother's ear. It was the song Anton always sang to her on their wedding anniversary.

Red wine seven years old.
Brandy from the jar,
Honey baklava in the sun
None sweet as you are.

Willing her mother to live, Rija gripped her hand tighter, until

Elena's eyelids fluttered as though she heard her daughter's words.

Rija awoke as dawn was breaking. As the sky outside the window slowly lightened, Rija stretched and yawned and was suddenly gripped by fear. She turned toward her mother, saw her staring back at her. Ever so slightly, Elena lifted her head off the pillow, pointing to a pitcher on the table. "*Voda*," she whispered. "*Voda*."

Rija held a plastic tumbler to her mother's lips. Elena pulled the oxygen tube from her nose to drink more easily. Her head fell back on the pillow, and she slept again.

When Dr. Singh stopped in on his morning rounds, his face loosened into a grin at the sight of Elena propped up in bed. "Mrs. Petric, good morning. I'm happy to see you awake."

Later in the hallway, Singh told Rija, "I'll tell you the truth, I was very concerned."

Through the day, Elena rallied, and the infection subsided, her legs and arms returning to normal size. The next morning, Rija met first with a social worker with little new information to share beyond continuing therapy and the promise of a visiting nurse once a week.

Walking off tension, Rija paced the hospital halls until she found herself outside glass doors that read, "George Constantine, Hospital Administrator." Beyond the vacant reception area, a heavyset man occupied an interior office, his bulk framed against a window. Anger welled up inside her as she pushed open the door and marched in.

Mr. Constantine looked up from his computer screen, his face a mirror of annoyance. "May I help you, miss?"

"My mother is a strong woman." She looked directly into his eyes. "She has survived many terrors in her life."

The administrator picked up the phone. "Margaret, send Security to my office, now!"

Rija continued unfazed. "She survived the bombs and snipers in Sarajevo to come to this country. Now she almost dies because of what? A bacteria? Can you explain this to me?"

For the first time, Constantine looked at her as though she didn't have two heads. "I'm sorry but I don't know what you're talking about."

"The nurse at the rehab hospital told me that many people become ill when they're in the hospital. She said she knows many people get the infection in this hospital."

Constantine raised his eyebrows. "And may I ask the name of that nurse?"

Even before Rija could answer, a security guard appeared at the door. Constantine caught the guard's eye, motioning his head in Rija's direction. "Miss, our hospital strives to provide the best care for all its patients. I am sorry for her illness. Perhaps her age and past history might have been a contributing factor to poor health."

"You don't care a thing about my mother, do you?"

"Excuse me, Miss. I have other matters that require my attention." He turned back to his computer screen.

Taking the cue, the security guard made his move. Firm hand on her elbow, he guided her to the door. "Sorry, Miss. You'll have to go now."

When Elena returned home three days later, Lili was waiting with a bouquet of flowers for her grandmother. Before anyone could say a word, she jumped up to plant a kiss on her grandmother's cheek.

Elena smiled weakly. "*Bacila me ne moze*."

Josef translated for Lili. "She says germs can't kill her."

Lili danced around the living room chanting, "Baba's home and germs can't kill her."

Josef helped Elena to the day bed of cushions and a quilt Rija had fashioned in the living room. As she watched her husband caring for her mother, a door opened in her thoughts and she remembered Josef with his own mother in Sarajevo.

After Doni was gone, Josef chose to let the Shadow fight on without him. He was needed at home. His family's apartment was shelled to ruins, and his mother, Anna, was gravely ill. His younger sister, Katja, was left to fend for their bedridden mother and for Dina, the youngest. Soon, Josef moved them to an abandoned flat on a different street. While there was no heat in the new building and the stove was gone, their days were quieter, the sounds of the artillery further away.

Whenever Elena could, she invited the Malacoviks for meals, and Josef never came empty-handed. Ever eager to see what Josef brought, Rija was seldom disappointed. But the night he appeared with a live chicken was the most memorable meal of those hungry times.

Even Elena, a master forager, was shocked. "Josef, where did you find this chicken?"

"The Dutch reporters gave me a bottle of gin. I traded it for a carton of cigarettes. For the cigarettes, I found a farmer in the market who gave me the chicken and some vegetables. He pulled two carrots from his pocket, grinning at his accomplishment. "And now everybody is happy, no?"

Before anyone could protest, Elena took the chicken up to the roof, returning thirty minutes later with a perfectly plucked and dressed bird. She added Josef's carrots and some wild onions to a pot of boiling water and soon a lovely fragrance wafted from the stewpot.

Josef, Anna, Katja, and Dina relaxed in the warmth of Elena's kitchen. That day, Elena took care to make sure that Dina and Anna were well fed, tempting them with the most nourishing morsels. Afterwards, Katja and Rija dutifully cleared the table, boiling water to wash the empty plates as 11-year-old Dina contentedly sucked on a chicken bone.

Little by little, Josef, Katja, Dina, and Anna moved into the Petric apartment. The girls arrived with bedding and their few clothes. Anna, suffering from stomach ulcers, took up residence on the old sofa and slept there most of the day. Katja made herself useful, carrying water from the barrel on the roof where rainwater collected for washing.

Dina's sprightly antics distracted Elena and Rija from their grief over Doni and Anton. There was comfort in watching the child as she sang to herself, spinning and dancing to music only she could hear. The presence of Dina's mother, Anna, was a blessing as well, and Elena threw herself wholeheartedly into nursing her. The two women sat by the hour, sharing stories of their lives, poring over old photographs, precious pictures of their children as babies. Anna kept her few treasures in a frayed brocade bag that never left her side.

Some days the guns were silent. But the Serbs, pressured by the foreign troops nearby, increased their shelling and sniper fire. Whenever Dina's blue eyes grew wide at the sound of guns, Josef took heed. In a silly girlish voice, he called out to her. "Oh Dina, my little Dina. Look at me, look at your Josefina."

He wiggled his ears and wrapped his kerchief around his head, crossed his eyes and stuck out his tongue until he was satisfied with the child's bursts of laughter.

Through dark winter nights Josef told stories of the war, of being chased by the Serbian White Eagle militia, trading with the UN soldiers, or translating for foreign reporters. He described long journeys through the tunnel carrying a backpack full of luxury goods to trade.

"The tunnel is sometimes the only way out of Sarajevo. You walk for miles. Sometimes there's not enough air to breathe. But you must keep going, because at the end, there is freedom."

They all profited from his hours spent trudging through the airless darkness like a pack mule. The cigarettes, the chocolate, and even a bottle of French brandy were coin of the realm in their ravaged city. On the streets or in the Alpasina marketplace it was not difficult to find someone willing to trade ten kilos of flour or a kilo of sugar for a prized carton of Marlboros.

Thinking back, Rija remembered the careless teasing she'd suffered at his hands as a child. Now that she was the object of his attentions, Josef both fascinated and embarrassed her. She wouldn't have admitted it to anyone, least of all him, but she felt more alive when Josef was in the room. One day he slipped a new tube of lipstick into her hand, and the gesture brought tears to her eyes. Despite her ragged attire and unruly hair, he made her feel desirable.

Ever since Mira, her best friend, had disappeared, Rija missed someone her own age to talk to. Though she was older than fifteen-year-old Katja, they were very much alike. Her lovely gray eyes and straw-colored hair resembled the coloring of her brother, but she had a different manner, and Rija trusted the quiet, sincere way Katja spoke. Rija blessed Josef for bringing his sisters into their lives. Using textbooks saved from her student days, Rija spent time each morning tutoring Dina and checking the work Katja did on her own.

A month after they moved in, Josef brought a nurse to the apartment to examine his mother. In exchange, he promised her a leather jacket as payment for venturing out into the streets at night. She examined Anna, encouraging her to eat, to keep her strength up. Able to do little more than a laying on of hands, the nurse smoothed the sick woman's hair before she left Anna resting on the battered sofa. Out in the hallway, Josef handed her the jacket. Her eyes had a faraway look as she stroked the soft leather with her fingers.

But when Josef asked her what she thought, the nurse shook her head. "I am so sorry. The hospitals are full. We have no supplies, no medicine. There is no chance of finding a bed for your mother. Without the proper treatment," she said, her eyes on Josef's face, "I'm afraid there is no hope."

Elena could see that the light was fading from Anna's eyes. Still she made dandelion tea and spooned it into Anna's open mouth. She found wild garlic growing in the park near the market place and ground it into a paste for Anna to spread on her bread. Having someone to care for gave Elena a reason to get up in the morning. It helped to ease the loss of her husband and son.

Eventually Anna could no longer sit up because of the pain it caused her. "You are so kind to us," she said one day as Elena rearranged the pillows on the sofa where the sick woman spent her days.

Josef popped into the room where Anna lay. His broad smile couldn't mask the apprehension around his eyes. "Mima, look what I have for you."

With a flourish, he pulled an orange from his knapsack. "Shall I peel it for you?" he asked.

He sat close by his mother and took her hand in his. Anna looked up at her son, love brightening her tired face. "An orange? Where did you find an orange?"

"Oh, Mima, you know me. I was helping the UN troops when they got a food shipment airlifted in. I have one for Dina, too, and a loaf of bread."

He began peeling the orange for his mother. Suddenly, she gripped his hand, crying out in pain. Hearing Anna's cry, Elena ran into the room. Josef moved away from his mother's bedside making room for Elena, who stroked Anna's hand and held her head up off the pillow for a sip of water. Forgotten, the orange rolled to the floor.

The next morning, Katja woke to find her mother's hands cold and stiff under the quilt. She called out to her brother, and together they knelt beside her, praying silently. Later Elena and Rija prepared the body, gently washing Anna's face, hands, and feet before clothing her thin frame in her only decent garment, a rose-colored dress with a frayed lace collar. After Josef removed Anna's wedding ring, Elena insisted that Katja take her mother's gold earrings and Dina take her gold locket with the broken chain.

Rija carried the gold chain out into the hallway where the child sat silently on the steps. "Dina, shall we open the locket and see the picture inside?"

Dina shook her head.

"Dina, please, may I look? I want see the picture inside."

Rija sprung the catch, revealing a curled wisp of blond hair and the tiny picture of a baby girl. She held the locket out. "Dina, I think this is you when you were a baby. What do you think?"

Dina's eyes filled with tears, and she turned away. Rija closed the locket, placing it in the child's palm and closing her fingers around it. She wiped away the tear that had fallen on her own hand. They both sat silent until Dina's head collapsed against Rija's shoulder and her back shook with her sobs.

Word spread quickly through the building, and neighbors came with offers of help. Down on the second floor, Marko built a simple pine box from wood Josef had bartered for in the market. Next morning, at dawn, before the day's shelling began, he and Josef loaded the coffin into a pushcart while the family gathered for the final walk to the Catholic cemetery.

After the homemade service, neighbors came and went, offering what little tokens of food they could and murmuring their respects. Josef sat on the sofa, his arms around Dina and Katja, who were mute and devastated by their loss. Finally, Josef broke the silence. He gazed at the photo of their mother as a young girl, one they'd found in her old brocade purse. "Mima was so beautiful. I always want to remember her this way."

Elena did her best to comfort the two girls, and Dina clung to her. But Josef chose to deny his pain. Once everyone had gone, he escaped into the streets in search of distraction. Late that night, he returned drunk. Rija heard him stumble and curse his way into the sleeping apartment before he opened her door, whispering, "Are you awake?"

Rija sat up in bed, a cover over her chest. Never before had he come into her room uninvited. He knelt next to the bed. When their eyes met, she drew him closer. His breath smelled of alcohol, but Rija didn't push him away. She was tired, she was sad, and the warmth of his body was comforting. She let him stay.

Elena grew even closer to Katja and Dina. She washed their clothes, hanging them to dry near the window. Dina followed Elena as she moved around the apartment, and when Elena sat to rest, Dina crawled into her lap. Katja offered to go with her as she went to collect wood. Rija tried to find time every day to sit with the girls, solving simple arithmetic problems and reading from the books they had read so many times before.

Two weeks after the funeral, a delighted Josef brought a stranger to the door. Tall, with a drooping moustache, dressed in a farmer's rough clothing, the man had to duck under the doorway to enter. "Katja, Dina," Josef called. "Look who is here."

The girls appeared, looking mystified.

"It's your Uncle Zoltan," Josef said, and clapped the man on the back. "I found him in the marketplace."

"Don't you remember me?" the stranger asked.

Despite his kind smile, Dina shook her head no.

"Katja, you must know me. Don't you remember your aunt Maida and your cousin Basha?"

"You must remember," Josef insisted. "Summers when we visited our cousins Basha and Milos in the mountains near Bijela?"

"Katja, you came and stayed with us before your sister was born. We took you and Basha for a ride in the pony cart. And you wanted to milk the goats. Don't you remember?"

Katja's eyes widened. "The pony, her name was Greta. I remember her."

Zoltan smiled, and Elena offered to make tea.

Zoltan looked at his watch. "I must go back soon."

Rija wondered why Josef had pulled his mother's bag from behind the sofa.

As though something had been decided, Zoltan pointed to the bag. "Pack your things," he said to Katja. You and your sister can come and stay with us. We'll go back through the tunnel tonight. You can help us on the farm."

"The farm?" Dina asked.

"Our farm is many miles from here, near Bijela. There is not so much fighting," Zoltan told her. "We have food. You can go to school again with Basha."

"You'll be safe in Bijela, Katja," Josef said. "When the war is over, I'll come and get you."

Though Josef stayed on after Katja and Dina left, the apartment felt empty. Rija missed her quiet talks with Katja, the songs of young Dina. But after a month had passed, another worry filled her mind. Josef had begun to talk of leaving as well. He told her of his dream of going to America. Rija tried to convince herself that she didn't care, but a sense of dread was enveloping her. She had to admit that his crazy talk, even his wildest ideas, gave her hope.

"Admit it," he taunted her as they lay side by side to keep warm. In the candlelight, she could see his eyes lit up. "You would miss me."

"I'd only miss the crazy things you manage to drag home with you."

"No, that's not all. You might also miss this." He turned to face her and his arms held her tightly as he kissed her slowly and searchingly with great expertise. She responded, knowing he was right.

Chapter 12

Marti looked up and smiled when she saw Rija. "Hey there, I didn't know you still worked here."

Rija smiled and blushed. It felt like an eternity since she'd last been on the 22nd floor. "My mother was ill," she said. "She's okay now."

"I'm glad she's better."

Rija emptied the wastebasket. "I wanted to tell you that I don't need the skip trace now."

"Why, did you find your husband?" Marti asked.

"No, he found me."

Marti scrutinized Rija's face. "Is that a good thing?"

Rija lowered her gaze. "I'm not sure. He sleeps on the couch. He helps my mother, he's a father to Lili, and he is kind to me. But does he tell the truth? That I don't know."

She thought about the white SUV. She wanted to ask him about it, but she didn't want to hear any more lies, so she had put off asking.

"Keep me posted," Marti said. She got up from her chair and grabbed her belongings. "I'm giving myself the night off. Tomorrow is my birthday."

"Happy birthday, Marti. I hope you enjoy yourself."

"Thanks." She gave Rija's shoulder a pat on her way out.

When it was time for her first break, Rija didn't spend it with Carlene and Luz. Instead, she grabbed her coat and ran across the street to the all-night newsstand, which usually had flowers for sale. She had only four dollars and some change, but it was enough to buy a single red rose, a birthday present for her young lawyer friend who worked so hard.

When she returned to the building, she stopped in the basement to put her coat back in her locker. As she headed toward the elevator to go back upstairs, the elevator doors opened and a tall, well-dressed black man emerged. Without acknowledging Rija, he headed for Fowler's office. There was something familiar about him, yet she couldn't place where she might have seen him before.

The man entered the office and shut the door. As Rija turned back toward the elevator, she heard a low rumble of voices from behind Fowler's door, then a thump, then silence. The office door opened and the visitor strode out, straightening his suit jacket on the way. The elevator doors opened, and the man got on without a word or even a nod to Rija.

She went to the office and peered in. Fowler was slouched in his chair coughing. His file folders, always meticulously stacked, were askew, the papers fanned across the desk. He looked up and saw Rija.

"Are you okay, Mr. Fowler?" she asked. "Are you hurt?"

Rija saw his glasses on the floor. She entered the office and scooped them up, handed them to Fowler. His right eye was tearing and there was a red mark on his cheek.

"Do you want me to call someone? The guard?"

Fowler waved her away. "No, I'm all right. But I better not see that son of a bitch around here again, or there'll be hell to pay."

He fixed her with a warning glance she knew well. "Aren't you supposed to be working?"

"I just came down to put something in my locker, but if you're okay, I will go back up."

Later, Rija puzzled over what it was about the man in the suit that seemed so familiar. She wanted to tell the others what she had seen, but it would have to wait.

The next day, Rija got up earlier than usual. She dressed quickly and waited in the bedroom until Josef and Lili had left the apartment for their walk to Lili's school. Rija peeked in on a sleeping Elena and then picked up Josef's car keys, which he had left on the dining room table. She ran down to the street and opened the SUV's rear hatch. Fast food wrappers, yellowed gas receipts, and old newspapers littered the interior. She opened the spare tire housing and saw a black canvas bag under the tire.

Rija opened the bag and extracted a small snub-nosed revolver. Dull and oily and sticky with dust, the gun's dark metal exuded a strange power. It was not the first time she'd held a gun, and it conjured up memories of an old desire for revenge.

If she'd had a gun that day, things might have been different. The snarling look on the soldier's face as he came toward her would have faded to shock as she pulled out the pistol, held it to his head, and squeezed the trigger. But that didn't happen.

The morning of Mira's sixteenth birthday, January 18, Rija rose early, leaving the apartment before Doni or Elena would be able to stop her. She and Mira had spent birthdays together ever since they'd met in their first-form classroom at age seven, and this year would be no different, even if she had to sneak out to do it. Inside her coat she carried a gift, a collage she'd made from pictures cut from an American music magazine Josef had given her.

Outside, frost had settled on the ground, and the steps were covered in a thin sheet of ice. The wind picked up, and Rija wrapped her gray woolen scarf more tightly around her head before setting off. Signs on every corner warned, "Pazi Snajper"-"Beware Sniper." She looked to the rooftops, hoping the snipers who controlled their comings and goings would still be asleep. But the snipers weren't her only worry. She knew that anyone on the street was a target for artillerymen in the hills above Sarajevo.

Rija took an erratic path through back streets and alleys, behind the red-tiled buildings of their quarter. She listened to the sound of her breath as she inhaled the cold winter air in a meditative rhythm. Like a long-distance runner, she sped past bombed-out concrete-flat blocks of Kalemova Street. The once bustling street of shops and offices, now empty, bore witness to Sarajevo's wasted economy.

Her pace slowed as she turned into Lozionicka Street. This was the corridor they called Sniper Alley. Rija huddled in a doorway, waiting for other pedestrians to appear. As the seconds ticked by, she wondered what it would feel to be shot. Do you hear the sound? Do you feel the bone shattering when the bullet hits?

Two young boys on bicycles sped past, giving cover. Rija ran across the street and turned toward the river. She knew the bridges over the Milajacka River were the most vulnerable spots. Out in the open, there was no place to hide. Just for luck, she carried her mother's rosary in her pocket. She'd need it now. In a defensive crouch, she ran over the bridge, knees bent to present the smallest possible target.

On the other side, an old man moved toward her, slowly pulling a baby carriage loaded with scrap. Oblivious to the danger or not caring, he plodded on, head down. Once across the river, Rija watched him turn unharmed into one of the ruined facades she had left behind.

Rija's heart was pounding, and she gave herself a moment to catch her breath before she turned into Mira's street. How different everything looked, she thought. She searched for familiar landmarks until she found the yellow brick building in the middle of the block. Mira's building, No. 17 Lipa, was once like a second home to her.

The houses on either side looked empty. The front door yawned *open. She looked back toward the street. It was quiet. A voice in her head told her to turn and run, but she persisted. Names on the mailboxes were gone, but she knew Mira's family lived on the fourth floor. She walked into what was once the lobby and saw the ruined elevator hanging suspended above the first floor. She found the stairway just beyond the elevator, and with wobbly legs she climbed the four flights to Mira's apartment. She knocked softly and then pushed open the unlocked door. A few empty boxes and sticks of broken furniture were strewn around the empty living room.*

Rija forced herself to go from room to room, moving toward the back of the apartment. She called out softly, "Mira, Mira."

Hunger reminded her to look for any scraps of food. Only a scratching sound in the back made her jump. The relief she felt when a mouse ran across her foot quickly turned to fear as the apartment door banged shut. Too late, she searched for an escape. A brick courtyard four floors down made jumping impossible. She crept into a kitchen closet and pulled the door behind her. Seconds crept by while she prayed for the intruder to leave. The door jerked open.

A young soldier in the black uniform of the Serbian irregular militia stared in at her. "Why are you hiding, little one?"

"I came to look for my friend, but she is gone."

The soldier's lip curled in a smirk. "Too bad, your friend is not here, eh?"

Rija straightened her coat. "Please, let me pass. I must go."

"You will go when I say you will go. Not before."

He touched her cheek. He was young, she realized, only a few years older than she, no more than 20. His skin would have been smooth were it not for the sparse beard straggling over his cheeks. And he was drunk. His eyes were red. She could smell the stale beer on his breath. Despite the chill of the abandoned building, Rija felt hot perspiration run down her back.

When he pinned her to the wall, she brought her knee up between his legs. A snarl hung in the air as she darted toward the door. He lunged forward and grabbed her hair, pulled her to the floor. He put his knees on her arms and held one hand on her throat as he pulled open his belt buckle and unzipped his trousers. Rija tried to scream but no words came out. He pulled up her skirt and ripped her panties. He cursed through the pain and rubbed himself until he was erect. He thrust himself into her and lunged forward grunting with the effort.

His breath was in her ear, harsh and rasping. The strong smell of sweat that rose up from his unwashed uniform made her gag. Her cheek burned as the rough wool of his jacket rubbed her face as he pushed forward, again and again, battering her body with his hatred. She prayed he would stop, and after a few minutes he let out a groan and rolled over.

Feeling a draft of cold air, Rija pulled down her skirt. Her limbs felt like stone. She wanted to get up, but her legs would not respond. As she struggled to regain awareness of her surroundings, her outstretched hand felt something hard and smooth behind her. Her fingertips explored the object until her palm closed slowly around the wooden leg from a broken chair.

Rija waited. One part of her mind wondered what the soldier would do next. She prayed he would get dressed and let her go. Sensing motion nearby, she realized he was rubbing himself. He moved back toward her, pulling himself up on his knees. He grabbed her head pushing her face toward his groin. When she resisted, he hit her.

He thrust his penis in her face. "Suck it."

When Rija turned away, he hit her across the mouth with the back of his hand. "Now, do as I say!"

She could taste blood. Finding a will she didn't know she possessed, Rija swung the chair leg with all her strength, hitting him on the side of the head. He fell back, howling in rage.

Rija found her legs as energy surged through her. She jumped to her feet and ran to the door. She threw the deadbolt, and grabbed the knob with both hands, fighting for balance as the door jerked open. She careened down the stairs, two steps at a time.

From above, she caught a glimpse of the soldier staggering after her, one hand holding his head, the other holding a gun. "I will kill you."

Near the first floor, a bullet whizzed by Rija's head and lodged in the wall. She heard him call her a whore as she stumbled out of the building and into the street.

As she ran back over the bridge, snow began to fall. Shells burst overhead, and a sniper's bullet broke the remaining window of an abandoned car under the bridge. Rija stumbled, tripping into a gutter. Her boot filled with cold water. Tears blinded her eyes.

Crouched on the stone curb, she tried to pull off her boot but her fingers, numb and frozen, failed her. Catching sight of a church door near Fra Filipa Street, she ran inside and hid under a bench for what seemed like hours. Gradually, her breathing slowed, but she *refused to allow her mind to return to what had happened in the apartment.*

Rija shook her head to clear away the memory. The sound of children's voices brought her back to the present as a school bus rattled down the street. Quickly she returned the gun to the bag, closed the trunk, and locked it.

"Fowler said Luz called out," Carlene told Rija when she arrived at work that night. "That means we'll have to split up her floors. Which ones do you want, the mortgage brokers or the accountants?"

Rija wondered what was wrong with Luz. This was the third straight night she'd called out. "I'll take the accountants, they're not so messy."

Carlene glanced toward the locker room door and then looked back at Rija. "Luz called me at home. She may not be back. Fowler trapped her in a corner in the basement. Grabbed her breasts from behind and tried to stick his hand down her jeans."

Rija's stomach knotted into a ball of anger. "He can't get away with that."

"Oh yeah? He told her if she went along with the program, she'd get a raise. She was too afraid to move, and he managed to pull down her zipper before one of the janitors came in and she ran away."

"In my classes, we hear that there are laws against this kind of thing. She can make a complaint."

"Yeah, well. Good luck with that."

It was after midnight by the time Rija finished work that evening. Josef was waiting for her, standing next to the SUV and smoking a cigarette. He smiled when he saw her come through the revolving door. He dropped the cigarette and opened the passenger-side door as she approached. "You look tired," he said.

"Luz was out sick tonight, and we each had an extra floor to do," Rija said as she climbed into the SUV. He shut the door, and she leaned back and closed her eyes. She wouldn't miss the cold, dark subway ride home.

"Would you like to stop for something to eat?" he asked. "A coffee perhaps?"

"I just want to sleep."

"Sit closer."

Rija stayed where she was.

Josef persevered. "Tomorrow, we could go for a ride, just the two of us. I want to show you something."

Josef's ways hadn't changed. He still knew how to entice her, but Rija resisted.

"I'd love to go, but tomorrow's Saturday. I have my classes, and I've missed so much time already."

Josef struck a match and lit a cigarette. Rija rolled down the window. They were silent for the ride home.

Chapter 13

On Saturday, Rija's class met in the school's computer lab to learn about online research. Mr. Sturgis, the legal investigator who conducted the class, passed around handouts and asked how many of the students had computers at home.

Rija glanced around. Half the class had raised their hands. She was relieved not to be the only one who hadn't.

"This is your password for today," Mr. Sturgis scrawled a string of numbers on the board. "Write it down."

Rija wrote down the password but had trouble logging on to her computer. The student to her left, a young man who often sat behind her in the back of the class, glanced her way momentarily and then turned his screen so that she could see it. She nodded her thanks and logged on successfully.

The logo for InfoSearch America appeared on Rija's screen. When all the screens displayed the logo, Mr. Sturgis told them to start searching. "Type in your own personal information, or search for a family member."

Rija stared intently at the screen, fully engaged. She keyed in her name and pressed enter. Moments later, her name, age, and address appeared. She smiled. It was almost like magic. She typed in Josef's name and waited, but the magic, for now, had abandoned her, and she met with no success.

Mr. Sturgis walked between the rows of students. "Anyone have a search they'd like to do?"

Rija had an idea. She glanced around. No one else had a hand raised. Although she didn't want to draw attention to herself, she didn't want to miss an opportunity, either. She swallowed and raised her hand. The instructor acknowledged her.

"Can you check the owner of a car?" she asked in a quiet voice.

"We'll give it a try. What have you got?"

Rija dug in her bag until she found the document that she'd discovered in the SUV's trunk.

He pointed to a number. "That's the vehicle identification number. They call it the VIN. Search that."

Rija followed his instructions and waited. The screen came to life, and the results of her search marched across the screen one line at a time. A woman's name appeared first, followed by an Ohio address. The final line, in flashing yellow capital letters, said, **"VEHICLE REPORTED STOLEN."**

73

Rija quickly minimized the search program and glanced around. She was grateful that her classmates, including the young man who had helped her, were all absorbed in their own searches. She took a final quick look at the vehicle report and then closed the program.

After class the following Saturday, the young man introduced himself to Rija. Tony Carabello, part-time bartender, was in training to be an investigator for a law firm. He also claimed to be good with computers and offered to give Rija a tutorial. Rija wouldn't mind some help, but she also knew she was smart enough to learn computers on her own. Besides, she had just realized that there might be another way Tony could help her.

"What did you have in mind?" he asked when she broached the subject.

Rija suggested that they go to a coffee shop, where she would tell him her idea and explain the details. A few minutes later they were seated at a small table in a nearby café.

"I might have an investigator job for you," Rija said. "Would you be interested?"

"I might be. What's the job?"

"I want you to follow my husband and find out where he goes. I'll pay you."

Tony looked surprised, and he took a sip of his coffee before responding. "You'll need to tell me why. What are your suspicions?"

She realized what he was probably thinking and quickly set him straight. "Josef isn't cheating on me. It's not that."

"What then?"

"I'm sorry. I know this must sound crazy."

He shrugged and smiled. "I'll let you know how crazy it is after you give me some details. But if you're not comfortable with that, I probably can't help you."

Rija nodded. "Josef just moved back in with us, with me and my mother and daughter. He has no job. He says he doesn't know anybody here in the city, but all of a sudden he has money. Where does it come from? I want to find out where he's going, what he does."

Tony frowned. "I'm not gonna get whacked am I?"

"Whacked?"

"You know, killed, snuffed. In other words, dead."

Rija thought about the gun in the SUV's trunk, tried to put it out of her mind. "No, no, no," she assured him. "He's not dangerous."

"Here's the thing, I don't have a lot of spare time," Tony said. "I mean, what kind of hours does he keep?"

"After he brings my daughter home from school, he disappears."

Tony thought about it. "My day job, I usually work eight to four. So maybe I could do a couple of hours before I go to my bartender job. That starts at seven-thirty."

"You work two jobs and go to school?" Rija thought Tony must be even more tired than she, but she kept that to herself.

"Yeah, it keeps me out of trouble."

Rija wrote her address on a piece of paper and pressed it into his hand. "Here's our address. He drives a white SUV with New York plates. It's not his car."

Tony raised an eyebrow. "Whose car is it?"

Rija hesitated. "It once belonged to a woman in Ohio. She reported that it was stolen."

Tony whistled under his breath.

Rija produced an old photo of Josef, taken soon after they'd left Sarajevo. "His hair's a little darker now. He's a little heavier, but mostly he looks the same."

"When do you want me to start?"

"As soon as you can. What is your fee?" Rija held her breath. She needed help, but in her heart she didn't know how she could make any more payments.

"I'll give you my bargain rate. That's $20 an hour, plus you pay for my gas."

Rija didn't know where that money would come from, but she nodded and reached out her hand. They shook and made the deal.

Chapter 14

What was he doing here? Josef smiled and waved to other parents as he left the schoolyard after dropping off Lili, and tried to ignore a familiar feeling rising up in his chest. A voice in his head urged him to pack it in, to jump in the car and take off. He took a deep breath and told himself to lighten up. He cursed himself for a fool and cracked his knuckles to release the tension.

It was boredom, nothing more.

Halfway home, he ducked into a corner deli for a quart of milk. He threw two crumpled bills on the counter and let his eyes flicker over the Asian storeowner. The man rang him up, barely pulling his attention from the TV screen on the wall where a talk show host was discussing the latest "get rich quick" stock market scam.

"Pretty good idea," the guy said, nodding to the infomercial.

Josef grabbed his milk. "Yeah, top notch!"

"Have a good day," the storeowner called out as Josef left the store and continued his way home.

As he walked, Josef wondered how the guy could stand it, how he could put up with staying all day in the same little store, just a crowded box, waiting for customers, exchanging a few inane words of fake conversation.

When he first got back to Philadelphia, what he wanted more than anything was to rest. He wanted to stay in one place, to spend his days quietly. He wanted to get to know his daughter, spend time with Rija. He had really wanted that, wanted it to be true. Yet now he felt himself growing restless.

He punched a 212 area code into his new cell phone. There was no answer, but he waited for the beep to leave a message. "Cousin, how are you? It's me, Josef. I'm in Philly. Give me a call."

When Josef got home he noticed a beat-up red Volvo station wagon parked on his block.

The next day, Josef looked out the window and spotted the red station wagon, a dark-haired man in the driver's seat. It was still there an hour later, and the man in the driver's seat hadn't moved. Josef didn't like it.

The car had Pennsylvania plates, so Nick couldn't have sent him.

And even if Nick had figured out where he was, Josef knew his old boss would never hire a loser who drove an old car with a bad paint job. Nick was sharper than that. Josef would never have spotted Nick's man, not until it was too late. So who the fuck was it?

Josef decided to wait him out, to sit tight and stay inside. The only time he would go out would be to take his daughter to school or help his mother-in-law into the van to go to therapy. Let the loser watch that and see where it got him.

But sitting around was starting to get on his nerves. He paced their four rooms trying to find a spot where he could blot out the sounds of *The Price Is Right* or *All My Children* or the million other shows Elena watched all day.

He jumped when his cell phone rang, excited to see the 212 area code. "Cousin, how are you? What are you doing?"

"Never mind what I'm doing," Milos shot back. "Do you have some free time?"

"For you, always"

"Good. Put some gas in your car, I have something for you to do."

Josef walked to the window and looked out. That fucking red Volvo was still there!

Milos was telling him he had to move now.

"OK, I can do it," Josef said. To hell with the damned Volvo. He grabbed his jacket and ran down the stairs.

Tony was having serious second thoughts about his chosen career path. For three straight days, he'd been parked on this crummy little street watching Rija's husband walk the little girl home, help the old woman out of the SUV, or pick up quarts of milk and loaves of bread. In fact, Josef seemed like a model citizen, at least for somebody who didn't have a job. At worst, he was a hen-pecked idler.

Nobody went in or out of the building who didn't look like he belonged there. Rija was throwing her money away, and he was wasting his time.

Tony drummed his fingers on the steering wheel and decided to wait till 6 p.m., then call it a day and be done with this useless time-suck of a job. He'd have to tell Rija. As for her husband, what could the guy be up to? The asshole barely left the house. Rija was a good kid, and he kind of felt sorry for her. It seemed like she had it rough.

Maybe living through a civil war in some miserable little country at the ass-end of civilization had made her paranoid or delusional. That kind of experience could change you up in serious ways. But, whatever. He had to tell her he couldn't do it anymore.

He flicked on the radio, hitting the oldies station by mistake. He usually hated oldies. But a snatch of "Come As You Are" by Nirvana sent him back in the day. Now that was a song! Many a night he and Bart, bored out of their skulls on guard duty, blasted Nirvana through their earphones even though it could have got them thrown in the brig.

Talk about changing you up. Saudi Arabia was the last place in the world he'd ever expected to find himself. What a hellhole! Like a million other stupid kids with no plan and no skills, he and his buds got caught breaking and entering. That cop wanted to kick ass and send them all to jail. He'd just turned 18, too old for juvie. But he got lucky. The judge gave him a choice, join the service or do 60 days in county. He took the enlistment. The judge kept his promise and sealed his records.

Thankful for the break, he straightened up in boot camp. Played it smart, worked out, bulked up, passed the test for airborne, got promoted to E-4 in less than a year, and got recon training. Once his hitch was up, the sky was the limit. But when Bart got killed and they covered it up, told his folks their son died in an accident, something shriveled inside. The guys on patrol that day talked about going to the State Department, but they let it drop, and he hadn't been there. If he'd been there that day, maybe Bart would still be alive. Who knows?

He still thought of himself as someone who wanted to play it straight but, really? Fuck it! If it came down to it, he knew he just might do whatever when the time came.

Tony must have dozed off for a few seconds. He blinked himself awake and checked his watch. It was time to call it a day. He turned the key in the ignition.

Then everything changed. Josef ran down the steps, cell phone to his ear. He hopped into the SUV, gunned the engine, and took off down Mercer Street. Tony took off after him, following fifty feet behind as Josef flew down Aramingo onto Delaware Avenue.

Tony floored it, thankful the Volvo still had some guts. The two cars stayed in sync past the tourist attractions of Penn's Landing.

Traffic thinned as they moved toward the warehouses and industrial piers above Packer Avenue.

When Josef made a left into Pier 48, Tony shot past cursing the big rig behind him. By the time he backtracked to the gate, he could make out a worker motioning the white SUV to the rear of the building. Ten minutes later Josef emerged, and the same denim-clad figure waved him out through the electronic entrance.

Seconds later, the white SUV was back on the expressway, heading north, Tony following behind. The SUV flew by Old Swede's Churchyard. At the entrance to I-95, the SUV made a left onto the Expressway. After a few more exits, it turned east at the Betsy Ross Bridge.

Tony looked at his watch. He had to be at the bar in half an hour. He made U-turn at the jug handle and headed back to the city. He looked at his watch again. Sorry, babe.

Josef returned to the apartment two days later with haggard eyes and an unshaven face. He barely acknowledged Rija before collapsing into a chair and closing his eyes. He began to snore softly, stirring slightly as his keys slipped from his hand and fell to the floor. Rija picked them up and squeezed them tight. She looked at Josef. His chest rose and fell as she listened to his regular breathing. She walked to the front door and turned the doorknob. She looked over her shoulder at him. He was still asleep. She opened the door, closed it carefully behind her, and ran down the steps.

She was on the street seconds later, spotted the car parked a few houses down. She popped the trunk and found the black bag. Inside, three packs of fifty-dollar bills were rubber-banded together. The voice in her head tempted her to take what she needed, but she resisted, only lifting a bill from each of the three packets. She zipped the bag tight and left the trunk of the car just as she'd found it.

"Litigation - The Discovery Process." The words flashed on the screen as Mr. Doyle began his PowerPoint presentation. Was it the seventh or eighth time the class had met? Rija had lost track. She'd missed too many classes and was behind in her assignments.

"Today, we'll go over the research and discovery phase of preparing for litigation," Mr. Doyle announced. He looked around and focused on the back row. "Mr. Carabello, what does that mean?"

Rija looked back. She could tell by the color flushing his cheeks that Tony hadn't expected to be called on.

"You try to find documents that will back up the facts of your case, I guess," Tony replied in a bored voice that Rija thought he was using to hide his discomfort.

"Okay, I guess that's a start." Doyle pointedly imitated her friend's low-key delivery to get a laugh from the class.

"So, people, what types of documents would they be?"

Determined to regain his composure, Tony shot back, "Letters, memos."

Doyle nodded. "What else?"

Rija raised her hand. It was the first time she'd responded in class. "Medical reports, doctor's records?"

Doyle nodded and Rija felt pleased.

After class, Rija and Tony met at the fast food restaurant across the street. Rija pushed an envelope across the table. She decided not to tell him where the three fifty-dollar bills came from. "Here's most of what I owe you. I'll give you the rest next week."

"No worries, forget it. I should pay you. It was great practice. I watched him drive down to the pier, pick up something, and head for the bridge. But I couldn't tell you what it was."

"I guess we can stop for now. But thank you for helping me."

Tony shrugged. "Hey, I'm hungry. How about a hamburger?"

Rija nodded and they got in line.

After missing weeks of classes, Rija was far behind in her courses. She hadn't opened a book, and the major project for their Litigation Support class was due in two weeks. She thought of asking Tony, but he had as little free time as she did. Running a vacuum cleaner over carpet on the 20th floor, she thought of Marti.

Two nights later, she saw the young lawyer's light on. A combination of fear and hope set her stomach quivering. Rija pulled her cart toward the light spilling from the office into the corridor and peeked in.

Marti's head was tilted back, and her eyes were closed. Rija wondered if she should wake her. "Hello, Marti."

Marti's head snapped up. "Oh, my God. I must have fallen asleep. Thanks for waking me."

"You should go home, Marti. Get some sleep."

Marti pulled her dark hair out of her eyes. "I know, you're right. And thanks for the thoughtful birthday gift. That was so sweet of you."

Rija thought back to the single red rose the newsstand vendor gave her that night. He'd told her just to take it. "It's the last one," he had said. "I was going to throw it out anyway."

Rija said, "Oh, I'm so glad you liked it. Did you enjoy your birthday?"

"Yes, I went out to dinner with some friends. It was great to take a little time off." Marti smiled. "And how are you doing?"

Rija explained about her assignment, how she needed to read and analyze some simple cases to see how they'd been handled. Then she took the plunge. "Do you think I could read some of yours?"

The young lawyer listened thoughtfully. "I'd like to help, but it's really against our code of ethics, you know, client privacy and all that."

Rija nodded, disappointment showing on her face. She turned to go.

"Wait a minute," Marti said. "I know I really shouldn't do this, but I guess it won't hurt anyone if I pulled a few they gave me for training."

Rija held her breath.

"I can pull some old case records out of my files. They were settled years ago, so I guess we'd be safe if you just want to take a look. See if anything helps with your assignment."

Rija felt some of the tension draining from her face. "Oh, thank you, thank you."

Marti patted the top of her filing cabinet. "I'll leave them up here."

"If I have questions, can I leave you a note?" Rija asked.

"Yes, use these." Marti pushed a pad of blue sticky notes across the desk. "If you don't understand something, leave me one of these on my telephone and I'll try to answer you the same way."

Tears welled up in Rija's eyes. "Oh, thank you, Marti."

Marti was gone the next night, but the young lawyer kept her word. Rija was grateful for the old case files on top of her filing cabinet. Careful always to put everything back as she found it, Rija felt at first like a trespasser. But she got over it quickly, and many times she found herself sitting at the desk, even switching on the reading lamp.

A week after her conversation with Marti, as she swiveled in the lawyer's leather chair, Rija noticed a folder on the desk with a tab that read "Northeastern Hospital." Rija felt her heart beat faster as she stared at it. She glanced through the open office door and peered into the hallway. All was quiet. She slid the folder from the desk onto her lap, glanced again at the open door. She looked down and opened the folder. The title read, "Deposition in the case of Flanagan vs. Northeastern Hospital."

She scanned the first page and saw the name George Constantine. She looked at her watch. It was 10:44. She'd be lucky to finish her work before Josef came to pick her up. Heart pounding, she took the folder to the alcove where the copy machine stood. She switched on the power, heard the machine start to hum. Her heart was racing as she waited for the copier to warm up. She glanced at her watch. It was 10:45. She wanted to scream.

The copy machine finally signaled it was ready. Rija slid the first page into the feeder, and then froze. What if the machine jammed? She wouldn't know how to clear it. She relaxed when the machine spit out the original and the copy, but she copied the remaining pages one at a time, lifting the copy machine cover and placing the originals on the glass. Finally, she was finished. She returned to the desk and arranged the papers neatly, then returned them to the folder.

She was seized by a sudden jolt of fear and dashed back to the machine. She cursed herself for a fool as she turned off the power. Blood was pounding in her head. As she stood there trying to calm herself, another thought flashed into her mind. She slowly lifted the copy machine cover and saw the last original page lying face down on the glass. Her hand trembled as she picked up the page. She started to cry. Her whole body was trembling. She walked back to the desk, returned the last page to the folder, then took her copies and quickly exited the office.

The next morning Rija was filled with anticipation as she kissed Lili goodbye and then waited until Elena finished washing and dressing. When her mother was finally settled in front of the TV, Rija sat down with the case file. According to the plaintiff summary, the patient, a Mr. John Flanagan, had received knee replacement surgery. During recovery, Mr. Flanagan contracted a serious staph infection but was discharged. After returning home, Flanagan developed blood poisoning, but when he returned for treatment, his skin rash was diagnosed as a case of boils for which he received an antibiotic. Later, Mr. Flanagan developed pneumonia and died. His widow was suing the doctor and Northeastern Hospital for several million dollars.

Next she read the deposition given by Constantine. As she pored over the administrator's words, the face of the arrogant bureaucrat with the dismissive manner flashed before her. Rija shook her head to clear his words from her mind.

Reading on, she learned that Mr. Flanagan and Elena had had the same surgeon, Dr. John Randolph. Rija learned that Randolph left the hospital staff when he moved to Florida. Dr. Randolph's deposition was taken there in Fort Lauderdale.

Rija read a series of questions posed to the surgeon by Robert Schwartz, the Flanagan's' attorney.

Schwartz: *"Dr. Randolph, please think back over your career and tell me if you have ever lost any patients as a result of medical malfeasance?"*

Randolph: *"To my knowledge none of my patients has ever suffered an injury as a result of my care."*

Schwartz: *"May I ask, Dr. Randolph, if you recall a patient, a Miss Melanie Caputo?"*

Randolph: *"Yes, I do recall Ms. Caputo, a most unfortunate case. But I assure you that there was no malfeasance involved."*

Schwartz: *"If I may, Dr. Randolph, I'd like to read a court transcript, with testimony to the contrary, from Ms. Caputo's father, Albert Caputo. But perhaps you'd like to tell us the details of Ms Caputo's medical history."*

Rija tried to picture Randolph's lawyer as he jumped to his feet to object. Following that exchange, the line of questioning stopped. Afterwards, the Flanagan's' attorney referred to the testimony of an operating room nurse, Laura Boone. She testified that on the day in question, Dr. Randolph came into the operating room, upbeat, almost exuberant. He announced that he'd come straight from the golf course where he'd shot a hole in one. That day she did not recall Dr. Randolph performing standard scrubbing procedures. Nurse Boone described how he washed his hands perfunctorily, looked at his watch, clapped his hands, and commanded everyone to look sharp as the patients were backing up and he was behind schedule. After his speech, Randolph went immediately to perform Mr. Flanagan's knee replacement surgery.

Still, Constantine upheld Randolph's reputation, saying that the hospital had been sorry to see him go. Nurse Boone's statement contradicted that, saying all the OR nurses were happy when Randolph left, taking his abusive attitude with him.

Rija noted the firm suing for the Flanagan family. She copied the name, Lynch, McKenna and Schwartz, along with their telephone number.

"Why wait?" Rija asked herself aloud. Her hand shook as she dialed. After a brief conversation with the receptionist, she was switched to Alan Greenfield, an associate. She told her story. "Your firm has a case with the Flanagan family against Northeastern Hospital. The same surgeon, Dr. Randolph, operated on my mother. She became very sick afterwards, and the hospital didn't help her."

"Miss, I'm sorry. May I have your name again?"

"It's Malacovik, but my mother is Elena Petric. She's the patient who was at the hospital."

"Please hold. I'll try to transfer you."

Rija listened to piped-in classical music, waiting for what seemed like hours before another voice, this time male, came on the line.

"Thanks for calling, Miss. I'll try to follow up on what you're telling me. Can I take your number and call you back?"

With growing doubt, Rija supplied her name yet again. "When will you call me?"

"Today's Tuesday," the young associate replied. "I'll call you back by the end of the week."

Rija checked the date on the kitchen calendar and circled February 12th. "Thank you. I'll wait for your call." Rija realized, too late, she'd forgotten to ask for his name.

That date, February 12th, had special meaning. Rija remembered a day when every face in Sarajevo beamed with pride. It was a time for the world to see how far they had come from the dark days of their country's past. The world would see why their city had been chosen.

On that day, February 12th, 1984, a morning snow fell on Sarajevo for the first time in more than a week. Less than an inch, to be sure, still, it was a good sign. In the streets and markets of the old town, already bustling with tourists and international visitors, everything was primed and ready.

Everyone was on holiday. Rija and her classmates, second-form students of the Kosovo Akademija, lined the streets from the airport, waving and offering flowers to the Olympic athletes. Older students, dressed in sleek skiwear, felt honored to help the visitors settle in at the Olympic village.

That night, the Petric family had tickets for the opening ceremony. Dressed in their finest, her father, Anton, her mother, Elena, and Rija sat with neighbors and friends, sharing the surge of pride that swept the crowd. Rija saw tears spring to her father's eyes when Doni appeared on the stadium floor marching with the other young men, each bearing the Yugoslav flag.

After the ceremony, shops and bars stayed open all night. Though it was well past midnight, Rija was allowed to stay up as Anton herded them all into the Danube Pastry Shop for tea and cakes. As she sat at the table waiting for her favorite dessert to arrive, Rija couldn't help but admire her own reflection in the mirrored walls of the pastry shop. She felt so grown up in the embroidered white dress and lace cap she and the other girls wore for the ceremony.

"Mama, may I wear this dress tomorrow to school?" Rija asked, giving her mother her best smile. "Mira's mother told her she could wear hers."

Elena cupped her daughter's chin in her hand. "No, my sweet one, Mira does not tear her clothes the way you do. If you wore your long dress tomorrow, it would be in tatters by the time you got home. You must wear your uniform."

Rija sulked but only until the food appeared. Her eyes widened in anticipation as the server arrived with the tray of pastries. The first bite of her favorite, a linzer torte topped with spun sugar, was heaven. Too soon, enthusiasm was replaced by shame as the raspberry-filled pastry oozed down her starched white blouse.

"Mama, see how our little Rija once again has proved you right," Doni said and laughed at the expression on his sister's face as she wiped red jam from her fingers and her clothing.

Rija looked at the calendar. Valentine's Day had come and gone. Despite leaving two more messages, there was still no word from the law firm. Thumbing through the Philadelphia telephone book, Rija scanned a long list of Flanagans. There were six John Flanagans listed in Philadelphia. She searched for a familiar street name. The third name had the East Thompson Street address she remembered from the deposition. She picked up the receiver. After three rings, a woman's voice answered.

"Mrs. Flanagan?" Rija asked.

"Yes, who's this?"

"My name is Rija Malacovik. I am trying to find the family of John Flanagan who was in the Northeast Hospital."

There was silence on the other end. "What's this about?"

"I'd just like to talk to you about ..."

The voice turned sharp. "Don't try to sell me nothing or give me a good deal on my house, I ain't selling! Now why don't you just leave us alone?"

"Wait, wait," Rija pleaded. "My mother too was in the hospital, and she got sick like your husband."

"How do you know about my husband?" the woman asked.

"One of the nurses told me," Rija lied. "Can I come and speak to you?"

"What? You want to come here? I don't know you."

Rija could hear muffled voices on the other end of the receiver.

"What do you want to talk about?"

Rija knew she must speak quickly before the woman hung up. "Please, Mrs. Flanagan, is there a way to make the hospital pay for what they did?"

There was more silence before the woman spoke. This time her voice was less harsh. "I have a lawyer. There's a lawsuit, but I don't know if I should talk to you. How do I know who you are? You could be anybody."

"Please let me come and talk to you. I'll bring proof. I live in Port Richmond too. I have my mother's papers from the hospital. I'll bring the medicines she takes. You can see them."

At the corner of Ontario and Thompson, men in Flyers' orange stood outside the bar, smoking and laughing as they waited for Sunday's hockey game to begin. Intent on the Flanagan's address, Rija walked past, oblivious of their appreciative glances. Mid-block she found the house she was looking for. Miniature American flags fluttered in an empty window box. Rija took a deep breath and knocked. After several moments, a woman with tightly permed blonde hair appeared.

"Mrs. Flanagan?" Rija asked.

"Ma!" she yelled. "Somebody here to see you."

An older woman in purple sweats squinted at her over her daughter's shoulder. "Are you the girl with the mother?"

"Yes, I called. My mother, Elena Petric, was in the Northeastern Hospital like your husband. I have the papers. May I show them to you?"

Mrs. Flanagan stepped aside. "Okay, come on in for a minute." Rija followed mother and daughter into the front parlor. The Flanagans settled on the sofa while Rija perched on the edge of a chair. Photos of a thin-faced man in glasses graced the doily-covered coffee table, and several others were on the mantel.

Knowing she didn't have much time, Rija pulled medical bills, prescription bottles, and her mother's release records from her handbag. She placed Elena's hospital bracelet on the table in front of Mrs. Flanagan. While the younger woman read the label on an empty pill bottle, Mrs. Flanagan kept her eyes on Rija's face.

"Where'd you say you live?"

"On Mercer Street, near the park. Mr. Gracek's my landlord. Do you know him?"

Mrs. Flanagan shook her head.

Ignoring the chitchat, the Flanagan daughter plowed through what was on the table. "Look here, Ma." She elbowed her mother in the ribs. "Her mother had the same surgeon as Daddy."

For the first time, Mrs. Flanagan looked at Rija with something other than distrust. "When was your mother in that hospital?"

"She was in the Northeastern two times. The first time was in the fall when she was hit by a car. Dr. Randolph performed the surgery to fix her leg."

Rija looked at the two women. "Then she had to go back because of the staph infection. She almost died."

Mrs. Flanagan made eye contact with her daughter.

"Ma, it's more than a coincidence, don't you think? The same hospital, same doctor, the infection. This Dr. Randolph is a real Dr. Death."

Mrs. Flanagan's features crumbled. She pulled a tissue from her sleeve and dabbed at her eyes. "Your mother is lucky she's still alive."

She motioned to a photo on the mantel. "My Johnnie's dead."

"I'm so sorry, Mrs. Flanagan."

Mrs. Flanagan took a deep breath and let it out. "I can't call the lawyer today, it being Sunday and all, but I'll call them tomorrow."

Holding tight to a promise that they would pass her name and phone number to the lawyers, Rija gathered up her things. At the door, she thanked the Flanagans again and again. With a tiny surge of hope in her chest, she sailed home thinking, perhaps, justice was possible in her life.

On Wednesday morning the telephone rang. The female voice on the other end said, "Please hold for Mr. McKenna."

Waiting for the lawyer to come on the line, she thought of other times they had waited for legal help, help that never came. It was soon after they realized Rija was pregnant that Josef did whatever he could, using his contacts, trying to get a visa for them to emigrate. As usual during the war, the quickest way to do anything was with a bribe, and Josef was willing to give whatever he could, but it never seemed to be enough. They could wait for the lawyers and the clerks at the immigration office to give them the right papers, or they could find their own way.

Josef never told her how he finally got the documents, and by that time she didn't care. When it was time to go, Elena needed to believe that there would be a way for Anton to find them. Rija assured her mother she'd left their names with the Catholic charity Caritas and with the Red Cross. Only then would Elena even consider leaving their apartment behind.

Any goods left behind had already been distributed among the neighbors. Markos gave Elena a letter she promised to mail to his son in Austria. His wife, Alia, kissed Rija's cheek and folded an embroidered kerchief into her bag. "I made it for the little one. So she will not forget where she was born."

Esmuda, Elena's friend for thirty years told her, "You are right to go. There is no future here."

When Elena crumbled against the door, Esmuda pulled her to her feet. "You must go with the young ones. Besides, how can we live together after this?" She pointed to the ruined streets outside. "Under Tito we were all Yugoslavs, now we are Muslims or Serbs or Croats who hate each other. Go!"

Lili held out her arms to be picked up. Her grandmother put down the canvas bag with her few possessions. She lifted the crying child into her embrace. "There, there, little one. Don't cry, my love." Then Elena wiped her eyes, blew a kiss to Esmuda, and waved goodbye.

Rija held Lili close. The truck bumped and shook over battle-rutted roads carrying them toward their goal-safety beyond the UN checkpoint. Rija heard laughter coming from the front seat as Josef entertained the driver, distracting him with an unending string of jokes and free cigarettes. In the rear, Rija and Elena made space for a gaunt young woman with two young boys, the smaller one sickly and pleading for water.

Abruptly, the truck pulled off the road. Two soldiers threw back the canvas. The younger of the two shone a flashlight in their eyes. "Out of the truck, all of you. Have your travel documents ready."

At the sound of his voice, Lili woke and began to cry. A soldier with gray-stubbled cheeks helped Elena from the truck. Though his face was kind, he paid close attention to the papers they offered. Clambering into the open, they stood waiting in the rain for what felt like hours. When Rija could stand it no longer, she crouched behind a bush to urinate while her mother stood guard.

At a second checkpoint, they watched in horror as Josef and two other men were herded away. The wind carried their questions to her, and she heard Josef, without a flicker of emotion, saying that he had never been part of any paramilitary group or any army. When a soldier asked him why he looked so familiar, Josef laughed before answering. "I have the face of everyman. I am everyone and no one."

Rija's heart was in her throat. Overhead, thunder broke and the rain began again. Lili wailed, and the two little boys added their voices to the protest. Anxious to be rid of the crying children, the soldiers waved everyone forward, allowing them to pass through the barricades.

Rija sought Josef's eyes as he and one other man returned to board the UN personnel carrier that would take them south to Croatia and freedom. The UN worker in a white-and-blue uniform instructed them to don bulletproof vests resting under the seats. Once they'd all wrestled them over their wet clothes, the engine sputtered to life. As they picked up speed, Rija felt her shoulders begin to relax. Silently she told herself, "Perhaps your life does not end at 21 after all."

Chapter 15

On Friday, Josef drove Rija and Elena to the lawyers' office, a four-story brick structure near Independence Hall that was sandwiched between an insurance company and a storefront museum. He let them out and found a parking space nearby where he would wait. Rija wondered if he'd be conducting business on his cell phone while he waited.

Elena, in a new wine-colored suit, navigated the entrance carefully, using only her cane. Rija, in her blue dress, walked behind her mother, alert and ready to help her should she need it. Rija hoped her mother would not be intimidated into silence.

A young associate in a blue blazer met them in the lobby. "Mr. McKenna apologizes. He's running a little late."

They took an elevator to the third floor, and the young man escorted mother and daughter into an airy conference room. A large walnut conference table surrounded by plush leather chairs stood in the center of the room, and expensive-looking Oriental rugs protected the gleaming hardwood floor. The room was illuminated by sun streaming in through high windows on two sides.

They took seats at one end of the conference table. Elena gazed around the room as if it were the Hall of Mirrors at the Palace of Versailles. Rija ignored the luxurious surroundings and concentrated on the young man in the blue blazer, nervously waiting for his questions. When he asked if they wanted coffee or tea or water, Rija shook her head and began to relax. One question down. She was gratified when Elena asked for tea. The room might impress her mother, but she clearly wasn't intimidated.

When the young man returned with the tea, he smiled and said, "If you don't mind, I'll just take down some information until Mr. McKenna arrives."

He produced a small recorder. "Do you mind if I record our conversation?"

"That will be fine," Rija said.

He wrote their address, the date of the accident, and a few other facts on a yellow legal tablet. Then he asked Elena to describe what she could remember from that day.

Elena began, "I walk to the street to pick up the tray. Then the taxi ..."

Elena looked at her daughter, and Rija picked up the story,

describing the particulars of the trip to the hospital, the emergency room, and the need for surgery to repair the broken leg.

"What was the name of the surgeon who worked on your leg?" the young attorney asked.

Elena looked at Rija, who responded, "His name was John Randolph."

The attorney nodded. "And what happened after the surgery?"

"For a few days afterwards, Mama's fever was high, so the nurses continued with the IV to bring it down. When she was better they transferred her to the rehab, but her leg began to swell up very bad. The rehab nurse told the doctor, and they sent her back to the hospital."

After a few more questions, the young attorney switched off the recorder and excused himself. He stepped into the hallway where Rija saw a young woman motioning to him. He returned a few moments later, "I'm sorry, but Mr. McKenna still hasn't returned from court. But based on what you've told me, I'm sure he'll want to know more. Mr. McKenna will be in touch soon."

They shook hands at the elevators, and Rija assured the young man that they could see themselves out. They went to the car, and Josef drove them home through city streets crowded with lunchtime traffic.

On Tuesday night at work, Rija saw that the light was on in Marti's office, but she didn't want to talk to her lawyer friend that evening. She pulled her cart to the other end of the 22nd floor and was careful not to turn on the vacuum. She didn't want Marti to know she was there.

Rija worked on her other floors, occasionally checking the 22nd to see if the lights in Marti's office were out. Halfway through her shift, she looked back down the corridor and saw that the office was dark. Rija strode down the corridor and went inside.

First she ploughed through a stack of papers on the desk. Next, she thumbed through the filing cabinet. Her back to the door, she struggled to extract a bulging folder when a cough stopped her where she stood.

"Rija, what are you doing?"

Rija slid the file folder back into the drawer and then turned to face her mentor. "I have my assignment to do, and I was looking for the cases you gave me."

Marti pointed to a stack of folders on the filing cabinet. "Those cases are in the same place where I've always left them, right there."

Rija didn't respond.

"I think you had better get back to work, Rija."

Rija moved past. From down the corridor, she could hear the sound of locks turning in the filing cabinet.

It was after midnight when Rija finally clocked out. She paced the sidewalk watching the wind whip a plastic bag down Market Street. After several minutes she went back inside and used the phone at the guard station to call Josef's cell phone, but the call went to his voice mail.

Carlene appeared in the lobby carrying a large bag. "Hey girl, how are you?"

"Tired. No ride either. Josef didn't come to pick me up. I guess I'll take the subway."

"No way," Carlene said. "I'll drive you. Just wait two seconds while I put these supplies downstairs."

Despite the late hour, Carlene was even more animated than usual. "Today was quite a day for me!" she said after she returned to the lobby. "There was a lot going on."

Rija followed Carlene to the parking garage. "Like what?"

"You know how we've been so short-staffed, right? Well, I just hired a new person, and she'll start tomorrow."

"You hired someone?" Rija asked.

"Yes, me!" Carlene laughed out loud. "Didn't you hear? Fowler is gone! Now it's Keep it Clean with Carlene. For real, all the time."

She dangled a pink shirt in Rija's direction, holding it so the logo was visible. "As of yesterday, I've got the contract for all the floors in the building. Didn't have to blow anybody to get it either! And that's what's new!"

"Is this true? What about Fowler?" Rija felt a little balloon of joy. "We won't have to worry about him anymore."

"You won't believe it. Somebody filed a sexual harassment complaint against him, and I heard it wasn't the first time."

"Who?"

"Our friend Luz, that's who."

Rija heart surged in her chest. "She really did it after all?"

"Did what after all?"

"Remember when I told you I was going to ask my teacher, Ms.

Spadafora, about Fowler and what he does? She gave me the number for Women Against Rape, and I gave it to Luz. She was afraid to go because of her immigrant status and all, but I went with her, and they told her how to file a complaint."

"I guess she did something right, because they transferred our man Fowler out of this building to a warehouse down by the refinery. Not exactly a prize location."

Between giggles, Rija and her new boss exchanged a high five in the middle of the parking lot.

"That's not all," Carlene said. "Watch this." With a flick of her remote key, the doors of a shiny black minivan clicked open. "You like?"

Now Rija understood why her friend was more than willing to offer her a lift. "Keep it Clean with Carlene" shone in small pink letters below the passenger's side window.

They climbed in, and Carlene pulled onto the expressway while Rija admired the vehicle's interior and inhaled its new-car smell.

"Not bad for a little girl whose mama worked three jobs," Carlene said. "I wish she could see me now."

"Your mother would be very proud."

"My mama tried real hard, but she couldn't always be there for me. And what I mostly remember about my daddy was that he came and went. Sometimes on Saturdays he'd take me out with him if he had work to do. We'd deliver circulars or papers. I loved those times. He would tell me stories about when he was young and how he got here. He came to this country from Jamaica, got off a boat in Florida."

Rija nodded knowingly.

Carlene's expression turned sober. "But what I remember most is when he drank, and then he and Mama would fight. Afterwards, he would leave."

"My father drank, too, but he only came home and cursed the Serbs."

Carlene nodded. "From the time I was eight, it was just Mama, Rollie, and me."

"Rollie, he's your older brother?" Rija asked.

"Rollie's my little brother, but he's not so little now. He's six two. He helped me get a good deal on this car. Told me how to handle Fowler, too."

"I'd love to meet him some day."

"Oh, you will. He'll be walking down the aisle with us at my daughter's wedding. Then you'll see why I've been working over-time every day for as long as you've known me."

The expressway took them away from the business district. Late-night traffic carried them along. Rija pointed up ahead. "Here's my exit. Make a right."

At the bottom of the ramp, a sign read, "Welcome to Port Richmond Empowerment Zone."

"Just a few more blocks, past that traffic light, then turn left onto Mercer. My house is the one with the red door, near the end of the block."

Carlene pulled the van to the curb and Rija readied herself to jump out. "Thanks so much for the lift."

"Hang on a second, Rija," Carlene said, and she turned off the ignition. "As your new supervisor, I have to tell you something."

"Okay, sure. What is it?"

"We have to change your floors. One of the lawyers said you were going through her stuff."

Rija's throat contracted, her tongue felt thick.

"Were you?"

She tried to sound casual. "You must mean Marti, on the 22nd floor?"

"That's right." Carlene pulled out a scrap of paper. "Marti Goldman."

"But she told me it would be okay."

"Okay to go in her file cabinet?"

"I did look at some of her cases, for help with my schoolwork. I looked at some things on her desk. I got curious, maybe I went too far."

"Well, I'm glad you told me the truth, but take this as a warning. Don't do it again. With a building full of lawyers, if that kind of thing gets around, there's trouble. Understand?"

"Yes, I understand."

"No more lawyers for you, then. From now on, Dee Dee, the new girl, will do those floors. You'll have 15 through 18. They're mostly insurance agents and the one floor of accountants. Just stay out of trouble!"

"Of course, no problem. I'm sorry that you had any trouble because of me." Rija hoped it was dark enough that Carlene wouldn't see the guilty flush on her cheeks.

"Where were you last night?"

"I meant to call you with the good news, but I didn't have time."

Rija noticed Josef's red-rimmed eyes. "What news?"

"I picked up some work unloading at a warehouse."

"You didn't have two minutes to leave me a message at the desk?"

"Sorry, I will next time. Now let me show you what I brought home." With a flourish, Josef opened the door to their refrigerator's freezer. Instead of frozen emptiness, it was filled with packages of Omaha Prime Beef.

"What is it? Where did it come from?"

"Steaks! Good stuff, too! It was left over on the job last night. They told me to take it."

As though that explained everything, Josef went back to the newspaper. Rija tallied a dozen wrapped steaks inside one package before she shrugged and closed the door.

Rija told herself to accept the bargain she'd made. She'd merely nod when Josef made his excuses, telling herself that as long as he helped her with Elena and took care of Lili, her husband's mysterious comings and goings were just a fact of life. And over the next few weeks, Josef's so-called jobs produced goods that benefited the household.

He enjoyed buying things for Lili, like the frilly dress he surprised her with. Yet Rija couldn't help but be uneasy. If she couldn't trust his words, she knew there were other ways to trace Josef's activities, and she became adept at using them. She would come to find money, a few pieces of jewelry, and once, a case of Cuban cigars.

Chapter 16

Rija checked the date on the wedding invitation, Saturday April 3rd. What in God's name would they wear? Josef couldn't understand why he shouldn't wear his black leather jacket to the wedding, but Rija insisted they go shopping for a new suit. Ever the negotiator, Josef agreed with conditions. "I'll buy a suit if you will buy something new to wear too. And you must let me help pick it out."

Surprised by her husband's newfound interest in her wardrobe, Rija dismissed any feelings of guilt as she and Josef pawed through sale racks at the outlet mall. She held up a black Calvin Klein with a low-cut back, marked down to a sensible fifty-nine dollars.

But Josef made a sour face at the dress and kept looking, sorting through row after row of women's sizes. Two aisles over, he found what he was looking for. "Here, try this one."

Though it looked like her size, Rija cast a wary eye at the leopard-print cocktail dress he was holding. Yet it might have potential. "Okay, I'll try it."

Even before Josef coaxed her out of the dressing room, Rija noted that with her hair and coloring, his choice was a good one. A clerk chimed in, "That dress looked fabulous on you."

Back in street clothes, Rija fingered markdowns on the price tag. At a current price of two hundred dollar, it was out of the question. "We can't buy this," she said.

Josef took the dress from her hand and carried it to the cash register. "Sweetheart, wrap this up for me, will you?" He pulled out a wad of cash. Winking at the salesgirl, he counted out two hundred dollars.

In the men's department, Josef found a Hugo Boss suit from last season. With his thin build, tousled hair, and bearded cheeks staring at her from the mirror, Rija could feel his appeal, in spite of herself. She wasn't alone. She overheard one of the two female salesclerks whisper to the other, "Check him out. He looks like a model."

Rija, astonished at the display of cash, couldn't resist asking about it. "How is it that you have this money from a job as a security guard?"

"I won some money at the casino."

"If you were to spend your time working instead of gambling, our family would be much better off."

"Don't tell me what to do."

"Did you forget? I took you in off the street. You had nowhere to go."

"That's not true. I came to help you. I take your mother to the hospital, I carry her up and down the stairs. I pick up Lili so you can go to work and go to school."

"Hush," Rija whispered when she noticed the salesclerks looking their way.

They walked from the store back into the mall, and Rija resumed the conversation.

"Tell the truth. You came back to us because you wanted a place to hide. I see the way you look out on the street to see who is out there. Who is it you are hiding from?"

Josef ignored her and picked up his pace.

Yes, that is what you do, she thought. You run away.

Rija turned around and walked in the opposite direction. The mall was unknown territory, but she found a snack bar and ordered a cup of tea. Rija waited for the tea and her temper to cool.

She had hoped that things might be different, that Josef had matured. But it was foolish to expect that he would grow to become a man like her father. He would never be a man who went to work at the same job each day. He would never be a man who returned home to his family each night and did the same thing over again the next day. If she had ever thought he might become such a man, she was dreaming. Josef was what he was.

The tea calmed her, and she decided to enjoy herself. She walked around the mall for another hour, window-shopping until she passed a pay phone that looked operational. She called Elena. "Mama, Josef and I had a fight. Don't worry, I'll take the bus home."

Near the bus stop, Rija spotted Josef's car. She toyed with the idea of ignoring him, but when he beckoned, she capitulated. As she slid into the front seat, Josef continued the conversation as though no time had passed. "You are right, there might be someone looking for me, but I didn't want to tell you."

Rija took advantage of the opening. "I want to hear the whole story."

Josef lit a cigarette. "I was in Las Vegas, working in construction, like before in Atlantic City. But I decided there was a better way."

As he spoke, his eyes had a faraway look. "I met a guy, Sergei, who worked with me. You might say we were in the personal banking business, mostly in collections. We were a good team. I was the talker and Sergei was the enforcer."

You were always the smooth talker, Rija thought. But she held her tongue.

"One night I collected twelve thousand dollars from a Japanese businessman. The plan was to turn the money over to our boss. But I was feeling good. I got drunk and went to the tables. Somehow, I lost the money."

"Oh my God."

"When Sergei found me in the casino, he agreed that we would try to get the money back. But there was no way. We tried a few things but ended up robbing convenience stores. It was a stupid plan, and it didn't work. The money was shit."

He threw the cigarette out the window. "At one store we got six hundred; at another store just seven hundred. One store only had fifty. Altogether it was much less than two thousand dollars."

"Thank God no one was hurt," Rija said.

Josef looked away. "I only wish that was true. They caught up with us. I had to leave town, and I've been running since then."

"Are they here? Have they found you?"

"No, but they might. I have to be careful."

"We have to be careful."

"Yes," Josef said.

Rija took a breath. "I'm glad you told me. And it's true you have been very helpful to us."

Josef looked relieved.

Yes, and if you'd found us at any other time, I would have shut the door in your face, Rija thought.

Josef turned the key in the ignition. "Let's go home."

After the confession, Rija felt her heart soften a little. No matter what, she told herself, he was her husband, the father of her child. While she didn't let him move into her room, some nights she let him sleep in her bed. On those nights she was surprised to find that anger could fuel her passion just as well as love, and she responded eagerly when she felt him reach out for her.

Chapter 17

Rija and Josef found seats on the flower-draped aisle toward the rear of the church. Above their heads, a soprano voice sang the final chords of Ave Maria. Pale pink garlands and dozens of candles reflected on the gold of the altar. When the organ swelled to a dramatic pitch, all heads turned to the rear.

Rija watched Carlene take her daughter Tamika's arm as they floated down the aisle. On the right, a tall, dark-skinned man with an air of authority was the second escort. The bride, swathed in tulle and satin, stared straight ahead to where the groom waited. All around, women dug for handkerchiefs to catch their tears.

In the midst of the glittering procession, Rija thought of her own wedding day.

The shelling was quiet on the Saturday that Rija, Josef, and Elena walked to what was left of the Sarajevo registrar's office. There were no candles, no flowers that day. Following a few words by the magistrate, Josef and Rija showed their identity cards, signed the license, and paid the fee in worthless dinars and three packs of American cigarettes before they ducked back out. Constantly checking the rooftops for snipers, they found their way home through deserted streets.

Indoors, Elena smiled in anticipation as they climbed the steps to a neighbor's apartment. Esmuda, one of the few tenants still in their building, invited them into her kitchen for a feast. Proudly she displayed an unlikely pizza of bread, cheese, and tomatoes, topped with sardines.

Josef, not to be undone, produced his own prize, a bottle of plum brandy. He uncorked the bottle with a flourish and poured a toast to his bride. Esmuda's son, Drago, tuned his guitar, and with brandy fueling their vocal chords, everyone joined in a wedding song until a distant roar interrupted.

Windows rattled and shook. A shell had hit the quarter, loud and close. Almost in unison, the party dropped to the floor and waited, listening for the sound of a shell tearing through the air. After several minutes, the wedding guests stood and dusted off plaster dust and bits of debris. At the stairs, they waited, listening intently for further gunfire. They inspected each other for damage, ready to run to the cellar if need be, before the next shell found its mark. After several minutes of quiet, Josef ran out and Drago followed.

Smoking rubble identified the shell's resting place. Across the street, men sifted through bricks and beams that once housed the neighborhood kindergarten. As if by signal, more scavengers scurried toward the wreckage, removing anything that could be used for firewood. Brushing dust from his hands, Josef shrugged. "No one was hurt," he said.

Back inside, the wedding party reconvened. Rija watched Josef lift the guitar, picking out the tune of an old folksong. She'd never heard him sing before, and his voice, a clear baritone, surprised her. She listened to his song.

"I wandered through the darkness of the world,
But you found me, and that's why I'm happy."

When they all joined in on the chorus, Rija found herself picturing the faces of Katja and Dina, wishing they could be with them.

Guitar in one hand, still singing, Josef picked up the bottle of brandy in the other. He offered the bottle to Drago, who shook his head. Josef held the bottle up to his new wife as though toasting her before he drained what was left in a long swallow.

Tamika's reception was in full swing. Wedding guests from grandmothers to toddlers crowded the dance floor. At the head table, Carlene held court in mother-of-the-bride pink.

Rija was enjoying her third glass of wine. She felt confident, her dress fit beautifully, her hair was piled up on her head. She admired her red nail polish. The manicurist had said, "Trust me, I can make your hands look beautiful, not like they spent the last week in a bucket of cleaning solution." She had kept her promise.

She and Josef found their names at a table with other members of Carlene's team. Josef, on his best behavior, was deep in conversation with Dee Dee's husband when Rija pulled him up to watch the newlywed's first dance. They'd even tried a few steps themselves before Carlene waved them over. Rija did the honors, and Carlene giggled when Josef bowed low and kissed her hand.

"Come over here. I want you to meet my baby brother." Carlene linked elbows with the brother who towered over her. "This is Detective Rollie Miller. He just got promoted to detective in the homicide division."

Rollie smiled and gave his sister a gentle shove. "Knock it off, Car, tonight's supposed to be about Tamika."

Carlene patted his hand. "Rollie's always been modest."

When Josef's smile froze, Rija stepped forward to make a toast. "We say good things come in threes, and your family has three things to celebrate, Tamika's wedding, Carlene's new business, and Rollie's promotion."

Glasses clinked, and they drained the contents in honor of the trio of happy events.

On Sunday morning, Rija groaned her way out of bed. Tired and headachy, she regretted the extra glasses of wine from the night before. She tried to ignore her pounding head, but the smell of breakfast cooking was nauseating her. She went back to bed and tried to sleep.

Starting on Monday, she checked the calendar every day that week, waiting for a period that didn't come. A week later, her breasts felt swollen and tender. Finally it was impossible to deny.

She had hoped to have another child some day when life was calmer, but not now. There was no room in their small apartment, and how could she pay a doctor? She remembered the shock of seeing the huge medical bills from Elena's injuries. She'd almost fainted before the hospital social worker told her that Medicaid would cover most of it. But now that she was working, Rija was no longer eligible, and her job offered no benefits, no insurance. She was as close as she'd ever been to embarking on a different life, the life she wanted for herself and Lili. With a new infant to take care, she would no longer be able to attend school, nor would she be able to work. The cost and chaos of a newborn infant would change everything.

Rija hoped she would feel better before her late afternoon shift began, but Carlene read her expression in a heartbeat. "What's troubling you? I can see something's going on."

"I'm pregnant." Rija blurted. "I love babies, but this is the wrong time for me and for us. Another child would be a disaster."

"Have you been to the doctor?"

"No, but I can feel it, and I had a pregnancy test."

"Have you told your husband?"

"No, I hate to even bring it up. I don't know what he would say. But maybe I'm wrong, maybe he would agree that now is not the time. What should I do?"

"That's something only you can answer. But you should do what your heart tells you. If you want a baby, let nature take its course. If not, then welcome to the modern world. Just walk a few blocks down to Planned Parenthood, they will take care of you."

Rija rarely ever set foot in church, but she surprised herself the next day by walking up the steps and into the sanctuary at St. Casmir's. She heard the big door close behind her, shutting out the sound of the city. Gazing at the altar, she considered every side of her predicament. What did it matter if women by the millions faced the identical situation every single day? Her problem was her own, and she had to decide for herself. What was more important, the life of her unborn child or her ability to create a life for herself and the child that she already had?

Hoping for a message, she added her candle to those in the nave already burning at the feet of the Blessed Mother. Struggling to quiet her inner thoughts, she looked up to the statue's unblinking blue gaze. "A baby?" She whispered.

Her question met with chilly silence broken only by a siren's blare in the street. And in her mind she heard Carlene's voice, "If you need help, they will take care of you."

Rija stood next to her mother at the kitchen sink as she rinsed the remains of Lili's breakfast from her Care Bear bowl. Rija's own breakfast was a piece of dry toast, and even that stuck in her throat. Still, she was thankful to keep it down. She sipped a cup of tea.

Elena frowned. "You don't look well. Did you not sleep?"

Rija avoided her mother's eyes. "I'm fine. Just a little tired."

Elena held Rija's face between her hands. "I had a dream."

Rija could feel herself coloring. "What was your dream, Mama?"

"In my dream, you were worried. You went from person to person, asking what you should do."

Rija leaned on her mother for support as tears fell. "Oh, Mama."

Elena cupped her daughter's chin in her hand. "Daughter, is there something you want to tell me?"

"Mama, how do you always know?"

"I know you, *draga*.

"I don't know what to do. Everything is awful, and I feel so bad."

Elena wiped away the tear that trickled down Rija's cheek.

"I'm pregnant, but this is not the time to have a baby. I know that in my heart."

Elena sat down in her chair. "I too know what it is to feel that way."

Rija looked at her mother with surprise.

"When you were just a little older than Lili is now, I was pregnant. But times were bad, your father wasn't working very much. It was right before he lost the business, and we had to take care of his mother too. Do you remember?"

Rija thought of the sickly old woman in black who lived with them when she was small. She'd always hated it when she had to kiss her. "Yes, I remember Nana."

"But it was hard for me. I couldn't take care of Nana and a new baby too. I never told your father. He never knew. He had enough worries. For women, sometimes, we must take care of ourselves."

Rija tried to hold the hospital gown together. One of her paper slippers fell off as she climbed onto the operating table. A shiver ran through her as she placed her feet in icy metal stirrups. The nurse who arranged the draping around her legs promised it would be over quickly. The light, round and pale, stared down like a single all-seeing eye.

She was still young, she reminded herself, still in her twenties. There would be time for another baby when life was less complicated, when things were more stable, and when they had their own home. At that moment, just as she had many times before, Rija created a wall in her mind. She put her fears and conflicts behind the wall.

The medical team entered the room. A dark-eyed woman approached. "I'm Dr. Riggs," she announced. "Just relax, you'll be fine."

The nurse gave Rija's hand a reassuring squeeze.

"You'll feel some pressure," the doctor said.

Looking at the light, Rija felt her thoughts turn fuzzy. The nurse smoothed her hair. Minutes later, as if from a distance, she was aware of a pulling sensation, pressure. When it was over, she slept.

An hour later, Rija was groggy, tired, and sore. She shivered with cold. The recovery room nurse came to check her vital signs. "How do you feel?" she asked.

Rija smiled weakly. "Okay." She fought against the sense of loss that welled up in her chest. Instead, she focused on counting all that she hoped to accomplish, and as she did, a powerful sense of relief flooded into her heart. Rija lifted her head from the pillow. "May I have some water?"

The nurse brought a few ounces of water in a paper cup. "Not too much, just a few sips," she cautioned.

Carlene's face registered relief as Rija emerged, pale and wobbly, from the recovery area. She stood, motioning Rija to take her seat. "The car's close by. You just sit here while I go bring it around."

Rija sat. She closed her eyes and put thoughts of the last two hours behind her. The receptionist helped her into the waiting car.

"How do you feel?" Carlene asked.

"I want to sleep for a week, then I'll be fine."

"Don't you worry," Carlene said as she patted Rija's hand. "We'll divide up your floors tonight. You just get some sleep and see how you feel tomorrow."

Twenty minutes later, Carlene edged the car to the curb on Mercer Street. Rija waited as her friend walked around to help her up the steps. At the door, Carlene reached out to ring the buzzer.

Rija stopped her. "No, wait! He doesn't know."

Carlene watched Rija pull her keys from her purse and unlock the door. She took Rija by the elbow and slowly, carefully, the two women made their way up to the second floor. When they reached the top of the stairs, the door opened and Josef was standing there. Rija cast a nervous glance at Carlene.

Carlene beamed a broad smile at Josef. "Hey, Josef, how are you doing? Rija's under the weather, so I brought her home. She needs some rest."

Josef took Rija's elbow and guided her into the apartment.

"If you want I can come in and help her into bed," Carlene said.

Josef started to close the door. "No, thank you. I can take care of my wife."

Still smiling, Carlene stopped the door with her foot. "Rija, call me if you need anything. And don't worry about the job. We'll take care of things, and I'll see you in a day or two."

Rija leaned against the doorframe. Her friend gave Josef another gorgeous smile. "Josef, you have a good weekend, hear?"

Josef closed the door and frowned at Rija. "What's wrong with you?"

Rija maneuvered past him and headed for the bedroom. "I got sick at work, and Carlene was kind enough to being me home. You didn't have been so rude to her. She was trying to help."

Elena appeared and took over, shooing Josef away and taking Rija into the bedroom.

Rija sank against the pillow. "Mama, my flannel nightgown is in the drawer." She allowed her mother to pull her shirt over her head. She crawled further into bed.

"Did everything go well?"

"Yes, they were kind. Now I need to sleep."

Elena wiped a tear from her eye. "I pray for your little one."

"Mama, sometimes, we do for ourselves what we think is best. I just couldn't go through all of that right now. You know that, don't you?"

"Yes, I know." Elena crossed herself.

Elena held a finger to her lips and slipped out. Rija heard Lili ask, "Baba, what's wrong. Is Mama sick?"

It was well past dark when Rija awoke. Her stomach growled loud enough to remind her that she hadn't eaten since the night before. For weeks the thought of food had made her ill, but now she was ravenous. She inhaled the aroma of onions cooking in the kitchen.

"Mama?" she called.

Josef opened the door. "What do you want?"

"I'm hungry." Rija smiled at him. "Can you bring me some tea or soup and a piece of bread?"

Josef returned with a cup of soup and some crackers on a tray. "Your mother made you supa piletina. Do you want me to feed it to you?"

Rija laughed nervously. "No, I can sit up."

Rija sat up, and Josef set the tray down next to her. She ate the soup as he silently watched. "Mama's soups are the best medicine," she said. "What was for dinner?"

Josef eyed her suspiciously. "For someone who is sick, you've made a miraculous recovery. What was the matter with you?"

"I met Carlene at work so she could show me my new assignment, the new floors I would clean. All of a sudden, I became very weak and she brought me home. I have my period."

Josef did not look convinced. "You were sick last week too, weren't you? I heard you vomit in the bathroom."

Anxiety shot through her. Did he know?

"It was because of my classes. I have so much work to do, and it's making me nervous."

Josef eyed the open handbag next to the bed. He reached into a side pocket and extracted a pink receipt with the words Planned Parenthood across the top. "What is this?" He looked at the paper briefly and then held it in front of her face.

Rija said nothing.

"Post-operative instructions? So this is the cause of your illness? You have an abortion? You destroy my child?"

As Rija maneuvered to the other side of the bed to get up, Josef struck her across the face. A thin trickle of blood snaked from her nostril to her lip. She threw off the covers, and the tray clattered to the floor. She stood up and glared at him across the bed.

"Your child? You care so much for the child you already have that you disappear and we don't hear nothing from you. Not a word. Now you show up here and you act like you're the perfect father and husband?"

Josef started to come around to the other side of the bed, and Rija picked up a heavy glass vase from the top of the dresser. She clutched it by its narrow neck and held it like a club. "Don't think I don't know that you left with another woman. What did she do, throw you out? Is that why you came back to us?"

Josef stopped and stared at her.

"Go ahead, hit me again. I dare you. I'll call the police, and what will you tell them?"

Josef stepped back. "Go ahead, call the police, I don't care. What have I done?"

"I have a job," Rija said, her voice rising. "I have a green card. I can apply for citizenship. What will you tell them you do?"

Josef spun around and strode out of the room.

"I hope they deport you," Rija called after him.

Lili began to wail. Her crying followed Josef down the steps and out into the street.

The first cop was already checking his Nevada license. The New York plate was a ringer, and he had no owner's card.

Josef cursed himself for a fool. Running the light was no big deal. It was late, the streets were empty, they would have let him go with a warning. But no cop would overlook the speeding, no when he'd been going over ninety. He hadn't seen the white car hiding under the trestle, waiting for him as he headed for the expressway. But they saw him, and once the lights came up behind him, it was too late. He could have kept going, but he didn't think the SUV had the guts.

Thank God he'd already delivered the pick-up to that guy up in the Northeast. Watching the red and blue lights flickering in his rearview, he felt sick at the thought of all those parking tickets thrown in the back seat and the gun he'd hidden in the wheel well. The second cop motioned him to roll down the window. "Sir, I'll have to ask you to step out of the car."

Two days passed with no sign of Josef. Rija stayed in bed for the first day. By the second day, she was tired of reading and watching television and felt as if the walls of the apartment were closing in on her. By the third day, her strength had returned, and she was ready to work.

It had rained overnight, and the late-afternoon sky was gloomy with fast-moving clouds. She could see tree branches swaying as a strong gust of wind whistled down the street, scattering leaves and litter. It felt more like March than April. When would it start to get warmer?

The telephone rang. Rija ignored it and continued to gaze out the window at the street scene below. Lili jumped up from her cartoons to grab it. She cradled the receiver against her ear, her head tilted to the side. "Yes, Papa, I'm fine, but I missed you. Baba came to school to pick me up."

She held the phone out to her mother. "Papa wants to talk to you."

Josef's voice was pleasant, as though he'd just ducked out for a minute and forgot to take his keys. "Hello, my little chicken."

"I'm just on my way to work, and I don't have time to talk to you," Rija said.

"May I say, I'm very sorry for what happened."

Rija cleared her throat but said nothing. She felt Lili's eyes on her face.

Ignoring her silence, Josef continued. "How are you feeling?"

Rija looked at her watch. "I'm feeling better. What do you want?"

"It's cold and I'm very sorry that I won't be able to drive you."

"Really, I don't have time. I'm going to be late."

"Please, listen. It seems there's been a little misunderstanding about my car."

"A misunderstanding?"

"Yes. I was stopped for running a red light. I didn't have an owner's card with me, and when the police checked, the car was listed as stolen."

Rija snorted.

He laughed and said, "Can you believe it? Of course, it's all a big

107

mistake." He laughed again. "And now I am in a holding cell at the police station. In fact, they are keeping me here in jail. Please, I need your assistance. Can you help me?"

"How can I help you? You know I have no money."

"Yes, yes, I understand that, but you know a lawyer, don't you? From your class?"

The last thing Rija intended to do was to get one of her teachers involved with Josef. Then she thought of Tony. "I know someone from class who might be able to help you. He's not a lawyer, but he works for one. Do you want his number?"

"I've already used up my phone calls. Can you call him for me?"

Rija sighed. "Yes, I'll call him, but only if you give me some money."

"No problem, I ..."

"You must pay. I won't pay any money for you. I have no money for you."

"You're not listening to me, Rija. Be quiet a minute."

She took a breath.

"Listen carefully. I need for you to do something. Go into the storage area in the cellar. Understand?"

"Yes, and then what?"

"Right behind the furnace, down near the floor, you will see a brick with blue paint on it. Pull the brick away from the wall. Behind it you'll find a packet with some money."

Josef had her full attention now. "Use that to pay for the lawyer."

When Rija returned home from work, she waited until after midnight. When Mr. Gracek's television went silent, she crept, flashlight in hand, down the steps, past his door on the first floor. Stepping over the landlord's sleeping cat, she padded toward the cellar stairs at the rear.

The cellar smelled of mildew and dust. Near the stairs, the well-used tenant's washer and dryer dominated the room. She pulled the string hanging above the laundry tub and a bare bulb flicked on, casting a dull glow. Beyond its dim circle of light, the ancient oil-burning furnace loomed out of the shadows.

Rija hit the flashlight against the heel of her palm until the batteries connected. She moved around the furnace. She crouched down under grimy ductwork and played the light from her flash up and down the bricks.

Near the floor, three bricks protruded slightly. The middle one was dabbed with a spot of blue. Rija's heart pounded in her ears. She pulled a screwdriver from her pocket. A mouse scuttled past her foot into the darkness, and she started and banged her head on the ductwork. Stars appeared behind her eyelids, and she crouched on her heels until the dizziness passed.

The flashlight dimmed. There wouldn't be much time before the batteries died altogether. Quickly, Rija dug at dried mortar, cursing as she scraped a knuckle. After what felt like forever, stale air wafted through the opening. Maneuvering the screwdriver back and forth, she loosened two bricks and pulled them out. Her fingers grasped a corner of canvas jammed in between strips of lathing where the bricks had rested. The slats gave up the packet just before the flashlight died. She felt her way in the darkness, tapping bricks back into place, feeling the wall to make sure the bricks didn't jut. Then she pocketed her prize and tiptoed up the stairs.

Rija turned the key and held her breath. Inside was silence save for the kitchen faucet's slow drip. She avoided the loose board and crept to her bedroom. She brushed away dust and grit and then unwrapped the canvas and stared. Ben Franklin's enigmatic countenance stared back at her. She fanned the bills over the bedspread and counted them, then counted them again. Making sure all the bills were face up, she stacked them in piles of five each. It came to thirty-five hundred dollars. Her brain reeled. She would work ten weeks to earn so much money, and Josef had kept it hidden from her. *She wondered how much more he might have-and where he might have it.*

The next morning Rija called Tony. "My husband's in jail for driving a stolen car," Rija told him. "Can you help him? I have three thousand dollars,"

"I can talk to my boss. I'll call you back," Tony promised.

They met on Tony's lunch hour in a small lounge overlooking the lobby of his building. Rija handed Tony an envelope with the bills and asked him to count it. He did and then gave her a receipt. He asked her if she wanted to join him for lunch across the street, but Rija just wanted to get the transaction over with.

"Once we get this to the court, we should be able to get him out on bail today," Tony explained. "Will you be meeting him there?"

"Where?"

"At the court building?"

"No, I'm going to work." The last place Rija wanted to be was in court waiting for a judge to free her husband on bail.

"I may not be there either, but when you see Josef, just make sure he knows to show up for the hearing. Our bail bondsman doesn't play."

"I'll tell him."

On her way home, Rija stopped for a pack of batteries for her flashlight. When she got to the apartment, she grabbed a load of laundry and took it to the basement. As clothes washed, rinsed, and dried, she methodically scanned every inch of the space. She searched dark corners with the flashlight, inspected the walls for loose bricks, and cleared away ancient cobwebs from the ceiling. Her search yielded nothing, but she felt sure Josef had hidden more cash somewhere. With the stolen car out of the equation, there must be another hiding spot.

Rija was still thinking about hiding places as she stood on the school grounds and waited for her daughter. When Lili emerged from the school building and spotted her mother, she broke into a run. Beaming, she thrust a gold-stickered paper up for Rija's inspection. "Look, Mama, one hundred percent on my spelling test. I got them all right."

Rija was so happy for her daughter that she had to fight back tears. "This deserves a treat. Shall we stop at the deli for something on the way home?"

"Yes, and we can put the test on the refrigerator like they do at Karen's house."

In the deli, Rija waited patiently while Lili walked back and forth inspecting her choices. After a few more moments of deliberation, she selected a box of chocolate cupcakes as her reward. Outside, Lili presented Rija with her book bag, insisting that she be allowed to carry the treat home.

As they waited at a traffic light, Rija said she had something to tell Lili. She tried to keep her tone light. "Lili, Papa's been away for a few days, but I think he should be home by the time we get back."

"Will you and Papa promise not to yell anymore?"

"Yes, I promise."

"I don't like it when you and Papa yell. It scares me. Timmy says he can hear it when you fight."

Rija wondered if Mr. Gracek did, too.

"We'll try not to. But married people do have disagreements. All families fight."

Lili's caution evaporated at Josef's wide grin. She squealed a welcome and rushed into her father's arms. Later, though, her eyes darted from one parent to the other as though searching their faces for clues.

"Lili asked me to promise not to yell," Rija said to Josef. "We're sorry. Aren't we?"

"Yes, it was a misunderstanding. Lili, there will be no more fighting. I promise. Now give me a kiss."

He smothered her smooth cheek with kisses. "Mm, you taste like cupcakes."

That night, Elena cooked a traditional meal. The four of them sat down to a roast with noodles, finished off with Elena's cherry strudel for dessert. Later Rija helped her mother clear the table. Out of Josef's hearing, she whispered tersely, "We still need his help, and that's why I let him come back, but why should we welcome him like a hero?"

Elena put the leftovers into the refrigerator. "He's Lili's father. And I'm grateful to him for the way he helped me."

Rija swabbed dishes in the soapy water and Elena picked up a dishtowel. "Since the time they took your father away, I wait, hoping to hear his footsteps on the stairs every night. Seven years and I still wait."

"But Josef isn't Papa. He left us once. He's only here because he's hiding and he needs a safe place. Now that the police know where he is, he may not stay much longer."

Josef left early the next morning. When Rija heard the apartment door close, she got up quickly and went to the living room window, saw the black town car parked at the curb. Across the street, a neighbor was peering out from her window. Josef appeared and glanced up and down the street as he walked toward the car. He opened the passenger-side door of the vehicle and got in. Rija watched the curtains across the street drop as the car pulled away.

Rija knew that little on Port Richmond's narrow streets went unnoticed, but until now she hadn't minded the scrutiny. Mr. Gracek joked that keeping track of neighbors was the most interesting part of the day for some people. He swore that despite buses, trolleys, and subways crisscrossing the city, the old-timers, born and raised in the neighborhood, rarely felt the need to venture further than the grocery store or to church for Wednesday night bingo or Mass on Sunday. Rija wondered if some of the neighbors knew more about Josef's comings and goings than she did.

After breakfast she called Tony at work. "When your boss got Josef out of jail, did he say anything about what happened?"

"I gave our lawyer the money, he made bail, paid the court costs and all that. I decided to tag along with him to the courthouse, and we waited around for a little while to see how things would go."

"So you were there?"

"Yes, I saw Josef come out of the courtroom. I'm not sure how much he knew, but he walked over to the lawyer and thanked him. He gave me a look, but I don't think he would have recognized me, do you?"

"No. How would he know you? Was there anything else?"

"Well, it got interesting afterwards, when Josef headed for the door. A short guy in a suit with a bag of Hershey's Kisses was hanging around. Like he was waiting for someone. When Josef walked by, he tagged him on the sleeve, pulled him aside. He got the funniest look on his face when the guy yanked him into a room. Does that sound like anyone you know."

Rija frowned. "No. This will sound strange to you, but I don't know anyone my husband knows."

Josef didn't come home till the following day. As Rija got dressed for work in the bedroom, she could hear his restless pacing as he talked on one of his cell phones. He carried two cell phones lately, one glossy black, the other silver. When he spoke into the silver one he used English, for the black phone, Russian. Though Rija knew little of that language, she could recognize a few words, and it seemed as if most of Josef's Russian conversations focused on *dengi*, slang for money. At the end of a call she'd hear the apartment door slam followed by Josef pounding down the stairs.

Today was no different. Rija turned the deadbolt behind him and returned to the kitchen. As his footsteps faded, she spotted the silver phone on the counter. She flipped it open and fumbled at the keypad. She found a list of contacts, but they were mostly initials, and the few full names were unknown to her. She wondered if Tony might be able to trace the telephone numbers. She picked up a tablet and pen and copied them down. When she was finished, she put the paper in her pocket.

Chapter 18

The train rattled overhead, shooting sparks as it screeched into the station to disgorge passengers. Despite the noonday sun, pedestrians on Kensington Avenue walked in shadow. Through a tinted windshield, Josef eyed two youths in Nikes and denim as they flew down the steps from the platform. He frowned as they jostled an old woman, almost tipping her shopping cart. He chuckled when she fought back, swatting them with her umbrella and cursing vigorously.

The black car, polished to a dull gleam, idled at the curb. Leon shot Josef a look that he took as his cue to get busy. When the Russian stayed put, Josef realized he would be on his own. He checked his reflection in the window of L & J Shoes. Inside, he smiled at the man behind the counter. "Good morning, my friend. How are you today?"

The shopkeeper turned to face him, and when he caught sight of the car outside, his sloping shoulders drooped a little further. "Things could be better."

"Yes, things could always be better, but my boss, Mr. Leon, says you owe him money. It's collection day, time to pay."

The owner edged toward the cash register. "Business ain't been so good. Nobody wants shoes no more. All the kids today are wearing sneakers, fancy styles. It's hard to keep up with what they want. But tell your boss I'm trying. Tell Mr. Leon I can get half the money by next week, okay?"

Josef smiled again. "Sorry. Not okay."

He hated to do what he had to do, but Leon was watching. He reached over the counter and grabbed the man by the collar. "Open the register."

The man choked and coughed. His glasses slipped off his nose and fell to the floor. "Okay, let me do it. Let me open it for you. You'll see for yourself."

Josef let go of the shirt long enough to pull out the cash drawer and empty its meager contents on the counter. "You're right, you don't have any money, but you better get it by next week." He poked the ashen-faced owner in the chest. "I'll be back on Monday. Have a nice weekend."

In the car, Leon headed west to the next pick-up. At the corner of Tioga Street, he pointed to a mural above a vacant lot bearing the words, R. I. P. John. Letters three feet high floated on a blue cloud. Below was a bleeding heart.

Leon gestured at the wall. "Look at this shit. Who is fucking John?"

Josef shrugged.

"Why his name is up on a wall? Who you think would be so stupid? To put this on a wall and call it art?"

Josef shook his head in silent agreement. He'd seen the wall before but never thought much about what it meant or why it was there.

Leon ranted on. "These people have no culture, they have no taste. They are animals."

Leon blew smoke from his cigarette. "Why do you live in this neighborhood?" He made a gesture that took in a wide area. "This is not civilized. You should move to the suburbs. Where I live there is less crime. Better schools. Your little girl can breathe the air. Your wife can go shopping. There you can live like a human being."

Josef nodded. "Yes, this neighborhood is a dump, maybe it is time to move."

Leon smiled. "Good, now you are being smart. Now you are thinking like an American. One more stop at that butcher across the street. Then you can drop me off at the restaurant. I'm meeting with my lawyer. We can finish pick-ups later."

That Saturday, Josef announced to Rija that they were going out that night.

Rija looked up from her magazine and frowned at him. "What do you mean, we're going out? Why didn't you tell me?"

"I wanted to surprise you. We're going to a party, a birthday party. At a fancy restaurant."

Rija considered. Surprising her-if, in fact, that's what he really intended-was a typical Josef move, but she had to admit it would be delicious to get out of the apartment for a few hours, to relax and shake off the draining work week. It had been a long time since she'd gone to a party.

"Why don't you wear the dress I bought you for the wedding?" Josef said.

Rija grinned and got up to see about the leopard-print dress.

With less than an hour to go before they left for the party, Lili peered wide-eyed as her mother teased her hair into a tousle of curls. "Mama, will there be games like we played at Karen's party? Will you have cupcakes? Please, can I go?"

"No, sweetheart, this party is for grown-ups. You wouldn't like it. There are no games, only grown-ups sitting around talking."

When Rija filed her nails and lacquered them with a coat of scarlet, the child held her small hand out to be polished as well, and her mother dabbed red onto Lili's wiggling fingers.

"Would you like to invite Timmy down to watch television with you tonight? I can ask Baba to make some popcorn."

Lili flounced from her bedroom. "No, I'm mad at Timmy. He acts silly."

Dressed and ready, Josef twirled Rija in front of the mirror, rewarding her last-minute efforts with thumbs-up approval. He steered her to the door. "Let's go. I want to show you something."

A shiny Land Rover waited curbside. Josef flicked the remote to beep the doors open. Rija stopped. "Where does this come from? Where does the money for this come from?"

"It isn't mine," Josef replied. "My friend Leon loaned it to me. You'll meet him tonight."

"Another car with no papers? Be careful or you could end up in jail for the second time."

Josef's face darkened. "Do you always have to look for trouble?"

Trouble was the last thing Rija wanted. It was Josef who had made all the trouble, Josef who had caused her no end of it. He had no right to put any blame on her.

Josef opened the passenger door. "Get in or stay home. It's up to you. I just don't want to be late."

Rija got in. Josef got in on the driver's side and started the engine. He turned on the radio, twisted the dial to find a pop station to his liking. He hummed along to a song as he put the car in gear and pulled away from the curb, oblivious to Rija's silence.

Rija regained her composure during the ride and began to look forward to the party. When Josef pulled into a humble shopping center parking lot, she wondered if it wasn't at odds with their Saturday night finery. But Josef pulled around to the rear of the strip mall where shiny high-end cars were clustered together.

Josef checked his hair in the rearview mirror. Satisfied, he opened the door for his wife and gave her his arm. They hadn't exchanged a word since they'd left Mercer Street, and as he led her toward Club Europa's flashing neon, he avoided her gaze.

Inside, Josef exchanged greetings with a burly man in a black jacket who crossed their names off the guest list. Rija smiled and nodded as Josef introduced her, surprised to feel his arm encircling her shoulders. From within, the sounds of music were exciting. Josef leaned in close and kissed her right earlobe. "You look beautiful."

"So do you," Rija said. They checked their coats, and Rija accepted champagne from a waiter's tray.

Lights bounced off an elaborate chandelier. Floral arrangements adorned the periphery. A cold buffet ran on for thirty feet, centered by an ice swan. Each table held its own frosted bottle of vodka and a champagne bucket. Music blared while a gyrating DJ worked the stage. Waiters circulated with trays of hors d'oeuvres.

Rija took in the surroundings, noting well-groomed women dressed in flashy ensembles of reds, purples, and greens. She wondered how her dress, so glamorous looking at home, had managed to turn shabby inside the club.

A barrel-chested man with thick salt-and-pepper hair motioned to them from across the room.

Josef took her elbow. "There's Leon."

Leon hit the shoulder of the young man next to him. "Yuri, Boris, get up. Let Josef and his beautiful wife sit down."

Two men wearing European suits and Rolex watches vacated their chairs, making space. Josef and Rija sat down. Introductions were made and names exchanged around the table. Leon's wife, Paulina, a platinum blonde in red silk, smiled and waved fingers twinkling with diamonds. Josef's charming side emerged as he traded shots of vodka, toasting his new friends in Russian. When one bottle ran dry, their host called for another.

Rija leaned across her husband. "Thank you for loaning us a car, Leon. That is very kind of you."

"My dear Rija, I have many cars." He gestured expansively. "Many people here work for me. Now that Josef will be driving for me, I'm happy to loan him a car."

"Well, thank you, just the same."

As the DJ played a Russian version of "Celebrate Good Times," Rija felt some of the tension drain from her shoulders. Holding her second glass of champagne, she began to feel more kindly toward Leon and Paulina.

Later, Rija and Paulina shared photos of their children. Paulina confided, "We are living here for ten years. We moved out of the city, and now we live in Bucks County. Five bedrooms, three baths colonial. Good schools."

"My Lili's school is also good, St. Casmir's."

"You have just one child?" Paulina asked.

"Yes, I'm working at night and going to school on the weekend. One child is enough for now."

Paulina laughed. "You are very busy woman."

Rija asked, "And you, Paulina? What do you do?"

"I shop. I am a very good shopper."

Conversation stalled as a tall red-haired waitress bounced on stage singing "Hot Stuff" in a combination of Russian and English. Her co-workers cheered her on until the banquet captain threatened them all back to work.

A gray-haired guest took the stage and changed the mood. As he crooned his rendition of the Russian folksong *Katusha*, the room came to its feet in a roar of nostalgia for the homeland that left the partygoers hugging, wiping their eyes, and drinking toasts to Mother Russia.

When the DJ finally regained control of the music by spinning a slow, romantic ballad, Paulina pulled a surprised Josef onto the floor. Not to be outdone, Leon turned to Rija extending his hand with a slight bow of the head. "Would you like to dance?"

Rija's lips smiled agreement but her insides quivered. She loved dancing as a young girl, but life had offered little opportunity since. "I haven't danced in many years," she said, but she stood up and went with Leon onto the dance floor.

Her steps were tentative at first, but when the music swelled, her feet took on a life of their own. She let her heart soar.

Leon leaned close. "You are a wonderful dancer."

She wasn't sure she believed him, but his graceful movement awakened memories of another time. Rija threw her head back, giving herself over to the waltz.

On the ride home, Josef waxed enthusiastic. "That Leon is a funny guy. And his wife is very charming. I like spending time with them. What did you think?"

"You're right. Paulina was nice. And Leon with his charming European manners was a gracious host. So kind and very pleasant. Still, I have a feeling he can be a dangerous man."

"Don't worry about it. He's a businessman." Josef blew smoke from his cigarette.

"Yes, but I wonder what business he's in."

"You think too much. Most of what he does is in finance. He's a smart guy. He puts his brain to work for him. Most of his money comes from investments."

Chapter 19

One morning Rija woke up to strange sounds coming from the living room. She threw on a robe and went to check. There, sitting proudly on the coffee table, was a new computer, its companion printer nestled on the shelf underneath. Josef, tapping happily on the keyboard, looked up at her.

"What do you think?" he asked. "I've already signed up for e-mail and sent a message. Now we can keep in touch with my sisters."

Rija's heart lifted at the mention of Josef's sisters.

"Last time I saw Milos, we called them," Josef said. "You know, everybody there has cell phones now. Maybe you should get one."

"I don't care about a cell phone. Just tell me about your sisters."

"I spoke with my uncle. Zoltan is well, and my aunt sends her love. And what do you think? Our little Katja is getting married to a carpenter in Mostar. They are building a house in the town."

"And what of Dina?"

"Dina is finishing high school. She wants to be a doctor."

Rija silently rejoiced at the news about Katja and Dina. For so long she'd been terrified to think about where they were or what might have happened to them.

"Why didn't you tell me this news sooner?"

"You didn't ask."

Rija spied her mother at her bedroom door. "Mama, come see. Josef can send messages to Katja and Dina on the computer."

Elena peered sleepily at the screen as though it might be magic.

"I'll send them some money when I can," Josef said. "Katja's wedding will be in the fall. And Dina, she uses the computer all the time at her school. We can communicate. You can send messages to Katja. They can send us pictures. You can even use it for your classes."

Rija agreed the computer could help her with her work, but she wondered what Lili would make of it.

Josef continued, "People in Bosnia are finding each other all the time. There are ways now to send messages and find people who are lost."

Elena's eyes filled. Rija read her mother's thoughts. She remembered articles in the papers. Tribunals sought justice for victims of Bosnian war crimes while archeologists excavated mass graves in search of the missing. Her father was just one of the thousands who had disappeared, never to be seen or heard from again. In her classes, she had seen how the computer could conduct searches. She wondered if there might be a way to find out about their father, what had happened to him after his enemies took him away.

A happier thought occurred. It might be possible to locate Mira. She had wondered so many times where her best friend might be and whether she had returned home. She pictured the last time they'd been together, the day shells fell near their school. From then on, Mira's father kept her home, and soon after, the family packed and left Sarajevo without a word.

Rija returned her attention to Josef and his continuing words of praise over the computer. When she was finally able to get in a word, she demanded a promise from him. "Lili can use it for educational things and for her homework when she's a little older, but no video games for her. Agreed?"

Josef agreed, and Rija padded into the kitchen to make coffee.

Josef slid behind the wheel of his new car. Before he even turned on the ignition a battered but familiar Ford pickup pulled into view. "Oh, fuck me," Josef whispered.

Zimmerman was driving. "Get in, dude." His partner, a man named Galter, opened the passenger door.

No choice but to do as he was told. Since these two had got their hooks into him, his life wasn't his own. Their messages on his cell phone, the way they turned up out of nowhere telling him what to do, it was making him sick. Right now, he didn't want to hear what they had to say. But they were calling the shots, and there was little choice but to go along.

They swung down Frankford Avenue, into an alley street facing a row of dilapidated garage fronts. Zimmerman parked and cut the engine. Galter straightened his baseball cap and gave Josef a level gaze. "So what's up?"

Josef turned sideways to face his handlers. Despite the cool temperature, sweat trickled down his side. "Most of the time I'm just driving Leon around. I help him and the others with collections, rents and loans, everyday things. That's it."

"What else?" Galter asked.

Josef shrugged. "From what I see, Leon is just a businessman."

Zimmerman sneered. "Yeah, he's a real civic leader, this guy. Now what else have you got?"

Josef mined his conversations with Leon, looking for details he could share, details he could give them without endangering his safety or his newfound livelihood. He didn't want to risk losing his share of Leon's lucrative operations.

Galter's face tightened. "Listen up, Malacovik. We know about you, and we know about Leon. Right now, you have three choices. You can go to jail, or we can turn you over to Immigration, in which case you go to jail or get deported. Or you give us some facts about the Russian's operation and you stay on the street. Understand?"

Josef understood.

"Okay. I'm gonna ask you again. What have you got?"

That evening, after Lili had been put to bed, Rija told Josef she needed to talk to him. Elena was watching television, so they went into the kitchen to talk. "Who were those men in the hats?" Rija asked.

Josef stayed straight-faced. "I don't know who you're talking about."

"Yesterday Lili and I were at the park. We went for ice cream at the drugstore. I saw you and those two men."

"What men?"

"The ones on Frankford Avenue. The men in the beat-up black truck."

"Oh, those guys? They're painters, they have some work for me next week."

Rija didn't pursue the conversation, but while Josef sang in the shower, she sifted through his pockets. She borrowed a few dollars from one pocket and found a key in the other. The key had "G-27" stamped on it and was attached to a tag that read,

"If found, drop in any mailbox, postage guaranteed.
U-Stor-It
2002 Rt. 13
Bensalem, PA 19003"

There was barely time to grab paper and pencil before steam billowed from the bathroom and a towel-draped Josef emerged. Cigarette dangling, he padded to the kitchen in search of a match.

"Did your mother iron my white shirt?"

Rija went to the closet. "Yes, it's right here. And you should thank her."

Josef dressed quickly and left. His so-called jobs now took him away from home most days and many nights. More often than not, he claimed his schedule prevented him from meeting Rija to drive her home from work. Waiting for the train on those nights, she wondered who benefited more from their arrangement. Josef had a place to stay, a hiding place that provided at least a minimum of security. Aside from his sporadic treats, the occasional envelope of cash on the kitchen table, or a bag of groceries, what did she get?

After class Saturday, Rija showed Tony the U-Stor-It address. "Can you tell me where this is?"

"It's just outside the city. Not far."

"I need to go there."

"Is this to do with Josef?"

She nodded.

"I'm off tomorrow. If you want, we could drive out together. Or we could go after class today."

Rija shook her head. "Thanks, but I don't want to take a chance going in the daytime."

"Do you want me to check it out for you?"

"No, I can't pay you this time."

"Don't worry. I'll put it on your tab."

"My tab?" Rija was puzzled.

Tony laughed. "It's an expression. I'll explain it to you some day."

The U-Stor-It lot was a warren of 6-feet by 8-feet cinderblock cubicles with bright orange doors. Tony pulled his car onto the lot, parked, and walked into the office. "I need a rental," he told the bald-headed man behind a battered desk.

"We have singles, doubles, and triples available. There's a three-month promotion on the double units. You get the first month free and two additional months at $75 a month. That's our discount rate. A great deal."

Pretending to think about it, Tony counted to ten. "I'm moving to a new place, so the three-month deal could work for me." He opened his wallet. "Cash okay?"

The clerk pushed an application across the counter. "Yeah, but I'll need to see some ID."

Tony flashed the fake ID he carried from his high school days and gave a name and address, which the U-Stor-It man wrote down. When Tony signed and took his receipt, the clerk produced a key.

"You're in Section D, in 19 and 20." The clerk circled units in red.

"What if I need to move in at night?"

"Someone's here from six in the morning till ten at night. We lock down overnight. Some people get the idea this is a motel. Know what I mean?"

It was full dark when Tony drove Rija onto the lot. The guard waved them through and Tony fiddled with his unit for a few seconds. Then they crept from section D to G-27. Rija crouched low holding an electric torch while Tony sweated through several tries at picking the lock. "These tools are useless." He threw down the pick in disgust. "The only way I can get this sucker off is to cut it. A hacksaw might work. What do you think?"

"No, better not do that."

Rija realized she would have to steal Josef's key if they were going to see what was in the storage unit. "We should wait. I don't want him to know we've been here."

They stopped for coffee at an all-night diner. Rija craned her neck at the sight of a familiar black town car nosing its way into a space. Sick with fear, she recognized the driver. She loosened her hair, letting it fall across her face. Tony played with the menu, oblivious to her drama.

"Don't look now," Rija hissed.

Thankfully, Leon was alone. She watched the door open. He shifted his bulk onto a counter seat. Chatting up the waitress, his restless eyes scanned the booths. Though Leon's eyes flickered over her, they seemed to register nothing. When the waitress brought his order, he paid for his sandwich, tipped several dollars, and walked out.

Tony spotted the black car, the driver, and Rija's silent transformation. He turned from the window. "That was him, wasn't it? The guy with the limo?"

Rija's ashen face answered the question.

Rija washed lettuce for Sunday dinner. She'd felt on edge since the night she'd seen Leon, and her senses were alert. An alarm went off in Rija's head when Josef stood close.

"Who is your friend?" he asked.

She knew that voice, soft yet threatening. She knew where this was going. She turned off the water and dried her hands. "Which friend?"

Josef grabbed her hair, pulled her around to face him. When he let her hair go, Rija jumped out of reach. Her eyes sought a weapon.

"Leon saw you in the diner with another man late at night. What was that? Was that a date?"

Silently, Lili emerged from the bedroom, her eyes casting about from one face to the other. Tears threatened to spill.

Josef's lips twitched. "How dare you? It shames me. You are my wife."

"He's a friend from my school, I was having coffee with Tony, from my school. Is that who you mean?"

"Yes, the friend from your school, the friend who follows me, the friend who knows the lawyer. That friend."

"Yes, that friend! He got you out of jail, didn't he?"

Josef slapped her across the face.

She returned the slap. "And you! How dare you? How dare you use the word shame to me?"

Elena pushed her granddaughter back into the bedroom but she stayed nearby.

Rija kicked at her husband and missed. "You have a nerve to talk. You desert us for years without a word. Who knows where you go or what you do. I wouldn't be surprised if you meet women every day, and I'm quite sure it is not for coffee."

Elena picked up a frying pan in case Josef decided to continue the conversation further. Reading the message in his mother-in-law's eyes, Josef grabbed his jacket at the door. They heard the familiar sound of the door slamming and footsteps down the stairs.

Chapter 20

Too late, Rija remembered Carlene's words. "I know it's hard, but you be sure to put a little something aside for when tax time comes around. It'll be here before you know it."

Since they were all outside contractors, Carlene explained that the company reported to Internal Revenue what the workers were paid. Rija remembered thanking her when Carlene told her that she paid something every three months. And did she want to be reminded when it was due for next time? But when the first 1099 form appeared in the mail, she put it in a drawer and tried to forget about it. Months passed and Rija hadn't paid any taxes. Tax day, April 15th had come and gone. When the next form arrived, she went looking for Carlene in the remodeled space that was once Fowler's domain. Though she could have guessed what the answer might be, still Rija asked what to do about her unpaid taxes.

Carlene thumbed through a binder from the shelf behind her desk, her long finger moving down the column of figures on the page. Finding what she was looking for, she scribbled a couple of numbers on a notepad and pushed the tablet across the desk. "It looks like you might owe the feds $1,140."

"No!" Rija gasped. The headache began working its way across her brow. It moved over the top of her head.

"And based on your weekly totals, you owe $650 to the city."

Rija remembered her father's negotiations with the tax collectors in Sarajevo. There, if you knew the right person, a small bribe could work miracles. "Is there any way I can pay less?"

Carlene shrugged. "You could talk to an accountant, but that will cost you money. The feds will let you use exemptions for your mother and daughter and maybe even that husband of yours."

"So there are different places to pay taxes to. The federal taxes and the city taxes?"

"That's right. And then there's the state too. But we don't need to worry about them right now. They're slow to collect."

"What can I do?" Rija's mind reeled at the thought of the unpaid bill.

Carlene leaned forward for emphasis. "The federal government is pretty efficient about getting their money. So you have to deal with them right away, especially for someone in your situation, if you know what I mean."

Rija scribbled as Carlene continued the lecture. "But the city, they don't care. Everybody's got to pay that five percent. Now the good news is, it takes the City of Philadelphia a while to catch up with you."

"So I don't have to worry about them?"

"No, I didn't say that. You can't forget about them, but you have to worry about that money for the feds first."

Rija hated to ask Josef for the money. She waited after dinner on Sunday night, hoping he would be in a generous mood.

She showed him the 1099 tax form. "Here's what I have to pay."

Josef's eyes narrowed. "When?"

"Carlene says I should pay it now, or it will only be worse later."

"What if you don't pay? Then what?"

Rija chewed her lip. "I could get in trouble. What if they checked those things before they renew your green card? What if they don't let you become a citizen? What if I get deported?"

Josef laughed at her fears. "You think they check everything?"

"You can't tell. All I know is we have this bill that needs to be paid."

He scoffed. "This is not Soviet Russia. I don't pay taxes. So what? Do they bother me?"

"I'm not you."

"Relax. Here, here is your money for taxes."

He counted out eleven one-hundred-dollar bills from his pocket. "Working for Leon, I can get this much money in one day."

Chapter 21

For the second time in five minutes his phone buzzed. Josef checked the number. Paulina again. He hesitated, but he knew he had no choice. He picked up the call determined to keep this strictly business. "Hello, Paulina. What may I do for you?"

"You didn't get this message?"

"I'm so very sorry. I meant to call you back right away, but Leon and I were busy."

He hoped the mention of her husband would interject some reality into the conversation.

"I'm hoping that you are free tomorrow because I need someone to drive me to Atlantic City. I promised my sisters we can go shopping and go to lunch at the casino."

"I would love to do this for you, but as you know I am only free if Leon says I am free. Perhaps we should check with him."

"Leon will be tied up tomorrow, so he tells me. He's flying to Florida."

Josef grimaced. "What time would you like me to pick you up?"

Paulina parked herself in the front seat while her two sisters took over the rear. Josef thought his day could turn ugly at any minute. But it wasn't just traffic that was grueling. The prospect of driving three chattering females back and forth on the expressway, waiting by the door as they shopped at the clothing outlets, and babysitting them as they indulged their three-martini lunch spread out dismally before him.

Thanks be to God, the sun was shining. Josef knew from experience that Atlantic City in the rain was an ugly sight. Early on, he'd worked cleanup crew in the casino where the ladies planned to have lunch. He'd left that job in a hurry and never looked back.

Josef found a parking space near the designer outlet. He leaned against the car, smoking and killing time on his cell phone. From where he stood, he could watch Paulina and her kin trolling the store aisles, picking up and setting back down one vivid ensemble after another. Once they emerged with their purchases, he hopped to attention, storing their loot while they resettled themselves inside.

"Where to now, ladies?" Josef asked, hoping his chirpy tone hid his annoyance.

"The Belle Epoch," Paulina directed.

At the hotel's gilded entrance, he left the keys with the valet and trailed his charges toward the restaurant.

"So Leon tells me that you spent a few years in Vegas before you came back East," Paulina said. "I love Vegas. I love everything about it, the shows, the hotels, the pools. There is always something to do. I would love to live there if it wasn't so hot all the time."

Josef nodded. "Yes, at first it's wonderful. The sun shines all the time. The skies are clear. Unlike the East Coast, there's no rain. Even the winters are warm. I loved that, but ..."

"But what?"

"I missed my family. I came back to see my daughter. So she wouldn't grow up without a father."

A sly smile played around the corners of Paulina's mouth. "You missed your daughter, not your wife?"

"Yes, of course. My wife too."

Paulina invited him to join them for lunch, but Josef begged off. "I'm sure you ladies will have much more fun without me. Call me when lunch is over, and I'll be happy to take you wherever you'd like to go next."

Josef left them and headed for the hotel's casino. It held the usual low-rent quotient of senior citizens and slots traffic. A banner proclaimed the Championship Middle Weight title fight that night. They would miss the crowd, Josef thought, but perhaps it was for the best. His credit card was no good, but he had some cash. A blackjack table might provide some diversion. He turned to head for the cage, and his heart stopped.

At the top of the stairs, he spotted three men looking like money. Scrutinizing the room with practiced eyes, the one on the right nodded to a cluster of Asian players in suits. Josef looked at the man on the left. A suspicious bulge ruined the fit of his Armani. The one in the middle was Nick Zhurko, his Las Vegas boss.

Josef felt bile rise in his gorge. He scanned the periphery looking for a way out. A door proclaimed Emergency Exit Only. Calling it a personal emergency, he barreled though. Sirens blared. He pounded down a cement corridor, oblivious to the shouts and footsteps behind. The corridor ended with a metal door into the parking garage, out into a dazzle of sunshine.

Josef leaned over a banister and vomited into the gutter. Then he got as far away from the casino as he could. The wind sprang up, pushing him past a quartet of new stucco villas and on toward a spit of beach. He slumped over a bench, sharing the view with an old man one bench over. Josef tried to look calm, but his guts wouldn't stop quivering. When his breathing slowed, the phone vibrated.

Paulina was summoning him back to the last place on earth he wanted to go. "We're waiting at the main entrance. Where are you?"

"I'm on my way."

He scrambled for options. A sudden gust blew the old man's porkpie hat toward the water. Josef chased it down and pulled out a twenty.

"Man, let me buy your hat."

"What'd you say?"

"I said I'll give you twenty dollars for your hat."

"No you won't. This hat ain't for sale."

He put the money in the man's spotty hand and slammed the hat on his head.

"Bring back my hat, you bastard. I'm calling the cops."

Josef's muscles didn't relax until they were halfway home on the Atlantic City Expressway. He vowed never to return to Atlantic City and its casinos again.

Rija examined Josef's keys, pleased to see the U-Stor-It tag warning "Do Not Duplicate" still there. She pulled out her office keys, looking for a comparable size and hue. One they used for the basement storeroom looked similar. Side by side, their size and thickness were so alike that when she held both to the light, notches aside, the two matched perfectly. She slipped the key off her ring, switched the two, and replaced Josef's keys on the dresser just as she found them.

At work, Rija flew down the corridors, hurrying through four floors of bathrooms and offices. Dee Dee had agreed to cover her for the rest of her floors. For the tenth time that night, she patted the keys in her pocket. By nine o'clock she was out the door on the street where Tony's car waited, motor running. She settled into the Volvo's passenger seat, more determined than ever to know what Josef had stored in the shed.

Tony stopped for a traffic light, and Rija pulled a sheet of paper from her handbag. "I didn't want to forget, so I wrote down these numbers from one of Josef's cell phones. Can you help me find out who they belong to?"

Tony glanced at the numbers and stuffed the paper into a pocket. "I have a buddy at the phone company. I'll see what he can do."

Rija went off on a tangent. "Since he became friends with Leon, all day long he gets calls, sometimes on one cell phone, sometimes on another. But whenever the phone rings, he jumps. Somebody on the other end gives him orders. Then he runs out and disappears for long time. It could be days until he shows up again. And he doesn't say a word. What kind of job is this?"

"Where is it exactly that he works?"

"Once we stopped to drop something off at a restaurant in the Northeast, on Bustleton Avenue, at a place called the Little Odessa."

Tony's eyebrows shot up. "I heard about that place. If his friend Leon hangs out at the Little Odessa on Bustleton Avenue, that's no joke."

"No joke?" Rija puzzled.

"What I mean to say is, those guys play for real."

"But they don't just hang out there," Rija told him. "Leon owns it."

Traffic thinned, and Tony headed out of town on the expressway. It was 9:35 when they reached the U-Stor-It. Beyond the glass, the guard dozed, head slumped forward. When he jerked awake at the sound of tires on gravel, Rija ducked.

"You'll need to make it fast," the guard warned Tony. "We close in twenty minutes."

Tony gave him a nod. "I'll just be a second. I need something outta my unit in section D. Be right back."

The guard lifted the gate and waved him through.

Tony stopped at Section G. "Here it is."

Rija slipped out, running into the shadows. For the guard's benefit, Tony went to Section D. He opened his own rental, transferred a few empty boxes from his trunk, pulled the orange door closed, and drove out the gate. The guard, barely taking half an eye off his TV, waved him through. Rija stayed behind shivering in the dark.

Tony pulled into a used car lot next to the U-Stor-It. From where he was parked, he could see the guard exit the office and make his final rounds before locking up. When the guard got into his car and drove off, Tony grabbed a duffel bag from the back seat and ran back to the storage facility.

Wishing that she too had a cell phone, Rija paced back and forth on the other side of the wall, staying out of camera range. At the sound of footsteps on gravel, she whispered, "Tony, where are you?"

"I'm around the back, I'll be there in five minutes. Just stay low."

Rija moved in a crouch toward his voice. She spotted Tony on the ground, bolt cutters in hand, systematically cutting links in the chain fence. He cursed with the effort, flattening himself against the ground as the headlights of a passing car flickered over him. Rija watched him extract pliers from his bag, which he used to twist the cut wires upward. Soon he'd created enough of a space to squeeze through. Once he was back in, they kept low, inching their way along.

"Wait. One more thing." Tony climbed up on a unit and covered the lens of the Section G security camera with spray paint. "Okay, let's go."

With the flashlight beam as guide, they moved toward G-27. Rija had the key in her hand, but when she stumbled on some loose stones, it slipped from her fingers. She groped in the darkness until she found it.

She cursed herself for her nervousness. In Bosnia she had survived snipers and artillery and even a rapist. She'd survived hunger and deprivation and the loss of loved ones. She'd been shot at. Surely tonight's adventure was nothing compared to such things.

At G-27, she fit the key in the lock. It turned easily and she pulled.

Tony whispered from behind. "Wait."

He rummaged in the bag for a can of lubricant and squirted some on the door. It glided open noiselessly. Together they grabbed the bottom handle, pushing the door up just enough for the two of them to squeeze under.

Inside was complete darkness. Rija found her flashlight and flicked it on. She played it on the walls, then began a more methodical search, aiming the light near the floor and working up. Tony's electric torch came on and illuminated the shed's four walls. Rija gasped. It was stacked floor to ceiling with merchandise.

"Oh, my God, look at this," Tony whispered. "What a stash. Flat screen TVs, computers."

"Yes, he brings one home and keeps the rest here."

But Rija's attention was riveted on the foreign address labeling a wooden crate. "Look here."

Tony looked at the crate, then at Rija. "What's **Zastava?**"

"It's the name of a gun."

Rija spied three metal boxes stacked in the corner. She tried to open them, but the first two were locked. She tried the one on the bottom. It opened. "Bring your light here," she whispered to Tony.

Inside, packets of hundred-dollar bills were banded together. Tony gave a low whistle. "This must be his walking around money. Not bad. Rija, in case you haven't guessed, you're married to the mob, but not the Italian mob, not like on TV. This is the Russian mob, the mafiya. Understand?"

Rija's face felt tight. She fought off not only waves of panic but also a surge of embarrassment. But she couldn't afford such pathetic and useless feelings. She drew a single one-hundred-dollar bill from each of the packets and slipped the money into her backpack. They put everything back the way they had found it and slipped out of the unit and back into the night.

City Hall clock showed twenty minutes to midnight, the normal time her shift ended. Though she didn't expect Josef to show up, she had returned with Tony to One Liberty Place to wait, just in case. They were sitting in Tony's car.

Rija, now with a cell phone of her own, dialed Josef's phone. "Will you come to pick me up tonight?" she asked after he picked up the call.

"No, I'm sorry, I must meet Leon. Can you take the subway?"

"Sure, no problem. Ciao."

"Not to worry," she told Tony. "He's busy. So if you take the Allegheny exit on I-95, I'll just get out at Richmond Street and walk home."

Tony started the engine and pulled out. "I'd love to bring this up in class, next time Doyle asks about cases, wouldn't you?" he said.

Rija shook her head. "No, I don't think so." She hoped he was kidding.

A black town car passed under the street light, heading in the opposite direction. It turned right on Westmoreland. Tony scanned its blacked out windows, but Rija looked down, let her hair fall over her face. She stayed that way until Tony assured her the car was gone.

The Number 15 trolley slowed in front of Wysocki's Hardware. A pyramid of shiny metal cans stocked one window. Red snow shovels fanned below a neon sign that promised, "Doors and Locks, Our Specialty".

The neighborhood deli next door was doing good business.

Customers might line up to buy coffee and sandwiches, but Rija knew their main business was the phone cards, money orders, and lottery tickets on sale there. For people with no bank account it was a portal, a source of day-to-day commercial transactions for the financially dispossessed.

Her stop was coming up. From the rear, three girls in parochial school navy giggled their way to the front of the car. Rija let them go ahead of her, wondering how their parents let them go out in their short skirts and skimpy coats.

When traffic slowed at the intersection, Rija grabbed her bag and made for home. At Al's Discount Appliances, the wind licked at a banner over the door. "Big Sale - Everything Must Go!" Outside, a family clustered around dented refrigerators, washers, and dryers displayed as though in an open-air bazaar. Rija watched the mother move from one washer to the next, inspecting each one thoughtfully. She and the merchant conducted a running conversation on the merits of each appliance, switching from Spanish to English and back again.

Rija felt sorrow for the family. She felt sorrow for herself. Often she felt alone in a country she hadn't chosen to come to. It was Josef who insisted they strike out for the United States. Rija had wanted to go to Vienna and wait until the fighting was over so they could return home to Sarajevo. But Josef's certainty of the opportunities in America convinced her.

She wished that things had been different, that she had been different. Now she felt strong, but in her heart she knew it was too late to go back. Lili was a little American now, with her Barbies and her sneakers that lit up when she walked. Rija knew she was of two minds when she thought of returning to Sarajevo. Doni was dead. Papa was gone. Her friends were scattered. She thought of her fellow students, of Mira, gone without a word. Drago, the first boy she ever kissed, killed by the White Eagle militia. The Muslim family down the hall who slipped away silently one night. No, she would know no one in Sarajevo now.

If she'd known how things would turn out, she would have made more of an effort to find her own way when they first arrived in this country. Still, would things have been different?

Six of them sharing a one-bedroom apartment made life difficult. Still, when tempers flared, Rija reminded herself they'd lived through much worse. With the funds from social services, Rija contributed their share for food and such, but living from day to day was wearing the patience of hosts and guests alike.

While the men smoked outside on the fire escape, Rija could overhear Milos tell Josef about a job he'd heard of in Atlantic City. A company, behind schedule on their new casino, was hiring, few questions asked. The immigrant's grapevine promised good jobs for anyone who was healthy, ready to work hard, and could speak good English.

Once at the construction site, the jobs turned out to be less than promised. They offered work in a nonunion clean-up crew for lower wages, and it would mean finding a place to sleep in a strange town. Still, to Josef, the money sounded good. He signed on even though Milos returned to Brooklyn in a huff.

On his first day, Josef left at 4 a.m. to catch the bus to New Jersey. That night he called to let them know he'd found the site, donned a hard hat, and put in a full day's work on the new job. While his muscles ached and the work was difficult, he vowed to keep going until Friday when they would be paid.

Rija congratulated him and told him all was fine in Brooklyn.

But things weren't fine in Brooklyn. Rija felt Milos and Valentina growing weary of them. And why wouldn't they? There were not enough chairs for them all to eat at the table, let alone enough places for them all to sleep. With each passing day, Rija's sense of unease increased. She couldn't avoid hearing Valentina whispering into the telephone and groaning over their clothes. Perhaps she should have listened when they tried to convince her to do some shopping, but Rija, unsure of their finances, was unwilling to spend a few dollars, even on clothes for Lili.

When a frustrated Valentina swore it was time for mother and daughter to get a new look, Rija finally agreed. One afternoon, Valentina returned from her manicurist job bearing an array of cosmetics. Making expert use of the borrowed scissors and hair products, Valentina gave Rija and Elena new American haircuts and makeup lessons. Milos told Rija and Elena they looked charming.

When Josef arrived home from his first week on the job, with money in his pocket and a bottle of wine under each arm, he stopped and stared at Rija. His eyes flashed from puzzled to bedazzled to proud.

Valentina stood behind Rija, fluffing her hair. "How do you like your wife now?"

Josef grinned. "She looks beautiful!"

"I thought it was time for them to have a fresh start."

Josef broke open the first bottle of wine. "Here's a toast to a new beginning for all of us!"

Sharing the wine, Rija felt tension slipping from her shoulders. Valentina found music on the radio, and they laughed and danced as long as the wine lasted.

Later, Rija tried to tell Josef it was time for them to go. "Why can't we move to be close to where you work?"

"That's not possible," Josef said.

"But why?"

"There is no place there for a family to live. I share a room near the construction site with another worker. The Wheel of Fortune Motel. We work 80 hours a week to finish the building on time. For now, it's best if you stay here in Brooklyn."

Things changed the next weekend, when Milos pulled his cousin aside. "Valentina lost her job. Winter is coming, and I need more help with the rent, moj brat, or we all have to move."

After Valentina offered to make appointments for Rija to talk with social services to explore the family's options, she called the Red Cross and the Bosnian Foundation. On the appointed day, the two women went together. After Rija explained her situation, a social worker made notes before she began flipping through a file on her desk. She pulled out a map and spread it out across the desk. While Valentina and Rija watched, the counselor drew an inky line through New Jersey. She tapped her pen at a dot and circled it. "Philadelphia. Have you heard of it?"

Rija was hesitant. She looked to Valentina, who remained silent, and the geography lesson continued. Unsure of the outcome, both women could agree the distance between the two points looked shorter. The social worker described a grant that would allow the family to move closer to where Josef spent his workweek. "It's not a perfect solution, but if you want to be closer to your husband, I think it's the best we can do. Would you be available to drive there the day after tomorrow?"

Spirits lifting, Rija nodded. Barely aware of the existence of the city of Philadelphia, she agreed to review available spaces.

After a whirlwind day trip, the trio reviewed a description of the most affordable apartment they'd seen. "It's three rooms, a combined family living space and kitchen with a stove and a refrigerator. And it's available now. What do you think?"

Rija thought for only seconds before answering. "I like it. The rent sounds very good. When can we move in?"

Come the weekend, everyone was pleased with the plan except Josef. "What do you know of this city, Philadelphia? Better to stay in Brooklyn where we can have help from Milos."

Rija pressed her case. "Can't you see? Milos and Valentina need help themselves. You must be blind if you can't tell that they want us to leave. Besides, we'll be closer to where you are working."

Reluctantly, Josef agreed, and Milos and Valentina volunteered to drive Rija, Elena, and Lili to Philadelphia. At eight o'clock on a Tuesday morning, the packed car headed south. They found the address, and Milos helped carry their bags inside. Valentina offered hasty hugs and good wishes, and they left as soon as they could.

Inside, Elena took charge. She inspected under the cabinets, picked at crusty spots on the linoleum floor in the kitchen, and scrutinized the windows. After one sniff of the musty bathroom, she got to work with a bottle of bleach and a scrub brush while Rija washed the windows and cleaned out trash the former tenants had left behind.

Rija bought food and filled their small refrigerator. Elena hand-stitched curtains and continued cleaning until every inch of the apartment was spotless.

On Friday night, Josef arrived. He knocked on the door and blew in with balloons, flowers, and a smile that quickly soured. He inspected the refrigerator and the cans of food in the cupboard. Rija's heart pounded as she watched him walk from one empty room to the next.

"Where does Lili sleep? Where will any of us sleep?" He asked.

A trip to the Salvation Army added a table and chairs, but they balked at the stained mattresses stacked against the wall. Instead, they walked three blocks to Discount Mattress City for a full-size mattress and spring set on sale and twin beds for the second bedroom. The storeowner promised delivery that afternoon, when Josef peeled bills from a bankroll.

At their Sunday night goodbyes, Josef promised to return the next weekend with overtime pay. But things changed when he called Rija the following Friday night. "I must work this weekend. But don't worry, soon we'll be together."

Josef made it home with some cash the following weekend. For several weeks after that, he called Rija every night. But as he worked more and more, the calls dwindled to twice a week. "There's overtime, we're on a deadline. I'm exhausted."

"Will you call me tomorrow?"

"I'll try. But sometimes I'm so tired after I get off work, all I can do is sleep."

His last call came on Thursday. When Rija telephoned the Wheel of Fortune Motel, a voice on the other end told her, "Sorry miss, no one registered here under that name."

A frightened Rija found the bus terminal downtown and bought a ticket to Atlantic City. On the other end, she asked directions of a uniformed woman at the information desk who pointed her toward the ocean. "Walk toward the beach, make a right and keep going until you see the sign for the new casino."

Blown by the wind, Rija peered at seagulls wheeling overhead. On the horizon, construction cranes were silhouetted against a gray sky. At the gate, posted signs warned of a "Hard Hat Area," but Rija ignored them and made her way inside.

A man whose hardhat read "Foreman" asked, "Can I help you, miss?"

"I'm looking for Josef Malacovik. He's my husband."

He looked into the distance, shifting from one foot to the other. "Sorry, miss, he's gone."

"Gone? Can you tell me what happened?"

"Not really sure."

"Please, I have to find him."

He pursed his lips and seemed to come to a decision. "Okay, come with me."

She followed him to the rear of the site, up steps into a trailer. Inside, a man looked up from his blueprints with a puzzled expression.

"Boss, you remember Malacovik?" the foreman asked.

The man at the table snorted. "Yeah, I think so."

"This here's his wife looking for him."

The man grimaced. "Sorry, I can't help you, miss. He's gone."

Rija's face turned hot. "Please, can you tell me what happened?"

"He left. That's all I can say."

"Please, I'm new here. I need to know where to find him."

The two men exchanged looks. Finally the man with the blueprints spoke. "What little I recall, Josef was more of a talker than a worker. One day, his supervisor called him on it. Malacovik got mad and just walked off the site."

"But he told me that he likes his job," Rija said.

"I wouldn't know about that. The next day, he showed up asking for his pay. The foreman brought him in here. I got the money from

petty cash. He didn't say another word, just grabbed the envelope and took off. That's all I can tell you."

"Was he alone?" Rija asked.

The boss shrugged and turned back to his work. "Sorry, I couldn't say."

The foreman stepped in, herding Rija toward the door. "Josef left in a car. Someone was driving. That's all I know."

Chapter 22

Lili and Timmy sat shoulder to shoulder in front of the computer, staring at the screen. Faces bright with excitement, they tussled over the controls. "My turn, it's my turn. Give it back," Lili demanded. Timmy waved at Rija over his shoulder, and Lili snatched the control out of his hand. She ignored everything but the bright images in front of her. Electronic blips and burps resonated across the room.

Elena's displeasure was clear. "Her father shows her how to play the game," Elena said. "Now she sits there all afternoon on the computer. She don't say nothing."

Though tired, Rija kept her jacket on. She caressed her daughter's shoulder. "Come Lili, let's all go to the park. Timmy, you come too."

Electronic bleeping sounds continued to bubble up from the computer.

"No, Mama, Timmy and I want to play this game."

Rija reached over the children's heads and turned the computer off. Wails erupted as the screen turned dark.

"Mama! No!"

"We're going to the park now, Lili."

Timmy groaned. "What about my turn?"

Rija got Lili's jacket from the closet. "Put it on."

Lili turned away pouting, and Timmy, in tears, jumped off the chair and ran up the stairs to the third floor.

The phone rang. Elena picked it up. "Allo." She handed over receiver and mouthed, "Josef."

Rija took the phone. "What do you want?" Her face flushed with anger as she listened. She drummed her fingers on the kitchen table. "You won't be home? You bring these video games here for me to deal with, and now you go out of town?"

Rija listened to Josef's wheedling explanation and became even angrier. "We agreed, no video games, remember? Lili should be doing her school lessons or playing outside. She's too young to spend her days in front of a computer. You broke your promise. Again."

Lili chimed in. "Papa told us we could play."

Rija made an effort to calm herself. "Fine, you do what you must do. Do whatever Leon says. But in my home, you do what I say. No more video games."

She slammed down the receiver.

Rija dragged a reluctant Lili out the door. On the landing, she called up to the neighbors. "Timmy, Lili and I are going to the park. You can still come if you want to."

At a corner table in The Little Odessa, Josef closed his phone and rolled his eyes at his three friends, who were smiling and shaking their heads at him. He shrugged and turned his palms up in a gesture of exasperation. "Women!"

"She's a good woman, but you need to show her who's the boss," Leon said before snapping his finger at a waitress and holding out his coffee cup for a refill.

Andrei, Leon's brother, turned to Yuri. "Stay a bachelor for as long as you can."

When the waitress returned with Leon's coffee, he asked for their table to be cleared. After the busboy brushed away the last crumb, Yuri set his laptop on the table and pulled up a spreadsheet. They all leaned in for a closer look as he highlighted a column of figures.

"These are numbers for the three gas stations we already have. If we can supply four more, that will take care of the shipment."

Leon caught Josef's eye. "I'll need you to do the persuading."

With Josef off to destinations unknown, Rija decided it was time to change the lock on their door. She told her landlord, Mr. Gracek, a story about losing a key and being worried that someone would find it, then she called the hardware store and made the arrangements.

When the buzzer sounded next day, she was surprised to see Mr. Wysocki himself carrying his tools up the stairs.

"Thank you for coming so quickly."

Wysocki nodded. "You can't be too careful these days," he said. He stopped at the top of the stairs and checked the thickness of the doorframe. "Let's take a look and see what you have here."

Rija looked on as Wysocki opened and closed the apartment door, testing the lock. "Even if you hadn't lost your keys, you'd be wise to get a new lock. This one is none too sturdy, and the neighborhood here has changed quite a bit over the years."

Mr. Gracek appeared on the landing. "What's all this talk about the neighborhood changing?"

Wysocki turned. "Not this block, of course. Here you have Bulldog Gracek to protect you."

Gracek clapped Wysocki on the shoulder. "I thought that sounded like a sales pitch. How are you, Ted?"

"Doing okay. Like everybody else, just trying to stay in business."

"Real estate, my friend. Bricks and mortar, always a good investment."

Wysocki wiggled the woodwork of the frame for the landlord's benefit. "Well, if you are ready to improve your investment right here, I suggest you reinforce this door frame and add a wooden brace for extra security."

Gracek frowned and then nodded. "You sold me. Send me the bill."

Gracek headed downstairs. "And now, I'm going out of town, spending the week-end upstate."

"A little fishing perhaps," Wysocki teased.

Gracek patted his ample paunch. "No fishing, not this time, but even better. I'm going up to visit an old friend. She's showing me around."

Wysocki grinned. "A little romance, perhaps?"

"Who knows? If the weather cooperates, we'll ride around and look at some properties, expand my real estate empire."

The landlord's words stayed in Rija's mind, and her thoughts flickered over the Real Estate Law course that would be offered next semester at the Paralegal Academy. But there were more immediate questions to deal with. She watched Wysocki set to work and thought about what would happen when Josef finally came home.

A fragrant aroma from the kitchen began to fill the apartment. Mr. Wysocki sniffed appreciatively. "Mm, that smell reminds me of my mother's kitchen. When I was a kid, she made a dish of sausages that I loved."

Rija called to Elena. "Mama, Mr. Wysocki says your cooking smells like something his mother would make."

Elena emerged from the kitchen, all smiles. She offered a small dish of sausage and a piece of bread. "Here, some lunch."

Mr. Wysocki stood. He pulled a clean handkerchief from his back pocket, as he wiped his hands carefully.

Elena held out the dish to him. "Please," she smiled. "Try my cevapi, it's special Croatian dish."

Elena gestured for him to sit at the table, and her eyes lit up as he gobbled down the sausages and nodded his approval. When he used the bread to make short work of the sauce that remained, Rija thought she hadn't seen her mother look so cheerful in years.

Wysocki smiled. "I'd almost lick the plate if it weren't rude to do so."

Elena took his empty plate. "We have plenty, I put some in a dish for you to take home and share with your family."

"No family, sorry to say. Just me rattling around above the store. My wife passed away from cancer two years ago, and my son and his family live in New Jersey."

Elena put her hand on his arm. "Very sorry." She said. "But please, you will take the cevapi and enjoy."

Josef hadn't been home for more than twenty-four hours, but Rija knew he might return any moment. On edge with nervous energy, she went through the house with an empty box.

"Mama, what are you doing?" Lili asked.

"Papa is going away for a trip, so I'm putting his clothes in a box for him to take with him." She placed the box on the landing and tested the new locks.

Later, Rija tried to watch television, but her stomach was tense. She cautioned Lili, "When Daddy comes, we'll play a little game. We'll pretend that we're not here. Then he'll take his box and go on his trip."

Lili's eyes were wide. "Will he go back to Las Vegas?"

"I don't know, sweet one. Maybe."

"But when will Papa be coming home?" she asked.

"Soon, perhaps. But I don't know."

It was after midnight when Rija heard Josef's footsteps pounding up the stairs. She sat upright on the edge of the bed, still dressed. She held her breath and waited for the sound of his key trying the lock. He tried it once, then again. Between curses, his fists pounded on the door, calling her name.

Lili appeared rubbing her eyes. Rija held a finger to her lips to say "hush" before Elena caught the child's hand, drawing her into their bedroom and closing the door. Rija prayed the new brace would hold.

Josef ignored Tess Gallagher's eyes peering down on him from the landing above. "Go back inside, troublemaker," he muttered under his breath.

He was surprised that the fat, big-mouth landlord didn't stick his head out the door. As he dialed and redialed from his cell, he heard the rings go unanswered, but he knew they were there.

The box of clothing at his feet bore his name in bold black

letters. He knew what that meant. First he kicked at it, then he pawed through the contents until he found what he was looking for, his Armani jeans and the good black suit still folded inside the garment bag.

Red and blue lights flashed up through the front door transom. A loud knock set Josef looking for a way out before he heard someone buzz them in. Above, he heard the neighbor's door open.

Cool air blew in, followed by a young policeman who peered at him from the stairwell. The cop walked up the stairs slowly and steadily, his eyes locked on Josef's. "How's it going, sir? How you doing tonight?"

Josef, suddenly calm, picked up the box of clothing. "No problem. I don't want any trouble. I'm just on my way out."

The first cop blocked his exit. "Just a minute, sir."

A policewoman stood below. "What seems to be the problem?"

Josef made his case to her. "My wife and I had a misunderstanding. She must have changed the locks. So I'm leaving, end of story."

The first officer moved past Josef and knocked on the door. Rija opened it, chain on.

"Everything okay here, ma'am?"

Rija's voice quivered as she spoke through the crack. "My husband is right, I want him to leave."

The policeman turned to Josef. "So, everyone agrees that you're leaving now, yes?"

Josef nodded.

"We'll just stay until you're off the premises. But before you go, sir, we'll need to see some ID."

Josef extracted a Nevada driver's license from his wallet and handed it over. The policeman recorded the information on his report pad. "Thank you, Mr. Malacovik."

The female officer moved aside, allowing Josef to carry the box downstairs. As the door closed behind, Rija took the chain off the door and stepped onto the landing. "Thanks to both of you."

The first cop scribbled a brief report sheet and handed her a copy. He pointed to a telephone number, name, and badge number. "Mrs. Malacovik, if there's any more problem, you give us a call."

A wide-eyed Lili emerged. She grabbed her mother's hand, and they watched the retreating navy backs descend the stairs.

"Mama, why was Papa so angry?"

"Hush, sweet one. Let's go to bed now."

Before she turned out the light, Rija pulled back the curtain, relieved to see the squad car sitting in front of the house for a time before they drove off.

Chapter 23

Josef sat in his car outside St. Casmir's school, waiting. He heard the bell ring twice and watched Ms. Gardner walk the first graders outside for afternoon recess. At the bottom of the stairs, the youngsters broke and ran, with Lili and Karen making a beeline for the jungle gym. He knew they would continue their daily contest to see who could hang upside down the longest.

Their competition ended quickly, and from the stormy look on his daughter's face he knew Karen must have won. There was Lili, bored, wandering over by the fence. When she spied him, her face brightened, and she waved. "Papa, Papa."

Josef leaned out the window and smiled at her. Putting a finger to his lips, he motioned her toward the gate. Lili looked around like she knew she shouldn't do it. The children weren't supposed to go to the gate, but Ms. Gardner was deep in conversation with Mr. Foley, and the aides were nowhere in sight. Lili looked back at her father.

Josef did a U-turn and pulled the car around to where the gate emptied into the sidewalk. He leaned across the passenger seat and opened the door. "Come, Lili, get in."

Lili looked over her shoulder. "I shouldn't. Mama told me that I can only speak to you when she's with me."

"But, my dearest Lili, I've picked you up from school many times, why should today be any different?"

Lili shrugged and remained where she was.

"Papa has a surprise for you in the car," Josef said. "Do you want to see it?"

Lili smiled and nodded and skipped through the gate. She jumped into the car, where a brand new Barbie waited for her on the passenger seat. She tore into the doll's bright packaging, oblivious to the sounds of the car's engine starting.

Josef pulled away from St. Casmir's and checked the rearview mirror. Satisfied no one was watching, he pressed the gas pedal. At the intersection they picked up speed. From there he followed the signs to the highway.

Totally absorbed with her new toy, Lili didn't look up as they flew over the bridge. Only when her father slowed the car to turn off the highway did she sit up straight enough to see out the window. "Where are we, Papa?"

"It's a surprise."

Trees surrounded a U-shaped stucco building situated around a tarp-covered swimming pool. Josef made a point of waving to the brown-shirted maintenance man riding a red mower back and forth over the grass strip that separated the complex from the highway. The man waved back as he slowed to maneuver the vehicle around a gold-lettered sign that read Heritage Gardens.

"We're in Cherry Hill, isn't that a pretty name?"

After parking the car, Josef held Lili's hand as he led her up the stairs to the second level. A row of forest-green metal doors matched painted iron railings. He could look down and see the swimming pool with its sign that promised, "Pool opens May 28th."

Josef went to a door and fit his key into the lock. Lili looked up puzzled as he held the door open for her. It was dark inside, heavy drapes blocking the sunlight. The room was furnished with only a black leather sofa and a large-screen TV.

Lili looked around. "Who lives here, Papa?"

"I do."

"Don't you want to live with us anymore?"

"Your mother and I need to have some time to think things over."

Lili took in his words. "But where do you sleep?"

Josef opened another door, and Lili peered inside the bedroom. A mattress took up one corner, and the box with his things from the apartment occupied the opposite corner. Lili walked to the window and lifted a corner of the blinds. She saw a wooded lot where a mist of new leaves covered the trees. She let the blind drop then turned to her father.

"Are you divorced?"

"No, of course not. Where did you get that idea?"

"Timmy says his father is divorced. He lives someplace else. Timmy goes to stay with him sometimes. Timmy said after you left he thought you were divorced too. But I told him you weren't."

Josef would have smiled at his daughter's prattling if it weren't so close to the truth. He brushed Lili's cheek with his fingertips. "No, Timmy is wrong. Mama and I love each other, we're not divorced."

Lili nodded and then wandered into the tiny kitchen and opened the refrigerator. "I'm hungry."

"We'll get some pizza later. Would you like that?"

"When will Mama and Baba come to pick me up?"

"Mama has to work a lot for the next week, and she wants you to stay here with me until she's ready for you to come home."

"Why didn't she tell me?"

"She forgot. Now why don't you sit down and watch television."
He picked up the remote and flicked on the television. Lili lay down
on the floor with her new Barbie next to her. Soon she was asleep.

Rija was trembling with outrage as she stood inside the principal's
office at St. Casmir's. Her hands were clenched, and her eyes bored
holes in Ms. Gardner. "How could you let this happen?"

"I don't know, Mrs. Malacovik, this never happened before," Ms.
Gardner replied. She swallowed and turned to the principal, Sister
Teresa, who sat behind a large oak desk. "We do the head count
before and after recess every day."

"But you're the teacher and you didn't even notice that my
daughter was gone?"

"I'm so sorry," Ms. Gardner said. "I'm so, so sorry."

Sister Teresa tried to soothe Rija. "Mrs. Malacovik, we're all very
sorry. Almost immediately, Ms. Gardner realized someone was
missing."

The teacher's voice trembled. "We asked the children if anyone
saw anything."

"It was Karen who spoke right up," Sister Teresa said. "She said
Lili got in a car."

"Karen told us your husband came to pick Lili up," Ms. Gardner
added. "She saw her jump in his car. And then-and then they just
left."

A police officer appeared in the doorway. The principal
motioned him in. "Ms. Gardner, would you please ask Karen to
come in."

Frantic, Rija turned to the cop. "Please, you must help find my
little girl."

"Ma'am, we'll do our best." He cleared his throat. "Can you tell
me what happened?"

"My daughter has been kidnapped by my husband, Josef
Malacovik."

"He would be your daughter's father?"

"Yes, we had a fight and the police came and told him to go. And
now he kidnaps my daughter. This is how he gets his revenge."

The officer pulled out his report pad. "Can you tell me when the
argument happened?"

"Saturday night. It should be in your records. One of the
policemen gave me his name. I think it was Officer John Anglan."

The officer made notes as the teacher escorted a frightened Karen into the office. The officer smiled encouragingly. "Don't be scared, sweetheart, we're here to help. Just tell us what you saw."

Karen tightened her grip on the teacher's hand.

The policeman gave Rija a ride to precinct headquarters, steering her to the front desk. He encouraged her to sit, explaining that the Domestic Affairs officer would be with her shortly.

She tried to sit, but it was no good. She paced back and forth until a round-faced officer approached from the other end of the hall. Sergeant Brady, his bulk stressing his shirt seams, introduced himself before he guided Rija back the way he had come.

The staff room was controlled chaos. Telephones rang constantly, and multiple conversations filled the room with a steady hum that was occasionally pierced by loud laughter or a shout aimed from one side of the room to the other. Cops came and went, some prodding suspects ahead of them into interrogation rooms. Others jockeyed for position at the captain's office door. Two female officers arranged photos on a bulletin board.

Brady led Rija to a cluttered desk where he gestured for her to take a side chair before tucking himself behind it. "Can I get you anything, miss? Water, coffee?"

"No, thank you."

He logged on to his computer and waited while its grimy screen ticked to life. "We'll do a missing persons report, but first, I have to ask you, do you have legal custody of your daughter?"

"Of course, I have custody, she is my daughter."

"I understand what you're saying, but legally, unless a judge awarded you her custody, I have to tell you that your husband has just as much right to have your daughter live with him as you do. Do you see what I mean?"

"No, I can't believe it. This can't be!" Rija sprang out of her chair. "My husband left us years ago. He only just came back a few months before now."

"But during that time, you weren't legally separated or divorced, is that correct?"

A black tunnel opened in front of Rija's eyes. Her ears buzzed. The voices in the room bounced back hollow and disconnected. She could hear the sergeant speaking to her, but his voice sounded as though it was coming from the bottom of a well. She felt faint and slumped back in the chair. "No, no divorce."

"Okay, here's the good news. As long as he doesn't leave the area, there's a good chance of finding him. Usually the easiest place would be for you to find him at work."

"The easiest way for me to find him? What about the police? Won't you be looking for him?"

"Like I said, we'll file a missing persons report. In the meantime, if I were you, I'd try to find him myself. Try to talk things out."

"I don't know where he is."

"I'd go to his job."

"My husband calls himself an entrepreneur, he works for himself."

"Who are his associates, who does he do business with?"

"He spends time at a restaurant near the Northeast shopping center called Little Odessa."

Brady's eyebrows shot up.

"Sometimes, he drives a car for a man named Leon Nemirov."

"You have any photographs of your husband and your daughter?"

Rija looked through her handbag. She thought of the picture of Lili she'd always carried, sorry that she'd hung it in her locker at work. "No, I'm sorry. I don't have anything with me. But I have their photos at home."

Brady turned his attention back to the computer. "Can you give me her description?"

"My Lili, she's a beautiful little girl. Her eyes are gray, and her hair is sandy blond. It's long, to her shoulders, and she likes to wear it in a ponytail.

The policeman looked up from the screen. "Ma'am, her height and weight?"

"She's small for her age, a little over three feet tall. At her check-up, the nurse tells me she weighs fifty-three pounds."

"And the father?"

"My husband's name is Josef Malacovik. He's six feet tall."

Rija tried to calculate his weight in pounds. "He is thin."

"His weight?"

She tried to calculate his weight in pounds and couldn't. She pointed to an officer across the room. "He is thin. Like him."

"Hair, eyes?" Brady prompted.

"His hair is like yours, you call it what, dark blonde? And his eyes are gray like my daughter's."

"Any photo?" Brady asked.

Rija shook her head. "I used to have his picture, but it's not here."

"What does he drive?"

"It's a blue car, new, I forget what it's called."

Rija remembered the card Carlene had given her. She pawed through her handbag until she found what she was looking for. She put Rollie's card in front of Brady. "I have a friend who's a detective, Detective Miller. Do you know him?"

Brady squinted at the name for a few seconds. "Just a minute, ma'am."

Rija took a breath as he stood.

"I'll be right back."

Rija watched the clock tick off twenty minutes, thirty minutes, while the walls pressed in on her, squeezing the air out of her body. Unable to stay seated, Riga headed back to the corridor. Down the hall, a female officer with short blond hair and bad skin fielded incoming calls. "Fifteenth District. Officer Parkinson. How can I help you?"

When Rija moved into her line of vision, the cop held up her index finger, mouthing the words, "One minute."

When she'd finished with the call, she glanced in Rija's direction. "Can I help you?"

"I was talking with Officer Brady, filing a complaint. He said he'd be right back. That was a long time ago. Please, can you find him? It's very important."

The desk officer opened her mouth, then stopped, when Brady appeared. "Sorry for the delay, Mrs. Malacovik, let's go back to my desk."

"Did you call Detective Miller?"

"I tried, but he's out. I left a message."

They sat back down. He hit the enter key on his keyboard, and the computer crashed. Brady swore under his breath and flipped his notebook open. "Tell me again what happened the last time you saw your husband."

"We had a fight, and I had the locks changed. When he came home that night, he took his things and moved out."

"What was the date?"

Rija wanted to scream. "Last Saturday. I think the date was April 19th. But what does it matter? While you're asking me these questions, we're losing time to find her."

"I'm sorry, but it's important. Was he arrested?"

"No."

"Did you file a formal complaint?"

"No, but the officer gave me a slip of paper."

"Did you get a restraining order?"

Tears welled, and she sniffed and shook her head. "No, no, no."

Brady pushed a box of tissues in her direction.

Rija wiped her eyes. "Please, we need to do something now. You can check the records later. We live at thirty-three forty-three Mercer St. My neighbor, Tess Gallagher, called the police. You can ask her. They came, Josef left, and they said he shouldn't come back if I asked him to stay away."

Rija realized the policeman was not looking her in the eye.

"Here's the thing. We've run your husband's name through the Pennsylvania DMV."

"DMV?" Rija asked.

"Department of Motor Vehicles. We don't have anything on file for him. Still, I'm going to file a missing persons report for your little girl."

Rija's body sagged. "That's all?"

"I can put out an APB on the car along with his description and the description of your daughter. That's all we can do for now. I'm sorry, but that's all we can do. You should go home, see if you can find him."

Rija stayed put. "Go home, just like that? Go home?" She leaned closer. "Do you have any children?"

Brady stood. "Yes, ma'am, I do have children, and I know what you're going through, but there's nothing further we can do right now."

"Wait, please," Rija begged. "There's one more thing I should tell you."

"What's that?"

"There's a place you can check. He has a storage locker on Route 13 in Bucks County."

"Ma'am, that's out of our jurisdiction. Now please."

Two men over by the water cooler watched as Rija gripped Brady's beefy arm. As if on cue, the blond front desk cop stuck her head in. "Brady, call for you from downtown. They said it's urgent."

He pulled away quickly. "Sorry, Mrs. Malacovik, I need to take this. We'll be in touch."

The blond cop turned to Rija. "Please, ma'am, if there was anything more Officer Brady could do for you right now, I'm sure he'd do it. Why don't you go home now?" She walked Rija to the precinct door. "We'll call you as soon as we hear anything."

Outside their apartment window, birds chirped and trees were sprouting green, but Elena was immune to signs of life reawakening. In her world was only silence. She sat waiting for the police to call with word that they found Lili. She asked Rija again, "Did you call them?"

"I called Sergeant Brady four times yesterday."

"Then call him, call Josef," she demanded for what seemed like the hundredth time.

"Mama, I called the telephone number he gave me before, but the number is no good. He changes phones all the time."

Rija decided to call Tony to see if he could help. She tried to ignore Elena's sobs as she made the call. When Tony answered, Rija explained the situation, and he agreed to help.

Rija put down the phone and turned to Elena. "My friend Tony is coming over to help us."

"Who? Who is that?"

Rija moved past her mother. She splashed cold water on her face and peered into the bathroom mirror. As though willing herself to move beyond what her five senses could tell her, she stared past her own reflection, straining to see with Lili's eyes. Part of her knew what she attempted was impossible, yet the other, the intuitive part emerged. She imagined what her daughter saw, hoping for a clue that might guide them to where Lili was. In her mind she called out to her. She closed her eyes, tried to find a calm place in her mind. "Lili, it's Mama," she whispered. "Tell me where you are. Mama wants to find you. She wants to bring you home."

When no answer came, she splashed more water on her face, ran a comb through her hair, and prayed that Tony could help them find her child.

Almost before the buzzer faded, Rija was at the stairs, smothering Tony in a hug. "Thank you, Tony, thank you for coming."

He took her welcome in stride. "I have a couple hours before I have to be at the bar. So tell me everything that happened."

Rija guided Tony to where Elena waited on the landing. "This is my mother, Elena."

Elena bobbed her head and tried to smile. "Nice to meet you."

They shook hands, and Tony accepted a cup of coffee, sliding into a chair at the kitchen table. He looked at his watch. "We don't have much time. Do you have any recent photos?"

"Not too many. Let me get them."

Rija went into the bedroom and returned with a brown envelope. "These are all the pictures that I have of her."

Together they pored over the small collection, searching for a good picture of the six-year-old. All agreed the first grader's school picture showed her best likeness. Above her St. Casmir's uniform, Lili's shining face gazed back at them. Her eyes brimmed with confidence as she smiled into the camera.

Elena kissed the photo. "Please, you will help us find her?"

Tony put his arm around her. "You know I'll do whatever I can."

Elena crossed herself, then wiped her eyes.

Tony looked at his watch again. "We should get going if we want to make some flyers."

Rija slipped the photo into her bag.

Tony held the door open. "Let's go, the faster we get these made, the sooner we can spread them around."

Within an hour, Rija and Tony were carrying stacks of flyers out of the copy center on Frankford Avenue. Lili's smile hovered above the words, "Have you seen me?" They cruised the neighborhood streets, taping flyers to light poles and distributing others in convenience stores and local eateries until it was time for Tony to go to his job.

Chapter 24

Josef awoke to the sound of his bedroom door slowly creaking open. Every muscle in his body tensed as he prepared to leap out of the bed and defend himself. He had no weapon, but if he could move before the intruder struck, he might be able to dash from the room and escape.

He jumped at the sound of a curtain grating against its rod, rolled the other way and hit the floor on his hands and knees, ready to fight or run.

"Where were you last night, Papa?" Lili asked as she walked around the bed to where he was crouching and trembling.

"Lili, my love, you scared me," Josef said as he slowly stood up. His mouth felt dry as dust, and his head reeled with the effects of last night's vodka. He'd meant to come home early and bring his daughter's dinner. Instead, he'd gotten pulled into the game, lost money, and spent the rest of the night trying to win it back. When he finally stumbled home he didn't remember that his daughter was there.

"I'm hungry. When is Mama coming to pick me up?"

Guilt and shame surged into Josef's already aching brain. He cursed himself for a fool. Snatching Lili from the schoolyard had been a stupid idea, and everyone knew it.

He had told Leon about it but was unprepared for his boss's violent reaction. While others in the restaurant pretended not to notice, Leon had slammed Josef's head against a wall and screamed in his ear. "What is the matter with you? The child belongs with her mother. Who will take care of her? You?"

True, Leon had thrown Josef out of the restaurant bodily, still, Josef considered himself lucky. Days earlier he'd seen a displeased Leon throw an employee down the stairs and into the emergency room.

He had wanted to get back at Rija and had caused himself nothing but trouble. He turned to Lili. "I'm sorry, my little one. Papa has been very busy. I had some important work to do."

"I have work to do too," Lili said. "I need to do my lessons or Ms. Gardner will be angry with me."

Josef patted her head. "Don't worry, don't cry. I'll go to Ms. Gardner and get your lessons."

Lili started to cry. "I want to go home."

Josef patted her head again, but she pulled away. "I'm hungry, Papa. All you have to eat is potato chips."

Josef recalled his forgotten plan to go to the store yesterday. He'd do it today, for sure. "Just a little more sleep, my sweet. Then Papa will get you something to eat."

"I don't want any more sleep," Lili said.

Josef sat down on the bed and closed his eyes. He told Lili to wait in the living room, then he got dressed. He stumbled to the bathroom, hoping to find the aspirin tablets he knew weren't there. Then he went into the living room, took Lili's hand, and headed for the door.

"Papa, where are we going?"

"Like I said, I'm going to get your lessons."

"Oh, goodie, I'm going to school."

"No, not today," Josef said. "I'll drop you off downstairs with Mrs. Garcia. She's going to watch you until I get back."

Lili followed her father down the stairs and around to unit 1-B at the rear of the complex. He knocked and a frowsy blonde woman in a pink tracksuit appeared, a baby on her hip. Inside, another child threw cereal from a high chair. A large-screen TV dominated the room. The woman opened the door wider and gestured for them to enter.

"You must be Lili," she said. "Come in, honey. You can call me Maria." She caught the child's hand, drawing her through the door.

"Maria, can you give Lili some breakfast? She's hungry."

The woman pulled Lili away from the door. "Come on, sweetie. Do you like Cheerios?"

Lili's face tightened, and she looked to her father. But Josef had already turned to leave. "When I get back, we'll go get you another Barbie. Would you like that?"

Lili shook her head as her face crumpled. "I don't need another Barbie. Let me come with you, please, let me come with you. I'll be good."

A blue road sign and a stretch of fast food restaurants welcomed Rija and Tony to Bucks County. Spring skies had turned dusky by the time they pulled off the highway onto Street Road. With time to kill until dark, Tony wanted a quick burger, and Rija picked at a couple of french fries before she threw them away.

From her vantage point in the fast food parking lot, Rija watched Tony cross over the highway to the U-Stor-It. His red Volvo headed to Area D where, for show, Tony made a perfunctory visit to the storage unit he'd rented.

Five minutes later, Rija walked into the rental office, nervous and excited. She was wearing her first pair of tight American jeans and a sleeveless sweater, and she'd let her hair hang loose and shiny. Tony had told her she looked hot. The young employee who looked up from the video screens seemed to think so too. "Hey there, can I help you?" he asked.

Beyond his eager face, she spotted Tony's car on one screen. A second screen switched to Area B. Music emanated from a third screen, and the credits for the Simpsons scrolled past.

Rija positioned herself so that he could only face her by turning his back to the surveillance monitors. "I need a place to store my things. My boyfriend and I are splitting up, I'll be moving out next week."

"Oh, sorry to hear it, but I'm sure we can help you," he said. "We're all about customer service."

"Can you tell me how much it would cost?" Rija asked.

Past his shoulder, Rija caught a brief glimpse of Tony's back on the middle screen as he slipped around the corner into Area G. She shook out her hair and fixed the clerk with a bright smile. By now, Tony should be making a hole in a chain link fence that separated Area G's storage lockers from the used car lot beyond the U-Stor-It.

The clerk handed her a clipboard with an application. Rija took it and moved away from the counter. The clerk followed as though pulled by a string.

"My English is not so good," she told him. "Can you help me fill this out?"

He offered her a pen, then hovered. "I sure can. By the way, my name's Johnny."

"Thanks, Johnny, I'm Alina."

Rija toyed with filling out the application. Checking the monitor, she caught sight of Tony heading back to his car. Then she looked at her watch and stood. "Oh, it's so late. I'll have to come back tomorrow."

The clerk's face lost its glow. "Don't you want to see the unit? I can show it to you now."

Backing toward the door, Rija cooed, "I'll come back tomorrow, I promise. Thanks so much for your help."

Tony pulled out of the lot, giving the clerk a beep and a wave. The clerk turned back to his cartoons.

After Tony watched the clerk lock up on schedule, he waited a few more minutes for his taillights to fade in the dark. Then he and Rija drove back across the highway, and he pulled into the used car lot next to the U-Stor-It. Rija urged speed as he parked the Volvo, positioning it to shield the hole he'd made from the lights of oncoming cars. They were ready to go back inside.

Rija got down on the ground and wiggled through the hole in the fence. Tony followed close behind. On the other side they hunkered down in front of unit G-27.

The hum of highway traffic masked the hacksaw's grate on metal and Tony's curses of frustration. Sweat dripped from his forehead and stung his eyes, and he mopped his brow with a kerchief. "This isn't working. Time to try something else."

He opened his satchel and removed a small acetylene torch. He turned the nozzle and lit the torch with a butane lighter. The torch flared from yellow to blue, and Tony went to work. A minute later, the lock fell onto the gravel. Tony killed the flame and set the torch down. He grabbed the door and pushed it up halfway.

The beam from Rija's flashlight danced on the shed's contents. "I want proof of all of this, to show to the police."

"There's even more here than last time," Tony whispered. He pulled a camera from his satchel and handed it to Rija. "I think it's time for a Kodak moment. Get a picture of this."

The flash punctuated the night. Pointing and shooting, the two of them moved around the perimeter, recording everything. Rija found the cash box, but a new lock secured the contents. She smashed the lid open, knowing this time there was no need for stealth or pretense. Methodically, she emptied all the bills into her backpack. A final box, empty of cash, held a small pistol. Rija picked up the gun and slipped it into her purse.

Other boxes yielded up their secrets as Tony forced lids off crates of weapons stacked one on top of the other. "What are these guns called again?" he asked.

Rija looked over his shoulder. "Zastava. I must take a picture of those."

Ten minutes passed, and they were done. They left the unit, and Tony pulled the door back down. Rija spotted the ruined lock on the gravel nearby. She picked up the still-warm lock and threw it into the tall weeds. Then she and Tony wriggled back through the chain link fence.

In the car, Rija's hands shook as she opened the backpack.

"When my husband finds I have taken his money, he'll come out of hiding to find me."

"You'll have his undivided attention," Tony agreed.

For what seemed like her entire life, Rija had felt the hands of the clock ticking off the seconds of her life. The responsibility, the need to be always present, always caring for others, had been the measure of her days. Tonight was different. Tonight, there was no need to rush home to her child, and while she felt a strange lack of constraint, it was not a freedom she relished. Still, Rija surprised herself when she agreed to stop at Tony's place. Silently, they turned off the expressway and drove past streets of two-story brick row houses and corner stores that looked much like the ones in her neighborhood. Past an intersection with a pizza shop, Tony found a spot on a tree-lined street. Car parked, Rija breathed deeply, inhaling the spicy aroma wafting from the pizzeria.Tony noticed. "It's always pizza time around here. I guess I'm so used to the smell, I don't even notice it anymore."

"It smells good. I love pizza."

"Are you hungry?" he asked. "Do you want me get one for us?"

Rija shook her head. "Not right now. Maybe later."

Tony unlocked a side door and gestured Rija up a flight of stairs. "This is it." He turned his key in the lock. "My little corner of heaven."

His apartment, a one-bedroom on the second floor, was spare and clean. Rija gazed at the living room's only furnishings, a futon, TV set, and weight bench. The only real sign that he actually lived there was a photograph on the mantel. Rija picked up the framed photo and took a closer look at a younger version of Tony and a buddy, both in camouflage gear. They grinned into a barren, desert landscape.

Tony answered before she asked. "Yep, that's me. And that's my buddy, Bart. We were in the Gulf together."

"I didn't know you were a soldier."

"No, I tried not to be. But I did serve, then, right out of high school."

"What did you do?"

"As little as possible." Tony laughed. "That's what everyone says. In reality, our unit worked recon."

"Recon?"

"We were part of Intelligence. We followed troop movements, went out on patrol, stuff like that."

"What was it like, your war?"

"Wasn't really a war."

"But, tell me."

"It was hot, mostly. Saudi Arabia, where we were stationed, it could easily get up to one hundred and ten degrees, one hundred and twenty. No fighting. They are our allies. Supposedly, we were there to help them keep the peace. But still." Tony shrugged, "That's not to say that people didn't suffer for it."

Tony thought about Bart. An investigation that never found real answers to why he died, a report that never mentioned how the patrol strayed over the Iraqi border or the landmine that sent Bart home in a body bag. Yes, his soldiering days changed him, all right. Removed the scales from his eyes, left him distrustful of authority. If he wanted to know the truth of a situation, he would check it out for himself, get to the causes, the secrets. And if he had to break some rules to get to the bottom of things, so be it.

Rija's eyes drifted restlessly around the room. She looked toward the window, peered through the Venetian blinds as though looking for something. Her mind felt blank. Her head ached. Now that she was here, she didn't know why she'd come. Suddenly, the money didn't seem so important.

Tony interrupted her thoughts. "Why did you take that gun?"

Rija didn't know he'd seen her. "I don't know why I took it."

"You don't?"

Rija tried to be casual. "An impulse, perhaps? But why shouldn't I take it?"

Tony held out his palms. "Don't get defensive. I just asked."

Somehow Rija knew she planned to keep it with her, at least until Lili was back home where she belonged.

It wasn't the first time she'd held a gun in her hands.

After Doni died, Josef brought guns to their apartment. He needed a safe place, he said, a place to store the weapons until he could find someone to carry them to the Shadow's men at the front. Elena agreed to keep them safe, took the wooden box from his hands and slid it into the bottom of their hall closet.

That night as her mother slept, Rija, curious to see what was there, searched the box. She selected a small pistol, drew it out, held it in her hands. Feeling its dark power, she pointed it around the room, all the while watching her own reflection in the hall mirror. She imagined what a bullet would have done to the face of the soldier who had raped her or what she would do if another soldier tried to stop her.

She didn't return the gun to the box that night. She placed it under her bed. The next day she decided to keep it.

The gun became her secret. Even as Elena begged her not to go out on the streets, Rija found ways to elude her mother's watchful eyes. She slipped out of the apartment and into the alleys of Sarajevo. Sometimes she ran, as though pursued by an invisible army. Rija found that she liked the feel of the weapon in the pocket of her coat. The pistol provided a sense of security, even if it was a false one.

Twice, on warm summer nights, she went up to the roof and stood in the darkness taking aim at the lights of the soldiers camped across the river. She imagined squeezing the trigger, firing bullets and watching them fall. Sometimes she felt her being consumed by a desire for revenge against all of them. The soldiers, who had destroyed their lives with their hatred, became her enemy. Her hatred came to match theirs, burning with an intensity that surprised her. But she had kept the gun.

"I don't want to talk about the gun."

"Okay, let's change the subject. What about that pizza?"

"No, my appetite is gone. Thanks, but I'm just not hungry."

Tony retrieved a bottle of wine from the refrigerator. "I don't know about you, but I'm thirsty."

"Thirsty?"

"I think we deserve something special after our work tonight."

He poured a few ounces of red wine into glasses. "Just try a sip, it's homemade."

Rija sipped. "It's delicious."

"Good, huh? My father makes it the same way his father did in the old country."

Tony drained his glass and tossed back a second, but Rija took only one more sip. She slid her glass back across the kitchen counter. Remembering what she was there for, she hauled the heavy knapsack onto the table and dumped out the packets of bills.

"Let's count the money." Once they'd tallied over nine thousand dollars. Rija felt her mood lift.

"Now what?" Tony asked.

She laughed nervously. "Yes. Now what? I need a place to hide it." The sight of that much money stacked high was a powerful antidepressant. She held out her glass. "May I have a little more wine?"

Tony poured and Rija drank. Holding out her glass again, she was grateful for even a few moments away from the stress of the night and the horror of the last days. The wine warmed her belly and went to her head. Rija looked deep into Tony's dark eyes. "Tony, thank you so much for doing this for me. I don't know what I would do without your help."

His lips found hers in a tentative kiss that grew bolder. She could feel his fingers twining through her hair. Gently, Tony drew her head back so that she met his gaze. "You don't know how beautiful you are, do you?"

Rija's stomach quivered with the fear that she might break down and sob. Without thinking of the money now, she pulled away. Before she could run, Tony caught her arm.

"Wait." He drew back her back.

Feelings of panic began to subside. She wavered, the tang of his kiss still with her. She met his gaze and felt his arms, strong and comforting. She wound her arms around his neck and they kissed again, hard and long. Tony took her hand in his and she nodded silently as he led her to the bedroom.

Elena sat silent, hour after hour. Lili was the joy of her life. Rija thought her mother seemed to feel the loss of her grandchild almost more than the loss of her husband or son. While Rija tried to keep occupied, bustling around the apartment, tidying the rooms and making small meals, Elena spent her day by the window, gazing at the street below. Her programs on the big-screen TV, once so interesting, held no allure for her now.

On the fifth day, Mr. Wysocki appeared at their door with flowers. He wavered at the threshold. "Anything I can do?"

Rija asked him to come in.

Inside, the locksmith handed her the flowers.

Rija took them and then turned to her mother. "Mama, look, we have a visitor."

Wysocki held up the flyer. "A dark-haired fellow brought this in the store. Asked me to put it up."

"That's Tony."

"He told me what happened. I'm so sorry."

Elena picked up the flowers from the table. "Rija, put these in water."

Rija did as her mother asked, returning with tea and cookies on a tray. Wysocki accepted the tea, looking relieved to have something to do with his hands. Rija put a cup next to her mother, but it sat untouched as the sound of a ticking clock filled the silence.

"Have you heard anything?" he asked.

Rija shook her head and moved to pick up his empty cup.

"Please, let me do that." He picked up the cup and took it to the kitchen. He sat back down and smiled hopefully at Elena. "How's that lock holding up?"

Outside, a squirrel skittered across the tree branch next to the window. Elena looked up but remained silent.

"The lock's fine, just fine," Rija said. She thought of the night Josef's anger turned to revenge. She blamed herself for what happened and vowed never to tell the locksmith that Lili was gone because she'd decided to change the locks on her front door.

Only when Wysocki stood to take his leave did Elena rouse herself. She stood then, taking his hand. "Thanks to you for coming, you're very kind man."

At the door, he turned to Rija. "Please call me if there's anything I can do to help."

After he left, Rija paced. It was difficult for her to stay in the apartment. Time passed slowly. When the phone rang, mother and daughter jumped to grab it. But it was only Tess, their neighbor, asking if they needed anything from the store.

In bed at night she stared at the ceiling, unable to sleep. Sitting during the day, she would nod off and then jerk upright. She barely ate. The most she could manage was a few crackers and some of Elena's soup whenever it was placed in front of her.

Mr. Wysocki appeared again several times over the next two days, with offers of help. He volunteered to run errands or help Elena keep watch. She finally agreed, letting him sit by the phone while she got some much needed rest.

"It's not summer yet, guys and gals, but today will feel like it," the radio announced. "Today's high temperature could reach ninety degrees in Philadelphia and eighty at the Jersey Shore."

Rija fanned herself with a folded newspaper. Despite the heat, she wore a hooded sweatshirt and sunglasses. In the rearview mirror she spotted Tony on his way back from what he called a pit stop at the gas station around the corner. She looked at her watch. Had they really been sitting here for four hours? Before, she hadn't believed him when he told her, but now, she knew that Tony was right. The job of an investigator is to wait, and the waiting can be tedious, boring, and hot.

Hands full, Tony tapped the window with an elbow and Rija reached over to open the door. Back in the driver's seat, he handed her an iced tea and kept one for himself.

Now that Mr. Wysocki had offered backup on the phone, Rija and Tony could spend their time parked on Bustleton Avenue, eyes glued to the door of the Little Odessa. The day was quiet. They watched a navy Lexus pull into the restaurant's loading zone. Rija thought she recognized the tall young man who climbed out the driver's side. He opened the passenger door for a blonde woman in heels and jeans.

"Who's the babe?" Tony asked.

"Oh my God, that's Paulina, Leon's wife. And that's Yuri with her, he's Leon's accountant."

Tony laughed. "It looks like he's her chauffeur."

"Yes, she likes to have a driver when she goes shopping. Josef always hated it when he had to drive her around."

Tony checked his watch and turned the key in the ignition. "Sorry, it was just getting good, but I have to go to my job."

Rija gave his hand a squeeze. "I know."

Tony sounded more confident. "He's going to show up sooner or later. His boss will give him his next assignment, then we'll see where he goes.

Chapter 25

The line snaked around the building. Those in front held their ground, fighting off newcomers. When it was nearly time to open, the guards appeared, and the collective posture straightened like flowers after a rain. At eight-thirty the doors were unlocked, and the crowd surged forward. Applicants funneled into the waiting area gripping precious documents they hoped would make their case.

Rija came empty-handed with no appointment. She told the guard, "I'm not here for a green card. I have one already."

"I'm sorry, miss. You'll have to wait like everyone else."

The receptionist repeated the question. "Do you have your appointment card?"

Rija flashed her permanent resident card. "I'm not here about my status. I'm here to report someone."

The receptionist eyed her quizzically. "Who is this person?" she asked.

"It's my husband."

Though they had both arrived in the country with legal refugee status, Josef often confessed that he'd never followed up with his paperwork. Rija was determined to call his crimes and failures to the attention of the authorities.

The receptionist pointed. "Sign in, please, and have a seat."

Rija found space on a bench next to a woman in a hijab holding an infant. She smiled at the baby and nodded to the woman. The woman nodded back, her dark-rimmed eyes staring back at Rija. At her feet, two little boys shoved a plastic yellow truck around the floor.

Rija tried to distract herself with a tattered magazine. Two hours later, her name had not yet been called. She decided to take a different tactic with the receptionist. "My husband is a criminal. He sells guns and he kidnapped my daughter."

"Someone will be with you shortly. Please have a seat."

Restless and thirsty, Rija forced herself to stay in the chair, certain that her name would be the next one called. It was nearing 4 p.m. when she lost hope.

The security guard reappeared. "Folks, the office is closing. We'll reopen tomorrow at 8:30. You're all free to return then."

The receptionist stood, looking relieved as the occupants readied themselves to file out. Rija tried again. "Please, can you help me? My husband, he's kidnapped my daughter. I'm afraid he might try to take her out of the country."

The woman's eyes softened a little. "Let me give you a number to call."

She flipped through a directory until she found what she was looking for. "Tomorrow, first thing, call Mr. Parnell. He's a lawyer in our enforcement unit. If you can get an appointment with him directly, you won't have to wait so long."

Rija took what she was offered and slipped out just as the guard prepared to lock the door behind the retreating army of applicants.

Mr. Parnell's voicemail message declared him to be "out of the office." Then, his mailbox was full. Two days later, a female voice answered. The voice gave Rija a 2 p.m. appointment with Parnell's assistant for the following day.

Although she knew it would do her no good, Rija arrived early and spent another hour waiting. At 2:10, she found herself looking across a table at Ms. Singer, a young agent in glasses, her blonde hair smoothed back in a headband.

With a manner that matched the crisp navy suit she wore, Singer wrote the date and time on a yellow legal pad. "Now, Mrs. Malacovik, you say your husband is involved in illegal activities?"

"Yes, he's ...," Rija began.

"We'll get to what type of activity exactly in just a minute. But first, why don't you tell me a little bit about yourself and your family."

Suddenly, Rija thought of her unpaid taxes. She'd paid half but still needed to send the balance. Fear swiveled down her spine. She took a breath. "First of all, we are from Sarajevo, in Bosnia. After the war, we fled and came to this country. We had help from the Bosnian Foundation and the International Refugee Committee."

"May I see your registration?"

Rija watched the agent scan her card. "Can you describe your living situation for me now?"

Tears welled up. "I live with my mother and my daughter here in Philadelphia, and I have a job."

Agent Singer slid a box of tissues in Rija's direction.

Rija decided not to talk about her time on welfare. She would concentrate on the recent past. "My husband recently moved back in with us."

"When you say he moved back in, had you separated?"

"Yes, he left us a couple of years ago and then he came back."

"So, you reconciled?"

"Yes, he moved back in, and we were a family again. For a while things were going well, but he got arrested. After that I didn't like many of the things that were happening. We had a big fight. He left, and then I changed the locks. Two days after that, he took her from the schoolyard without permission."

Singer looked up from where she'd scribbled Josef's name on her legal pad. "And now?"

Rija flattened out creases in the flyer with Lili's picture. "I don't know where my little girl is, and the police aren't helping me find her."

She dug an envelope from her handbag and laid out a trio of photos from the storage locker. "Please, look," she said.

"What are these?" Singer squinted, moving the photos around in an effort to make sense of the murky images before her. "What are you showing me, Mrs. Malacovik?"

Rija knew there was no turning back now. "These are the guns and other things my husband has in a storage shed. I can show you where it is. This is where he keeps crates of weapons and other things he steals."

Singer sat up a little straighter. "Where does all of this come from?" she asked.

"My husband, he works for criminals, for gangsters, Russian gangsters."

Rija stared into the woman's cool blue gaze. "He drives a car for the boss, Leon Nemirov, and they pay him with TVs, computers, guns, maybe drugs. All of those things."

Singer stood. "Wait here, Mrs. Malacovik. I want to see if my supervisor is available."

She picked up two of the clearer photos and walked out, closing the door behind her. The hands on the wall clock moved slowly. It was quarter to three. Half an hour later, Ms. Singer returned with a man in a gray suit and glasses.

"Thanks again for coming in, Mrs. Malacovik. This is Agent Parnell," Singer said.

The man in the suit stepped forward. "We're going to investigate, and we'll be in touch when we've completed our investigation."

Ms. Singer nodded as though that were the definitive word. Parnell turned, indicating that the interview was over. Desperate, Rija followed after him. "But you don't have all the information about this stolen weapons. Don't you want to know where they are?"

She made a grab for his retreating back, pulling at his jacket. "Wait, please. My husband has kidnapped my daughter. She's tiny, only six."

Parnell shook her loose. "That, I'm afraid, is a local matter. You'll have to go to the police."

Red-faced, Singer slipped between Rija and her boss. "What we can do on this end is check your husband's immigration status."

"But I have gone to the police. I call them every day, and they have nothing. They've done nothing."

Ms. Singer walked to the water cooler. She filled a paper cup with water. Grateful for the water, Rija drank, oblivious as Parnell disappeared.

Chapter 26

Josef drove over the bridge, cursing himself for being such a fool. His wife had shamed him, hurt his pride. In a rush to get even with her, he just reacted without thinking things through. Still, people should mind their own business, people like Timmy's mother, that ignorant red-headed woman upstairs who butted in, called the police. Tess was her name. He'd like to get even with her. At least the fat-ass landlord, Gracek, hadn't been there to stick his big head into the middle of things. He cursed them all.

Taking care of Lili was more than he could handle. He'd make more of an effort to leave her with Maria from the day care while he was out in the daytime. Still, Lili was alone at night way too much. And then there was school. He didn't know what to do about that. Lili wouldn't be able to finish first grade, and now summer was coming. It was all too much. Josef made himself a promise to do better. Tonight he'd pick her up on time. They'd go to the grocery store, get something nice for dinner.

He parked in front of the Little Odessa and went in. Yuri was sitting in the back drinking coffee. "Boss was looking for you."

When Leon appeared, his sour expression boded ill. "Every time my wife gets behind the wheel, I pay! Look at this fucking insurance bill." He waved a paper in front of Josef's eyes.

"Go pick up Paulina. She hates to drive. And to be honest, I hate for her to drive. She has one cocktail and then, boom, crash!" Leon banged the table for emphasis. "She hits a car in the parking lot, my insurance goes up."

Paulina gave the mirror a pout before adding a layer of gloss to lips already pink and glowing. Satisfied with her look, she settled into the Lexus passenger seat and turned toward Josef. "And how is your busy wife? With her job and her classes?"

"She was angry the last time I saw her."

Paulina's eyebrows shot up. "The last time? That doesn't sound good. What happened."

He confessed that he had moved out and taken Lili with him.

"You put her in a new school so close to the end of the year?"

"No, not yet. I haven't found a good school for her in Jersey."

"Where is she now?"

He remembered Lili's tear-stained face as she begged him to take her. Still, he'd shut the door, running, guilty, down the stairs. These were images he didn't want in his head.

Paulina stared at him. "Who is taking care of your daughter while you're working?"

"Sometimes she stays with a neighbor. Right now, she's watching television and playing with her doll. She doesn't mind being alone."

"Josef, I thought you would know better. You are like these thoughtless American parents who leave their children alone. What do they call them, latch-key children?"

He shrugged.

"No, no, no! This will not do. Turn this car around. You will bring her with us right now."

All the way to the bridge to New Jersey, Paulina scolded him for being a careless parent. "A child has to eat. She needs clean clothes, she needs someone to play with."

She glared at Josef as he carried the tearful child down the steps and tucked her into the back seat. Paulina smiled over her shoulder. "Hello, Lili. My name's Paulina. How are you, sweetheart?"

Lili looked down. "Where's Mama? Are we going home, Papa?"

Josef nosed the car out of the apartment complex. He turned to Paulina. "Do you still want to go to the mall?"

Paulina shook her head. "No, I have an idea. Lili, would you like to come home with me?"

Silence from the back seat.

"You can spend the weekend with my Tasha. She's getting to be a big girl, nine years old, but she still loves Barbies, just like you. And you can play dress-up too. Would you like that?"

Tony choked down a bite of cold pizza. *It's your day off for Chrissake. What the fuck are you doing, sitting in front of a crappy restaurant on a crappy street in Northeast Philadelphia waiting for God knows what?* Disgusted, he threw the rest of the slice back in the box.

"What the hell are you doing?" he said aloud.

This was not like him, not like him at all. To be involved with a woman, married, and with a kid no less. And a no-good husband who hangs with the Russians? This was totally against his "don't get involved" game plan, but it was too late now.

Tony put down the binoculars and rubbed his eyes. His back hurt from sitting so long. You never knew how things would work out. He faced himself in the mirror, silently ticking off the milestones in his life since he'd come home from the army.

By the time he'd finished his Associates in criminal justice at community college he'd decided he didn't want to be a cop. Then he'd gotten a job, the only one he could find, in the mailroom at the law firm. The firm's investigator turned out to be a vet. They had a lot in common, and the guy schooled him, told him if he took the paralegal course and finished it, he'd help him find a way out of the mailroom. So he signed up for the course, and that's where he'd met Rija. *But where the hell was this going?*

When he looked back, the blue Eclipse pulled up. Tony grabbed the binoculars, glad he'd swapped cars with his buddy.

Tony's name flashed on Rija's newly installed caller ID. "He's here," his voice tight with excitement.

"Where are you?"

"Down the block from the Little Odessa."

Rija's heart pounded, she could hardly speak. "Is Lili with him?"

"No, he's alone. He just pulled up in a blue Eclipse with Jersey plates. I've got the license number now. He nabbed a parking ticket off another car and put it on his windshield, so I think he plans to be here a while."

"Hang up." Rija told him. "I'm going to call the police."

"Wait, no, wait. Let's think this through," Tony said.

"But I have the policeman's card."

"It might be better if we wait. Better if we don't involve them. They might not even show up."

"What's happening?" Rija asked. "What do you see now?"

"The door's opening. They're coming out."

"Who is he with?"

"Tall guy, thin, sandy hair."

"I'm not sure who that is."

Tony slunk down in the seat. "Josef's opening the door of a black town car. Here comes the heavy-set gray-haired guy getting in the other side. Looks like he's calling the shots."

"That's Leon. He's the boss."

"Rija, they're all leaving in the black car. Josef's driving."

"Tony, they are going to work." Rija' voice was hoarse with

emotion. I know it's a lot to ask but can you stay where you are? I'll be there as soon as I can."

Tony decided he would call in sick for his shift at the bar.

Hours later the black car nosed back to the curb. From where she sat in Mr. Wysocki's white van, Rija watched her husband shake hands with Leon and the tall man. Across the street, Tony kept the vigil in an old Ford.

Josef walked back to his car, and Rija held her breath. He removed the ticket, threw it on the pavement and slid behind the wheel. The car idled for a moment, then he made a U-turn and headed east, oblivious, as he flew past Wysocki's van.

Tony started his car and settled in two cars back. Wysocki pulled in behind Tony, and they all stayed on Grant Avenue until signs for the expressway directed them to I-95.

Rija's emotions soared with hope of finding Lili, then plunged. Perhaps following Josef would not lead them to the child, perhaps, he was heading elsewhere. But this was the closest they'd gotten so far. She felt like her heart would burst. Blood pounded in her ears.

Without taking his eyes from the road, Wysocki told Rija, "Hang on, we're on to him now."

"I feel like I'm going to faint."

"Take deep breaths," he told her. "Breathe in, count to five, then let it out slow."

Rija tried to do as he said. Oxygen filled her lungs, and the light-headed feeling subsided. At the top of the ramp, she could see Josef pull onto the expressway with Tony three cars behind. Wysocki pressed the gas pedal in an effort to hit eighty miles an hour, but Josef's car moved out of sight. The white van began to rattle and shake.

Tony tried to keep count as they blew by the exits. Josef was flying now, taking advantage of the Eclipse's powerful engine. Tony strained to keep the Eclipse in view. With no warning, Josef shot off at the next exit. Tony pulled behind him, cutting off a pick-up truck. In the rearview he saw Wysocki jerk the wheel to the right and then to the left, swerving to avoid a collision first with the pick-up and swerving back to miss the guardrail. The pick-up driver blasted his horn, flipping the bird as both vehicles careened onto the ramp toward the bridge. They were going to New Jersey.

Josef hit the bridge going ninety. Tony kept going but the old Ford was no match for the Eclipse. Tony figured Wysocki's van was having an even harder time. He looked in his rearview and saw it was half a football field behind. Josef pulled through the EZ Pass, but Tony was stuck in the cash lane behind a truck. He saw Wysocki a few cars behind.

Rija beat her fists against the passenger seat in a steady tattoo as she yelled, red-faced at the drivers ahead, "Go! Move! Hurry up. Get out of the way!"

Wysocki's face was red and perspiring. "I'm trying, I'm pushing the van as far as I can." He wiped his overheated brow with a blue bandana.

They watched Tony ahead at the tollbooth. Now he was through, waiting on the shoulder for the white van to catch up. Wysocki pulled next to the Ford.

"Where is he?" Rija leaned across the driver's side, begging. "Please, let's keep going, see if we can catch him."

"Let's do it." Tony made eye contact with Wysocki. "I'll flash my lights when I see him."

Wysocki wiped his glasses and put them back on. He turned to Rija. "You go ahead with Tony. I'll try to keep up."

Rija jumped out of the van and climbed into Tony's car. He hit the gas and pulled the Ford out in front, pushing it to the limit and beyond. If he burned out the engine there'd be hell to pay, but he had no choice.

Tony looked to the right. Rija stuck her head out of the window. She motioned at a convenience store they'd just passed. The Eclipse was parked in the lot. From a distance they waited, watching as Josef emerged, box in hand.

Rija crowed with excitement. "That's Lili's favorite cereal! He's taking it to her."

The caravan moved east for another three miles, past an unbroken line of strip malls, fast food restaurants, and car dealerships. Josef slowed as a state trooper went by and put on his blinker. An overhead sign read "Cove Road Exit," and they followed it. Two more lights, Josef turned right, drove another quarter mile to the Heritage Garden Apartments. Rija blessed the darkness that hid them from view. Tony pulled into the dry cleaners across the street. Wysocki pulled the van around the side.

Across the road, lights reflected on glass as the door of the blue Eclipse opened and closed. Josef moved quickly, his white shirt visible when he darted upstairs to the second level. He vanished around the corner to the rear of the complex.

Wysocki slid into the Ford's rear seat. He rubbed the Saint Christopher medal around his neck and crossed himself. "What do we do now?"

"We need to be careful. He may have a gun," Tony said.

Rija didn't wait for them to finish the conversation. She jumped out and darted across the road, ran past the swimming pool to the stairs. She scanned the second level for any visible signs of life. Tony appeared behind her and took cover behind a utility shed. Wysocki crouched near the trashcans.

Minutes later Rija heard Josef's voice from above. "I may have to go back out again tonight." Josef followed a blond woman toward the stairs. He pulled out a roll of cash. "Here's fifty for this afternoon and another fifty if you can you come back later."

"Okay. Let me feed my husband some dinner and I'll stop back to put her to bed in an hour."

The trio held their breaths as the woman padded past them down the stairs and disappeared around a corner. All was quiet as they pondered a next move.

Rija waited as long as she could. Maybe they should just go up, knock on the door, and take Lili out of there. They'd beat Josef up if they had to. But he might have a gun. Perhaps they should call the police? Rija stepped from the shadows for a better look at the second level. A glimmer of light flickered as the drapes at 2G opened and closed with a whoosh. The door opened. Rija's heart stopped.

Lili's small form rushed forward. "Papa, wait. Papa, take me!" her little one cried out.

Josef's reply was inaudible from where Rija stood. Despite Lili's pleas, he shut the door and locked it behind him. Tony pulled Rija back into the shadows as Josef pounded down the stairs and ran to his car, cell phone to his ear. Tony watched Josef's taillights turn back out to the road.

Rija was already up the stairs, knocking softly, her ear to the door. "Lili, Lili, it's Mama. Can you open the door for me?"

There was silence.

Rija tried the doorknob, but it was locked. "Can you open the door, love? Mama's here to take you home."

Wysocki brought out his locksmith tools. "Just give me a minute and I'll get her open."

In less than a minute, the door was open and Rija was inside the apartment. She burst into tears at the sight of her six-year-old hiding under the sofa. Rija scooped Lili up in her arms, wrapped a sweater around the sobbing child, and bundled her out.

Tony pulled the Ford up next to the stairs. Wysocki jumped into his van and turned it around. Within minutes the two vehicles were headed back to the bridge.

Lili cowered in her mother's arms, quivering like a wounded kitten. Her voice was barely a whisper. "Mama, where were you? Why didn't you come get me?"

"My love, I didn't know where you were, but now that I've found you, I'll never let you go again. Let's go home.

Chapter 27

When Paulina called Josef late, he expected it would be to make arrangements for a trip to the mall the next day or to ask him to be the designated driver for her next three-martini lunch with her friends. Instead, she demanded that he come and pick her up right away. Josef wondered where she wanted to go at such an hour and hoped he wouldn't be gone too long.

Paulina usually waited for him at her front door, ready and eager to go. This time she ushered him into the kitchen and poured him a cup of tea. "I want to ask you a question."

"Yes, of course."

"What are your plans for your daughter?"

A warning light went on behind his eyes. "Well, of course, I want everything the best for her."

"And of course, the best must mean that she goes to school, correct? Have you registered her in a new school?"

"Not as yet. I am waiting for her records to arrive," he lied.

"Okay, good. Let's go pick her up." Paulina grabbed her handbag and pushed Josef to the door.

"What about the shopping?" Josef asked.

"But, Josef, I never said anything about shopping."

Neither one of them spoke as the blue Eclipse ate up the miles from the Nemirovs' suburban enclave to the Betsy Ross Bridge. Finally, Josef broke the silence. "You want my Lili to come back and play with Tasha, is that right?"

"No. I want Lili to come and live with us. We love her and Lili is happy with us. She cried when it was time for her to leave on Sunday night."

"I'm sure she was sorry to leave her friend. Paulina, you know I try to do my best for her. Still, it's difficult. I'm a single parent, but I do have someone to watch Lili during the day. She stays with the wife of the maintenance man, who runs a day care. Lili has been staying there with her when I go to work. She feeds her meals and puts her to bed for me when I have to go out at night, like now."

"Lili told me all they do is watch TV and the babies cry all day long. She hates it there."

Josef had no response. He knew the way he was treating his daughter was wrong. It wasn't what he had planned. In fact, when he took her from school that day he had no plan beyond making his wife furious. He hadn't thought of all the things a child needs. And most of all he hadn't realized that it would be his job to provide them.

"What is she doing now?" Paulina asked.

Shamed, Josef stared straight ahead at traffic, unable to meet Paulina's look. From the corner of his eye, he could see the bounce of her blond hair as she turned to face him. He squinted in the rearview mirror to avoid the sight of her manicured fingernails tapping an annoyed tattoo on the leather dashboard.

"Where is she now?"

"She's probably sleeping. I had to leave her at the apartment when you called."

"We're going to go pick her up, and she either goes home with me or she goes back to her mother. Whichever she wants. You agree?"

"Yes, I agree."

Relieved, Josef was ready for this to be over. He hit the gas as they pulled onto the exit that would take them to New Jersey. And it was over, but not in the way that he and Paulina thought. When he unlocked the door to 2G, all was silent. The television was dark, the living room empty. Dreading what he might find, Josef searched the bedroom closet. After a final look behind the shower curtain, he reported back to Paulina, who screamed, "Call the police! Now!"

Chapter 28

From the moment Rija carried her daughter up the stairs, Elena did not leave her side. Even though Mr. Wysocki urged Rija to take Lili to the emergency room, Elena would not hear of it. Instead, she ran a warm bath, easing Lili into the sudsy water. Slowly and gently she washed the grime from Lili's face. Carefully she wrapped her in a soft towel, pulled a nightgown over her damp curls and carried her to bed.

Elena stayed close. Knowing what her granddaughter needed, Elena lulled her to sleep, stroking her hair, whispering softly. Sometimes Lili woke with a cry and looked around with wide, fearful eyes, but Elena comforted her with sweet words. "You're home, my little one. You're here with Baba."

Rija fell asleep in a living room chair. When Tony called the next day, she barely had strength to talk for a few minutes.

Carlene arrived with a bag of groceries. At the door, she enveloped Rija in a hug and then pulled a pink teddy bear from her handbag. "How did you get her back? You have to tell me what happened. But first, how's my little girl? How's she doing?"

"She's doing okay, she's sleeping now." Rija took the food and set about boiling water for tea.

Carlene settled herself at the kitchen table, listening wide-eyed as Rija described their trip to New Jersey.

"You know you did the right thing getting your daughter back the way you did. I mean it."

"There was no other way. I had no choice. I went to the police. I went to Immigration. No one would help me. What else could I do?"

"Good on you, girl. Lord knows, heaven helps those who help themselves."

Rija gave her friend a hug.

"Now that I think of it, you should have called my brother," Carlene said. "You should have called Rollie."

"I gave his name to one of the policemen. I showed them his card. They told me they couldn't reach him. They said they left a message."

Carlene chewed her thumbnail. "He was probably on assignment. But if you should ever need him again, don't you hesitate. You call him yourself, and if you can't get through, you call me, hear?"

"I could use his help now. I want nothing more than for Josef to get deported."

"I don't know how that works, but I'll ask my brother to run a rap sheet on him and see if he's been arrested. See if that will help."

Rija set two cups of tea on the table. "I can tell you right now, he has been arrested. When he first came back, the car he drove was stolen. They picked him up when he ran a red light and held him overnight. He called me to bail him out."

"Why didn't you tell me before?" Carlene asked.

Rija gave her a look. "I was embarrassed to tell you, afraid I would lose my job."

Carlene laughed. "Honey, in my neighborhood, it happens all the time. If every black man in this city who got arrested were to stand up and be counted, you wouldn't have many people sitting down!"

"What do you mean?" Rija asked.

"Our men get arrested all the time, just for nothing, it's called driving while being black."

Carlene laughed at her own words and Rija joined in. But once the joke was over, she held her breath, waiting while her friend pulled out her own cell phone and placed a call to her brother's private line.

When Rollie Miller returned his sister's call an hour, Carlene passed her phone across the table to Rija.

"Hi, Rollie. Thank you so much for looking this up for me. Did you find anything?"

"Your man's got someone watching out for him," Miller told her.

"What does that mean?"

"It means that your Josef has an arrest record, but the details are deleted. I showed it to my boss. It made him think that Josef could be working with another law enforcement agency. Maybe even the FBI. Here's a name for you."

Rija worked hard to get her mind around what the detective was saying. She found a pen and some paper and asked Rollie to repeat the name. She thanked him and hung up.

Rija looked at Carlene. "Your brother told me Josef's file was changed, and it has a card with a name and number stapled on the back of it."

Carlene frowned. "What's he up to, this Josef of yours?"

"Rollie thinks he might be working with the FBI. He gave me the name of an Agent Branoff."

"Unbelievable," Carlene said. "This just keeps getting weirder."

Rija flashed back to Josef's behavior before all of this started. She thought about how he'd helped Elena. She remembered many afternoons when he picked Lili up at school and walked her home. Back then she thought things could work out between them, had hoped they might have a future. But after Josef got arrested their lives changed. After that, two cell phones ruled his life. One phone, the black one, connected Josef to the Russians. What kind of trouble did the silver one connect him to?

Rija showed Carlene the scrap of paper. "Where do you think I should look for this Branoff? I need to talk to him."

"If he's in the FBI, he could be in the Federal Building."

"I know where that is. I've already been to the Federal Building."

"You have?"

"I had an appointment with Ms. Singer."

"And?"

"Nothing. She did nothing for me. Nothing at all."

Carlene peered at the name scrawled on the paper. "You should try to get in contact directly with this Agent Branoff."

After many telephone calls and much searching, Rija found a phone number for the FBI. An operator answered, "Federal Bureau of Investigation, how may I direct your call?"

"I'd like to speak with Agent Branoff."

"Please hold."

"Central Services Unit. How may I help you?"

"May I speak with Agent Branoff?"

"Joel Branoff? He's not here, may I take a message?"

"My name is Rija, Rija Malacovik. My husband is a criminal, and I want to report this to the FBI."

"Well, ma'am, I hear what you're saying, but perhaps you should call your local police department."

"I already did. Now I need to speak to Mr. Branoff."

"I'm not really sure who would be the right person to talk to you, but let me take your name and we'll call you back."

Rija wondered how long it would take her daughter to recover from the lost days. Elena and Rija took turns sleeping next to the frightened child, changing her sheets when she wet the bed, soothing her cries when she woke in the middle of the night. During the day she trailed one or the other of them as they moved through the apartment cooking, cleaning, reading, or watching television. When Rija went out, Lili threw herself on the floor, distraught, until Elena distracted her with an offer to make cookies.

Come the weekend, Lili was by her mother's side, sitting on the bedroom floor while Rija sorted through the hamper. It seemed like weeks since she'd done their laundry. She held up a pink shirt and denim jeans, the clothes Lili had been wearing when they took her from the New Jersey apartment. She turned to the child. "What happened to your school uniform, my love?"

Lili shook her head.

"Where did you get these clothes?"

"From Tasha."

"Tasha? Who is Tasha?"

"She's my friend."

"How did you meet her?"

"Daddy took me to stay over with Tasha and Alex."

"Where do they live?"

"You know, with Aunt Paulina and Uncle Leon."

After Lili's first week at home, the faraway stare that had so frightened Rija began to fade, and the child's eyes once again began to focus on the everyday things around her. Knowing how Lili adored Ms. Gardner, Rija prayed that her teacher might be able to help. She had informed St. Casmir's the day after Lili's return home, but now she wanted to speak to Ms. Gardner herself.

She called St. Casmir's and waited for the teacher to come on the line. When she did she asked how Lili was doing.

"She is doing better, Ms. Gardner," Rija said.

"Thank God! We were so worried about her. Sister Teresa has been praying for her every day since she disappeared. We've all been praying."

"The day she disappeared, I said some unkind things to you," Rija said. "That was wrong, and I'm sorry. Please forgive me. I know it wasn't your fault. I want you to know that I do not hold the school responsible."

"Mrs. Malacovik, I understand completely. It was the stress of the moment. Anyone else could have done the same."

"Thank you for your kindness. I wonder if I can pick up some work for Lili so she can catch up. She's worried about that."

"Would it be better for her if, after school tomorrow, I come to you?"

Rija smiled and felt her eyes well. "Yes," she whispered. "That would be nice."

Ms. Gardner arrived at their door with a parcel and a hug for Rija. They stepped inside, and Rija called softly to her daughter. "Lili, someone is here to see you."

No response. Lili, whose greatest joy had always been to welcome anyone who came to visit, stayed where she was. They waited patiently, making small talk until Rija called again. "Lili, you have a visitor. Come see who is here."

Lili peeked around the corner. Rija could see the curiosity reflected in daughter's face. The child inched down the corridor, edging closer. She looked on as the teacher extracted several workbooks from her briefcase and placed them on the table. Curiosity overcame fear. Lili's trepidation evaporated, and she moved to the table to see what was there.

The tall blond teacher smiled. "I have something else to give to you. Close your eyes." Silently she unfurled a roll of brown paper, pulling the scrolled ends as far apart as her arms would allow.

Lili's eyes popped open, and she cocked her head from side to side gazing at her name written in large, uneven letters.

"Lili, everyone made this for you. There's a message. Can you read what it says?"

Lili nodded and, for the first time, smiled. She moved her finger over the letters, whispering each one.

Ms. Gardner said, "Let me read it to you. It says, *To Lili from Room 203. We miss you. Come back soon.*"

Below the greeting, her classmates had fashioned a world of houses on sunny hillsides, surrounded by cheerful flowers and birds in flight. Each piece of artwork was autographed in bold first grade letters. Lili continued tracing her finger over the letters of her name. But when the teacher smoothed back the child's hair, she flinched.

Ms. Gardner looked at Rija and took her aside as Lili continued to examine the gift from her classmates. "She's been through a lot," Ms. Gardner said. "And even though it was her father, she's obviously not herself yet. She should talk to someone; maybe you should too. It's been traumatic for all of you."

Tears welled in Rija's eyes. "I will try."

Ms. Gardner wrote the name of a therapist on the back of a card. "Don't worry. Until Lili is ready to come back to school, I'll bring her lessons and spend a few minutes with her while she does her work. I hate to see her fall behind."

Chapter 29

Leon soaked up the last of his borscht with a crust of pumpernickel before he turned his attention to the white fish salad. Watching Leon eat is not a pretty sight, Josef thought. He opened the newspaper to block the view.

"So how is little Lili?" Leon asked. "My Tasha asks for her."

"She's fine. Back with her mother. Paulina convinced me that would be best for her. I wasn't ready to be a full-time parent."

Leon gave him a knowing glance. "And so, when you went to take her home, she was gone?"

"Yes, it was surprising. But the maintenance man told me that my wife came to pick her up right after I left. He heard her say, "Mama's here to take you home.""

"Tasha will miss her."

"I appreciate all that Paulina did for Lili. But everything ended for the best."

Leon chewed silently. He washed down the remains of his meal with a glass of seltzer, wiped his lips, and belched softly.

Josef pointed out a headline from the newspaper. "Waiters Jailed for Drug Sales at Nightclub."

"Here, give me that." Leon stretched a meaty arm across the table. "Stupid Ukrainian asses, they are even dumber than I thought." Leon swatted the newsprint in contempt.

"You know them?" Josef asked.

Leon pushed his plate back and motioned for the waitress to take it away. "Yes, of course, I know them. Who you think got them the job at the Europa?"

Josef was all ears.

"First, they sell X in the club, make me look bad. And not only that, do they even come to me? No! They do business with a new guy in Jersey, Nick Zhurko, from Las Vegas. Ever hear of him?"

Josef struggled to keep his face blank. "Never met him, but a friend of mine did some work for him, called him a liar. Said you can't believe a word he says."

"Who knows?" Leon shrugged. "But maybe this could work for us."

"How?" Josef was eager to change the subject.

"Perhaps I will have my lawyers bail out our stupid waiter friends, find out what they know. Then maybe we go pay this Nick a visit, yes?"

Josef's head felt like it would burst. He struggled to keep his voice even. "It's an interesting idea."

"Perhaps I don't have to go myself. What do you think? Maybe, it's a job for you and my brother, Boris." Leon lifted his paw for a high five. "*Molodets*, very smart, no?"

Josef agreed. "Yes, very clever, boss."

Leon lowered his voice. "But that's not what I wanted to talk to you about. I have something more important to tell you. Come closer. Pay attention."

For a day in May it was cool and breezy. Still, Josef could feel himself sweat. Wedged between Zimmerman and Galter in the front seat of their pick-up was, perhaps, his least favorite spot. He prayed they didn't already know what he was going to say before he said it. Sometimes he wondered what the point was.

The three men watched Branoff pull his black sedan off to the side of the parking garage. "Let's go." Zimmerman nudged him out of the truck.

Branoff motioned Josef to join him in the front seat. Galter and Zimmerman got into the back. Was this the chance he'd been waiting for? The chance to find a way out? His stomach tightened, then relaxed a little. They all listened as he described Leon's new business venture. When he finished, Branoff got right to the point. "Josef, my friend, sounds like you are ready!"

The agent pulled a device from the pocket of his windbreaker and threw it into the back seat. "Galter, show him how it works."

The handler pulled up his jeans to display a hairy ankle and mimed a demonstration. "Just snap the Velcro together and you're good to go. Try it on."

Branoff exploded. "For Chrissake, I don't want it on his ankle, Galter. It needs to be on the upper body, so we can hear everything they're saying."

"Sorry, chief." Shamefaced, Galter took the transmitter back and showed Josef how to position it under his arm while Branoff watched.

Once they'd got it right, Branoff turned strategic. "So who's driving? And where?"

Josef sat up straight. "I'll be driving, but I don't know where. Yuri will only give me directions when I pick him up. I won't know which car Leon wants us to use or where we're going until I get there. Yuri has the instructions and the contact names. Jakov is the muscle. He only knows to shoot if anything goes wrong. That's how Leon works. Everything is separate."

"Our boy Leon likes to compartmentalize," Branoff said. "He's smart. But not smart enough."

"Most probably Yuri will get the money from Leon," Josef said. "I'm picking up the other payment today."

"What's the other payment?"

"The AKs."

If Branoff was surprised he didn't show it. Josef watched the agent scoop a candy from a bag on the seat next to him. He removed the silver foil, popped it into his mouth.

"There'll be two cars on the detail," Branoff told him. "We'll put you on a long tail, one car ahead and one behind."

"After this, I want out," Josef said, staring straight ahead. "It's getting too dangerous."

Galter snickered. "I thought you wanted to be the big-time gangster. Guess I was wrong."

"I never wanted to be a gangster."

"Yeah, right," Zimmerman said.

"I just tried to survive, like everybody else. To become an American businessman, that was my dream."

"The American dream, that's very heart-warming," Branoff said. "And now you want out?"

"Yes, I'm asking you for a way out of this."

Branoff shrugged. "We'll see how it goes. If we can get Leon with a big score, we'll talk. See how much you can find out before the meet and get back to me."

"I'll try, but like I said, Leon keeps the pieces separate. Only Yuri has the details. He trusts him."

Josef was behind the wheel of the Bronco heading north on I-95 with Yuri in the passenger seat and Jakov in the back. A deal was about to go down, a deal that Josef hadn't liked the sound of. But he couldn't think about that now. It was time to get chatty.

"So, Yuri, you must have worked on some big scores with Leon, eh?"

Yuri nodded.

"That Leon, he's a smart one," Josef said. "It's good to have a smart boss."

Yuri nodded again. "You know Leon, he doesn't like things messy. He thinks of himself as a businessman first."

"That's what I like about him," Josef said.

"I remember when his garage caught fire, and most of his vehicles and all of his taxis were destroyed," Yuri said. "He replaced a few of them with the limos, but then he moved into the fuel distribution business."

They were crossing the I-95 bridge into New Jersey. Josef tried to relax his muscles and breathe. He stared straight ahead at the lights of oncoming traffic while the sluggish brown current of the Delaware swirled below. Ahead, a billboard welcomed them to the State of New Jersey. "What kind of fuel?"

"Heating oil. He bought tankers of diesel fuel and declared them as heating oil. It looks the same, pretty much smells the same."

Josef checked the rearview. The only car behind him was a silver Audi two cars back. A woman was driving, and she was alone. His hands began to sweat.

"He sells the diesel to the Russian gas station owners he has in his pocket. He charges them the gasoline tax but he don't give it to Uncle Sam."

"Why not?"

"He don't pay the tax because the government thinks he's selling home heating oil. They don't tax it. See?"

"Sweet!"

"There's no federal tax, and it costs less per gallon. He shows less profit and no tax!"

"*Molodets*," Jakov laughed out loud in the back seat.

Josef felt newfound respect for Leon's intelligence. "He's smart, for sure. How did he come up with that one?'

"He heard it from a friend in Brighton Beach. The first year, he made enough to buy the Little Odessa for cash, but there's one problem."

"What's that?"

"You can't sell heating oil in July. So now, summer's coming, it's getting warm, and he's looking for other opportunities. So here we are."

They had barely crossed the river when the woman in the silver Audi pulled ahead of the Bronco and stayed there. She kept going as Yuri directed Josef to take the first exit. He pulled off the highway and entered Route 29, heading north. Yuri told him to get off and take the frontage road. They went under the bridge and past a sign that read, "**No Admittance**."

Josef pulled in and cut the Bronco's lights. The black Mercedes loomed ahead, its darkened windows reflecting lights off the bridge overhead. This is it. Josef prayed the agents were on their way.

He turned to Yuri. "I'm glad you're here. I *no hable Espanol.*"

"No worries, I speak many languages. That's why I am Leon's business advisor."

In the back, Jakov patted his sawed-off. "And I am Leon's security advisor."

Yuri seemed tense. "Sitting in a car under a bridge is not my style," he said. "I'm an accountant. This is not what I do."

It wasn't what Josef had planned to do either, but Yuri's uneasiness had made him a little less nervous. He put his game face on and gave Yuri's shoulder a playful punch. He peered at the giant sitting in the back seat. "We do what we must, eh, Jakov?"

Jakov grinned. "We were immigrants. Now we're entrepreneurs, making success in the U. S. A."

"Ten years ago, I was Leon's bookkeeper," Yuri said. "Part-time. I arrived on a student visa and never went back to St. Petersburg."

Yuri's phone buzzed. He fished it out and checked the number, put it to his ear. "*Hola, como esta?*"

Josef could hear rapid-fire Spanish on the other end.

"*Si, comprendo.*" Yuri disconnected. "They're ready."

The lights of the Mercedes flashed on and off twice.

"Let's go do this," Josef said.

Three men emerged from the Mercedes. The driver was dressed all in black, the other two wore white shirts over jeans, visible in the headlights. An Uzi swung at the side of the last man to step out of the car.

"Wait, Jacov. You get out last."

The big Russian grunted his agreement. He asked Josef, "Where's your gun?"

Josef tapped the small of his back, hiking the leather jacket from behind so that Jakov could see the Beretta stuck in the band of his jeans. He heard Jacov work the slide on the shotgun, and the sound shot fear into his heart. Josef searched the shadows under the bridge, eager for a sign that he wasn't alone, that Branoff, Galter, and Zimmerman were there.

Jakov, weapon down, walked between Josef and Yuri. In the light of the Mercedes high beams, Yuri stepped out, hand lifted in greeting. "*Señor Guillermo, soy Yuri.*"

"Encantado." The voice was clipped.

Yuri continued, *"Presenta mis amigos, Jose y Jaime."*

Guillermo bared his teeth in a grim smile. "Please spare me, I speak English."

"Excellent, A-plus," Yuri said. He extended his hand.

Guillermo ignored the gesture. "You have the money and the rest?"

"We have everything for you," Yuri said. "Once we test the product, we'll take delivery and everyone will be happy, no?"

Guillermo waved Yuri forward. Then he turned to one of his companions, a younger man with dark hair slicked back in a ponytail. He walked Yuri to the rear of the Mercedes and popped the trunk, standing close while Yuri counted the twenty bricks inside. When he was finished counting, he nodded to Guillermo.

Guillermo gave the go-ahead, and Yuri motioned for Josef to join him. Jakov stayed put as Guillermo's man opened the rear door of the Mercedes. Josef and Yuri got in the back, and the man shut the door.

Inside the car, Guillermo's other man pulled out a small blade. Efficiently, he slit plastic sheeting on one of the bricks and held out a bladeful of white powder for Yuri to try.

The accountant held up his hand. "With your permission." From a shirt pocket, Yuri produced a small plastic container. It held a test tube half filled with amber liquid and a tiny spoon. He removed the cork and scooped granules of the powder into the liquid. He reinserted the stopper and shook the test tube. The liquid inside changed color.

"A-plus, number one," Yuri said, and he stuck up a thumb in approval. "Josef, please bring these gentlemen their payment."

Josef and Jakov walked back to the Bronco. Josef cursed his nerves. He hoped Jakov didn't see his hands shaking. He unlocked the Bronco's trunk and handed the bag of cash to Jakov before he slid behind the wheel. He decided to back the Bronco toward the Mercedes to transfer the two crates of weapons.

Alone in the car, Josef waited, sweating and fumbling with the keys. Hoping for a sign that his handlers were nearby, he prayed aloud into the wire strapped to his chest. "Branoff, if you can hear me, please, make your move now."

Jakov lumbered back toward the Mercedes, money in one hand, gun in the other. Guillermo took the satchel, balancing it on the hood of the car. He fanned packets of hundreds, nodding his approval. Only then did Jakov give Josef the signal to pull the Bronco into position.

Sweat dripped down the inside of Josef's shirt, and he hoped it wouldn't short out the wires under his arm. He felt all eyes on him as he inched past the black car, ready to back the Bronco into place. The rear of the SUV faced the open trunk of the Mercedes with a yard in between.

Josef got out and opened the Bronco's hatch. He nodded to the man with the Uzi. Guillermo gave Josef the nod, and he used the crowbar, prying off the lids of the two crates of AKs. The Colombian's eyes lit up at the sight of the weapons. He ran his hand over the snub nose of the gun. "All is as it should be."

Jakov stood watching, gun pointed down, as Josef and Yuri wordlessly transferred the guns to the Mercedes and the drugs to the Bronco.

A rustle in the brush broke the silence. Jakov's eyes narrowed as he tracked the sound, and his head whipped back to Guillermo. Alert for betrayal, the Colombian snarled a command to the man with the Uzi. "*Matarlo*! Kill them!"

Jakov fired at the man who held the Uzi, then at Guillermo. He hit the leader in the hip, then in the torso. The Colombians blazed fire at Jakov, and a round from the Uzi tore through his shoulder. Russian curses poured from the big man's lips. His shotgun pulled two more rounds before a bullet from a Magnum toppled him face down into the weeds.

Josef ducked around the side of the Bronco, drawing the Beretta from his waistband. "Please, God," he prayed out loud. Had Branoff loaded the gun before he gave it to him? In his heart, Josef knew he was a mediocre shot at best. He'd seen some combat, but his war experience rarely involved face-to-face fighting, and the few bullets in the Shadow's meager cache of munitions meant target practice was an unknown luxury.

He took aim and squeezed the trigger, fired off a shot at Jacov's killer. The bullet missed its mark and shattered the windshield of the Mercedes.

Crouched behind the Bronco's bumper, Josef searched for Yuri, finally spotting him sprawled on the grass. His stomach turned at the sight of the dark blood spilling from a wound that had ended the young accountant's dreams of success. This time, Josef took careful aim and his second bullet wounded the man with the Uzi.

A bullet slammed into his hand, and he fell to the ground. His

186

hand was on fire, and blood was seeping through his sleeve.

A sound came from the bushes, and Josef ducked his head down. A deer jumped out and ran off. An acrid smell hung in the warm night air. Josef caught sight of the black FBI van and the silver Audi as they moved in from behind the bridge pilings.

The driver of the Mercedes, wounded twice, raised a hand in surrender. Guillermo lay face down, unmoving. The gunman with the ponytail made a run toward the river. Atop a chain link fence he froze, skewered by spotlights from two New Jersey State Police cars. The last thing Josef saw before he passed out was the Colombian kneeling on all fours while three uniformed state troopers pointed weapons at his head.

The black cell purred, rocking gently on the stand next to Josef's hospital bed. Branoff scanned the caller ID. "It's Leon, you know what to say."

Josef nodded as he took the phone with his good hand. "Leon, babolinka, I'm sorry." He waited as the curses on the other end of the line subsided. "I know. It's this fucking phone. I got no reception. We were under the bridge, and then my phone died."

The Russian fired out questions and curses. Josef rolled his eyes at Branoff. "Sure, Yuri's here, he's taking a leak, he'll call you back. Yeah, we got everything. We'll meet you at 6 a.m."

Still in her robe, Rija pulled her hair back, smoothing sleep-tangled curls behind her ears. She cupped her hand under the kitchen faucet and splashed water on her face before she hit the buzzer that would unlock the door.

Tony bounded up the stairs, two at a time. His lips brushed her cheek. "Did you see this?" He stuck a newspaper in front of her face. "Here, page one of the local news. I stopped for coffee, and it was sitting on the counter."

Rija struggled to understand. "Please, let me read it."

"Nobody called you? I can't believe you don't know." He pointed. "Three killed in drug bust. They don't mention Josef anywhere, but his two buddies were killed, Yuri and Jakov."

Rija gasped. "Yuri? I know Yuri. I can't believe it. He was so young, so smart."

Tony read aloud. "Drug Deal Goes Bad - Business Owner Held. According to this article, the FBI and the ATF were both involved."

The sun's rays shot red off the river before it disappeared in the west. To the east, a tugboat pushed oily waves ahead of the barge it towed. Three blasts of its horn carried across the water.

Josef lit a cigarette and waited for the mournful noise to fade. He wanted to make his point with no distractions. "I need protection."

Branoff raised his eyebrows but remained silent. He dug in his shirt pocket. He held out two wrapped chocolates. "You want a Kiss?"

Josef shook his head. He blew a stream of smoke through his nostrils. "We had a deal. I need protection."

"Not to worry, you'll have it." Branoff kicked gravel at his feet. "Once this is over, you'll be well taken care of."

Josef was unconvinced. "You know I can't testify against him. I'll be dead before the thing gets to trial."

"Trust me, we'll send you someplace nice, like Vegas or Seattle, maybe Florida."

"Florida sounds good. You'd get me a job? A real job?"

"Sure."

"What kind of job?"

"How should I know what kind of job? What can you do?"

"I have skills as a businessman."

"We'll make you president of a corporation." The agent laughed. "How's that?"

Josef ignored the sarcasm. "I need paperwork."

Branoff patted Josef's good shoulder. "Don't worry, we'll fix you up," he said. "Who knows, you might turn out to be a solid U.S. citizen after all."

From the street, a car backfired and Josef fell to the ground. Branoff pulled him to his feet. Turning solicitous, he brushed gravel dust from Josef's shirtfront. "Take it easy. Leon's in jail. His soldiers are dead."

"But don't forget Boris. Even worse, Leon and his brother are hooking up with Nick Zhurko, who moved into the Jersey territory."

"That name rings a bell. But what's that to you?"

"Nick's the reason I left Vegas."

"Yeah? I guess you're no help with him, then." Branoff laughed.

"I have another idea," Josef said.

"Let's hear it."

"I've been thinking. Maybe it's not too late to go back to Bosnia. To Sarajevo."

Branoff snorted. "Are you for real? Forget it. We can't protect you there."

Josef shook his head. "No need. I give myself a new name, a new identity. I blend in. No problem. I'll be safe. What do you say? You give me some of Leon's money as a reward?"

Chapter 30

No tears in the schoolyard this morning, thank God. Rija prayed while Lili lined up with her class. Two by two they marched into the school building. She decided it was safe to head home. Only one more week, then school would be over for the summer, and life would be a little easier. True, Lili's bedtimes were painful still. Either she or Elena needed to stay close until she fell asleep. Even then the poor kid might wake screaming with nightmares that would keep them all from sleeping. But thank goodness Lili was able to stay in school now without crying, and Rija was even more grateful to Ms. Gardner.

She could never repay the teacher's kindness. She had helped Lili get better, stopping by most days on her way home after school, spending time with her on assignments, encouraging her so that she could catch up with the class. Now that Lili was back in school, Ms. Gardner continued to watch over her, making sure the children were gentle with their newly returned classmate. Most important of all, the teacher made an appointment for Lili with her therapist friend. After only four sessions, the psychologist said she was making progress.

Their last appointment on Saturday had been a good one, and Rija felt a little more comfortable now that she knew what the treatment was like. Rija understood that Lili needed to go into the therapist's office alone. Instead of going in with her, she was able to watch though the one-way glass in the observation room. Although she hadn't been able to hear, she could see the doctor speaking softly and gently, using toys, games, and picture books to help her child move through the ordeal. Once Lili began to open up to her feelings they all agreed she looked the happiest she had been since "the rescue."

Rija would pay whatever she must for the treatment. She knew it was important, but she was delighted when the doctor told her they soon might be able to cut back to one appointment a week. Rija thanked her, and together she and Lili made their way home to the trolley stop. Once they found a seat, Lili craned her neck, engrossed in the cityscape as the trolley slowly churned it way through rush hour traffic.

Rija thoughts drifted. She wished there was a therapist she could talk to. She was confused. Her brain, her heart, and her emotions were at war with each other. A new life loomed in front of her, life as a single, more independent person. She wanted to be that person, to be strong and open to opportunities that might come her way. She knew Tony wanted their connection to move beyond friendship to something more intimate. He was attractive and fun, but he moved too fast, made her heart pound. True, he was more than a friend, and without his help, would she have found Lili and gotten her back the way she had? She couldn't be sure.

She tried to return their relationship to where it was before, to avoid being alone with him. Was that wrong? While she knew his feelings were genuine and sincere, she wasn't ready to return the emotion, and she felt sorry if she'd given him the wrong impression. Who could blame him? She certainly hadn't done anything to restrain his whole-hearted assistance. She'd leaned on him more than she should have, and now it was time to stop. Still, part of her regretted what happened that night. She felt torn. She needed time.

Rija balanced groceries on one knee, maneuvering her front door key toward the lock. But the sound of a familiar voice calling out to her, sent the bag flying, oranges cascading down the stairs. Fury sent heat radiating from her core through the top of her head. She turned toward the sound. "How dare you?"

Ignoring her anger, Josef retrieved spilled food from the sidewalk. Smiling, he offered up the bag of fruit like a gift.

Rija hit his hand away. Words tore from her throat in a slow progression of rage. "How could you face me?"

Josef lifted his eyes in supplication, "Wait, wait. Listen."

"No, you listen. Do you not know what you did? Leaving your daughter alone for hours and hours. A child is not a pet to be kept caged until one remembers to feed it. How dare you show your face?"

"Don't worry, I came to say goodbye."

Slowly, Rija walked down the front steps to face him. "Why would I want to say good-bye to you? I hoped you were in jail. I wished you dead."

"Oh, so you know?"

"Of course I know. I felt sad about Yuri, but I was almost sorry you weren't killed with your friends."

Josef held up his bandaged arm, cradled the sling. "As you see, except for a small scratch, I am still in one piece."

He smiled again.

"I heard about Leon." Rija said. "I saw his name in the newspaper. Why didn't they arrest you as well?"

"Me, get arrested? No worries. I was working with the FBI."

Rija snorted derisively. "Do you expect me to be impressed?"

"Impressed? That doesn't matter now. But I came to tell you that I'm going home."

Rija's voice rang hollow. "Home? Where is home?"

"I'm going back to Bosnia, to Sarajevo."

"It was your dream to come here, your dream of America. You dragged us here with you and now you want to go back? Why? The city is destroyed, the country's still divided."

"I've heard that much of the city is still damaged, it's true. But now, there's a lot of money coming in. They're rebuilding, and the EU and the United Nations are sending millions, and it's just the beginning. It's perfect for someone with the spirit of an entrepreneur, someone like me. I want to go back and start a business."

Rija's anger buzzed until she felt the top of her head would explode. This was the final insult. It was his dream that brought them here, a dream that failed. And now, again, he would disappear. "You're lying. I know you."

Josef let the comment pass.

"And why do you come to tell me. Did you think I would care? I never want to see you again."

"I came to ask a favor. I want to see Lili before I go."

"I will kill you first! How dare you ask for such a thing after what you did?" She marched toward him with a fierce expression as if she were about to make good on her promise.

Josef turned away and put up his good arm as a shield. "Listen to me. I know what I did was terrible."

"No you don't. You don't care about anyone, not even your own child."

"I was crazy. I lost my head."

She lunged again.

This time, Josef caught her wrist with his one good hand, and as she struggled, he managed to encircle her and hold her against an iron railing. "Wait, wait. Just listen to me."

Rija tried to twist away but Josef held her. "I will make you a promise. If you let me see Lili, I'll give you all the money in my storage locker. I'll give you the key too. You can have everything in it."

"Why do you think there's anything in it that I would want?"

"There must be something. I know you've been there anyway."

"How do you know?"

Josef laughed. "An FBI agent showed me the pictures you and your boyfriend took."

She wanted to kill him. "*Jebi se*, fuck you!"

"Please, I know you must hate me."

"Hate is too simple a word."

"Forgive me. I still love you and Lili, and I just want to take a picture of her. To remember her happy."

"You have no shame. Now you want to see her. You could have spent plenty of time with her. Instead, you left her locked in your dark apartment."

"That's not true. Not really. I didn't want to keep her locked up. I did my best to take care of her, but I just couldn't do it."

Josef stepped away from his wife as a police car sped past, siren blaring. He relaxed again as the white car turned a corner. "I took her to Paulina's. She stayed with them and played with their Tasha. They had a good time together. Didn't she tell you?"

"Yes, that's wonderful. You let her out only to take her to the home of your gangster boss."

"Please, I was stupid, I was wrong. But I just want to see her."

"Yes, of course. It's always what you want. Do you know that after we rescued her, Lili was sick in bed for two weeks. She sees a therapist. She's only now feeling herself again. If she saw you, it would be awful for her."

"She doesn't have to see me, I just want to see her."

"And just how should that happen?"

"You walk her to school. I wait in my car across the street. She won't even see me."

By the time Josef called, Rija had made up her mind. "No, I don't want you to see her. You don't deserve it."

"But in five days, I'll fly from Newark, New Jersey, to Vienna, then to Sarajevo. Please, I just want to see Lili once more. Please. I have almost twenty-three thousand dollars. Like I said, it's yours if you want it."

On Rija's end there was silence for several seconds. Then she took a deep breath. "You'll give me the money and the key to the storage locker first."

"Yes, I'll go get the money tomorrow and meet you afterwards in front of the church."

"And one more thing. When we meet, I'll bring divorce papers for you to sign. After you sign, after all of the business is taken care of, then you can see Lili."

"Okay."

"Instead of the schoolyard we'll go to the playground. You'll be able to see her easily from the street, but I don't want her to know you're there. Afterwards you will never see us or get in contact with us again. Do you agree?"

"Yes, I agree."

"And you promise to stay in your car, and not try to speak to her or touch her, correct?"

"I promise."

Once her anger subsided, Rija felt shame that she had let the lure of Josef's money change her mind. But she was so tired of being poor, having nothing. She wouldn't take all of the money. Just enough to give themselves a little comfort, to pay off her school loan, perhaps something to put toward a house. Something to give them a future.

Sleep was elusive that night. Tossing from side to side, Rija heard the word divorce resonate in her mind. She wanted it to be finished, and though she didn't yet have Josef's signature on a legal divorce agreement, she wanted to feel that it was over in her heart. Wide-eyed and restless, she remembered, years ago, hearing her mother and her friend Esmuda whispering about a neighbor who wanted to divorce her husband.

Fearing what neighbors in their Catholic neighborhood would say, and wanting to avoid the disgrace of hiring a lawyer, the determined woman consulted a neighborhood fortuneteller. It was the first time Rija heard of a country divorce. In hushed tones, Esmuda described a folk ritual that ended with the words, *Ja razvod te*, I divorce you, to be repeated three times.

It was well past midnight by the time Rija gave up on sleep. She got out of bed, tiptoeing past the room where Lili and Elena slept soundly. Through the kitchen window, the full moon cast light onto the floor. Rija flicked on the light over the sink, rummaging in the kitchen cupboard until she found what she was looking for. With a glass saucer in one hand and a candle stub in the other, she returned to her bedroom and closed the door.

Rija tore off a fresh sheet of writing paper from her tablet. Across its smooth white surface she inscribed Josef's name and his birth date. Then she drew a heavy line through what she had written and folded the paper three times. Next, she placed the saucer on the dresser, struck a match and lit the candle stub. When the flame burned bright, she held the paper aloft, watched the corner ignite. She whispered Josef's name. "You cannot hurt me anymore. I want you gone from my life." Three times she said, "I divorce you." Gray ash floated down and the paper was consumed.

Chapter 31

Rollie Miller's ass was dragging by the time he finished his shift. He'd spent the day out in the hot sun, chasing down leads on a murder suspect, leads that went nowhere. Right now the only thing he wanted from life was a chance to grab a six-pack, a shower, and a chair in front of the television for the Phillies game.

He hoped this favor for his sister and her friend wouldn't take more time than it had to. He remembered Carlene asking him to run a rap sheet on this guy, Josef, a while back. They'd met at the wedding, but he didn't remember much except that the guy seemed phony, maybe a little too charming for his own good. But that was before he heard of the drug deal with the Russians. Now that he'd seen the article in the paper, heard talk about the FBI, he'd do what he could.

He was doing it on the side, what he called extracurricular activity. Hell, he worked Homicide now. This interview wasn't really an official department interrogation. But he'd called ahead anyway to make the appointment, telling the federal marshal, "I need to talk to Leon Nemirov about a robbery. Can you make him available?"

He found a parking space half a block from the courthouse. At the entrance, he flipped his badge at the guard who waved him through. At a second checkpoint, Rollie flipped his badge again and signed in, glad they hadn't made him check his gun.

The guard found his name on the clipboard. "They're waiting in Room 197."

His footsteps echoed down the corridor to where a third guard waited to unlock the door. Inside, two gray-haired white guys whispered together at a government-issue table. Their conference ended abruptly at the sight of the tall dark-skinned detective. The shorter one stood. "I'm David Abrams, Mr. Nemirov's lawyer. And you are?"

"Detective Rollie Miller." He flipped his badge for the third time in ten minutes. "I'm here to interview your client about the sale of stolen jewelry."

Rollie watched Leon and the lawyer exchange glances. Then he turned to Leon. "The Diamond Factory on 7104 Torresdale Avenue, do you know it?"

Leon sat up straighter in his chair and looked Rollie in the eye. "No, I don't."

"It was robbed on December 18th of last year. Some of the stolen merchandise turned up in your office."

Leon's demeanor was cool. "I know of no such robbery. I often accept precious metals in payment for other transactions. Perhaps there was a mistake."

"There was no mistake, Mr. Nemirov. The owner was able to identify the pieces from photographs."

Leon growled, "I don't know what you are talking about. I am a respectable businessman. I am a member of the Northeast Philadelphia Chamber of Commerce. What do I know of this jewelry?"

"I wonder if someone planted it in your office, someone who wanted to put you away. What do you think?"

Leon snorted. "You are trying to trick me."

"Maybe somebody else tricked you. Maybe somebody on the inside."

Leon was stonily silent.

Unsure of the facts, Rollie played a hunch. "I heard somebody might have been wearing a wire."

Leon jumped to his feet. "You are lying!"

The lawyer grabbed his client's arm. He put a finger to his lips and whispered in Leon's ear. "My client has nothing further to say. This interview is over."

Rollie ignored him. With a smile, he walked to the door and knocked for the guard to let him out.

"The big Russian got all riled up. That's what my brother told me. But he didn't mention Josef's name, just left him with something to think about."

Elena put plates and cutlery on the kitchen table. "Carlene, you like something? Tea or beer?"

"No thanks," Carlene said. "I'll wait for my brother. He's on his way."

At the downstairs buzzer, Rija jumped to her feet. Seconds later she ushered Rollie into the apartment.

"Hey, bro." Carlene swiveled around and winked before she gave the detective a hug.

Rija pulled out a chair. "Come in, sit. What can we give you? Some food? Are you hungry?"

Carlene laughed. "Rollie's always hungry."

Looking surprised by all the attention, Rollie sat. "I'll never say no to a good meal."

Elena produced a beer from the refrigerator and placed it in front of him. She followed up with sausages and plenty of bread, looking on as the detective made short work of the food.

Rollie wiped his lips with a napkin. "Thank you, ma'am, that was delicious."

Elena glowed. "Thank you."

Carlene asked, "So tell us. What happened? How did it go?"

Rija, Carlene, and Rollie went into the tiny living room.

Rollie lowered his voice. "Leon knows that he's been double-crossed. He just doesn't know by who. He didn't like the news, but he got the message." He described the high points of their interview.

Afterwards, Rija said, "I want to give you something for doing that for me."

Rollie's face clouded. "No way, don't insult me, girl."

"I'm sorry."

"I didn't do it for money, and I didn't really mention any names. I just gave Leon something to think about.

"I am so sorry," Rija said. "It's not my wish to insult you. Please forgive. Carlene, I am so sorry. Please explain to your brother."

Rollie stood. "I gotta go." At the door, he called out to Elena, "Thank you again."

Following her brother out, Carlene looked back over her shoulder to where Rija stood. "Don't mind him. He gets a little touchy when it's hot." She blew a kiss. "You give me something for him later. He'll cool down."

Chapter 32

Josef exited the tollbooth at Exit 14. He was glad the rain had stopped, and it looked like the clouds were breaking. He thought back to the rainy day, years earlier, when Milos met them all at the airport and brought them to Brooklyn. His heart had been full of excitement, his brain teeming with plans for a new life. America was the land of his dreams. And yes, he had learned its lessons well, but this America, the real America, had been a difficult teacher.

The flight would take off in less than three hours. Anxiety mingled with expectation rose up in his chest. His mind soared with thoughts of escape. What would he find in Sarajevo? Where would he go to make a new start?

The war was over. He'd heard that the people of Sarajevo refused even to talk about the past. For them, the future was all that mattered. With his new skills and new ideas he would be part of that future. Josef made a promise to himself. He would not only survive but also prosper.

Traffic streamed around the curve to Newark Airport International Terminal. He peeled off for long-term parking, pressed the yellow button for a ticket. The lot in long-term parking was almost full. As he pulled onto the top level, the sun broke through the clouds.

Though he would leave the car behind, he found himself a corner space out of habit. Ignition off, he pulled the Lufthansa envelope from his pocket and placed it on the dashboard. He sat for a minute, absorbing what he could of the New Jersey landscape and the New York skyline beyond. At the edges of the marsh, discarded machinery crumbled into rust. Nearby, port cranes loomed like metal elephants, their tusks raised to the sky.

Would he ever return to America? He touched the crisp edges of his new passport like a talisman. Nothing was holding him back. Branoff even surprised him with an offer to call the U.S. Embassy and make contacts for him once he arrived in Bosnia, hinting that his special skills might be needed. With no ties and no one else to worry about, he was truly free to control his own destiny.

He checked the name on the airline ticket for the third time before opening the passport to look at his photo. Josef ran his finger over the name. With a glance at the rearview mirror he smiled at himself. A new name would take some getting used to. Practicing the feel of it in his mouth, he repeated, "Andrei Popovic, Andrei Popovic."

Josef turned off the air conditioning and rolled down the window. The rain had washed the sky clean. Breathing deeply now, he wanted to inhale his last breaths of American air. He put on his new Italian sunglasses. Feeling upbeat, he cocked his head and smiled into the side mirror. "Hello, my name is Andrei Popovic."

A shadow at the side of the car blocked the sun. Josef pulled off the glasses. He squinted up into the sun where the face of Nick loomed over him, his gun six inches from Josef's head.

Smiling slightly, the tall Russian reached in. He snatched the passport from Josef's hand and flipped it open. "Andrei Popovic, eh? Surprised to see me?'"

Josef shrugged.

"I had the pleasure of meeting your friend Boris. Charming fellow, we have much in common. He told me where I could find you."

"We do what we can do."

Nick smiled. "Yes, we do what we can do."

Nick threw the passport to the asphalt. Josef saw his dreams of escape face down in a puddle. "Sweet dreams, Andrei."

The shot exploded in Josef's ear.

Chapter 33

Rija awoke to a pillow wet with tears. What was the dream? She squeezed her eyes shut, struggling to hold on to a wisp before it slipped away. The image of her brother, Doni, brought the dream's substance back to her.

Her dreams of Doni were often dreams of their childhood. In those dreams, they laughed, chasing each other through the streets of Sarajevo or the hills beyond. It might be Doni standing above her, always teasing her with the toy she wanted just out of reach. Those were dreams of the past, but this was different.

Pieces of the dream returned, Doni was calling out to her. She answered him, following the sound of his voice as she ran though a dense wood. At the edge of a clearing, she found him dressed in the brown uniform of a soldier. She ran eagerly to where he stood only to have him point to a body lying face down. She turned and ran, crying, afraid to look back.

Later she got the call. The man's voice was soft and deep. He spoke slowly, identifying himself as a representative of the Newark, New Jersey coroner's office. He asked her name and when she gave it, he cleared his throat and said, "Ma'am, Agent Branoff gave me your number. I'm sorry to have to ask you to identify someone we believe to be your husband, Josef."

While she refused the offer of a train ticket to Newark, Rija agreed to give him her address and he promised to send photos by Federal Express. Following up next day, Rija confirmed that the pale, smooth, lifeless features in the photos were indeed those of her husband.

The man on the phone told her that she was not required to accept the body. If she chose not to, the responsibility need no longer be hers. But he sounded relieved when she told him she would make arrangements and call him with details on where Josef's body should be shipped.

Tony suggested sending an e-mail, but that felt wrong. It seemed important for the letter to travel the long miles to Bosnia, to the farm near Bijela, the village where Josef's sisters, Katja and Dina, had built new lives. Thinking of what she would write, Rija bought special stationery. She made a special trip to the post office to obtain the appropriate international stamp. Still, only after she sat with a cup of tea at the kitchen table did she realize it had been years since she'd written anything more than a word or two in her own language. She could easily have written in English. Katja and Dina would have no problem with that, but it would be wrong. And so she labored, slowly selecting her words, all the while remembering Katja and Dina as they were when she'd last seen them and picturing them as the beautiful young women they surely had become. She wondered how they would receive her letter. Would they mourn the final loss of the brother who had vanished so abruptly from their lives?

Satisfied finally with what she'd written, Rija folded the fragile pages into the envelope. She walked into her bedroom in search of the carved wooden box tucked in a dresser drawer. She withdrew the tiny battered photo of Anna, their mother, a keepsake Josef stored away and then forgot. She smoothed the corners of the photo in which a young Anna in a thin summer dress smiled into the camera, her short curly hair lifted by the breeze. The photo's reverse side, provided a context, the place, Split, and a date, July 19, 1961. She slipped the photo into the crease of the letter and sealed the envelope.

Elena insisted on a small service for Josef. "He is Lili's father. And we do it not just for Josef, we pray too for Doni and for Papa."

Rija agreed, hoping that her mother might find closure for the funerals denied them, the funerals for Papa and Doni. They decided on a service at the church, after which Josef's body would be cremated. Elena was reluctant to agree until Mr. Wysocki helped Rija convince Elena that it was the best thing for them to do, the only thing for them to do. They agreed that sending Josef's ashes to his family in Bosnia would grant his final wish, to return home. Once the plan was settled, Wysocki called friends at O'Leary's Funeral Home to make the arrangements.

Rija knew she would have to tell Lili what happened to her father when she was a little stronger. She would give her the few possessions he'd left behind, an old shirt, a handkerchief, the ring he'd taken from his finger when he signed the divorce papers. One day when she was older, Rija would give Lili the photo of her father holding her in his arms, a photo taken on the boardwalk in Coney Island just days after they arrived in Brooklyn. But today was not that day. Uncertain about how her daughter would react, Rija decided to say nothing. Only after Lili skipped upstairs to play with Timmy, did Rija and Elena dress for the funeral.

Not counting the two men from O'Leary's, it was just the four of them in St. Casmir's sanctuary. Despite the humid July heat bearing down on the streets of Philadelphia, the church interior was cool. From the front pew, Rija took in the closed pine casket in front of the altar. She stared, hypnotized, as the priest swung the censer back and forth like a pendulum, inhaling the whiff of incense hanging in the air.

It felt unreal, all of it. Josef's last moments in her life felt disconnected, anti-climactic, an afterthought to all that had gone before. Her head began to fill with images of a young Josef as she first knew him, brash, mischievous, and complicated. Always three steps ahead of everyone, even himself.

Rija twisted in her seat as his cousin Milos and his wife, Valentina, arrived and slid into the row behind them. She smiled her thanks and signaled the priest for the service to begin. After a beginning prayer and a hymn, the priest warmed to a discussion of the trinity and everlasting life. Rija was thankful that Josef and his story seemed to be a complete unknown to the priest. He didn't ask her the cause of death, and she didn't volunteer. Rija heard a rustling in the rear. Grateful for any distraction, she turned, surprised to see a round-faced man wearing glasses and a rumpled beige suit. The stranger met her gaze, pausing briefly in his removal of silver foil from what looked to be a piece of chocolate.

Carlene whispered to her. "Who is that?"

Rija shrugged and shook her head. When the two women turned for a second look, he was gone.

Rija emptied laundry from the bathroom hamper. The telephone's ring was insistent, but why, she wondered, did she have to do everything? "Mama, can you get that?" she called out.

Elena, still reluctant to initiate a conversation in English, was more eager to answer the phone now that some of the calls were for her. Hundreds of hours of TV viewing during her convalescence had been her mother's classroom, and Rija, grateful for the progress she'd made, could hear her mother answering in English. "Hallo, yes. Yes, this is Elena. I am Elena Petric."

From the doorway, Rija watched Elena's expression change as she listened intently to the voice on the other end of the line. "Please, wait. Please, can you say again? To my daughter?"

Elena passed the phone across to Rija, who listened as a

confident voice asked her name before introducing himself. "This is Alan Greenfield from Lynch McKenna and Schwartz. We have an offer for your mother."

Circumstances, the lawyer explained, were working in their favor. The hospital was in the midst of negotiations for a merger with a large university health system. Northeastern's administrators, he said, were anxious to clean the slate. To avoid a trial, the hospital was ready to make a settlement on their case. The original plaintiff, Mrs. Flanagan, was more than ready to accept what he described as the insurance company's offer. The number he described for Elena was $140,000. "We think it's a good-faith offer. I advise your mother to take it."

Rija tried to do a quick calculation in her head. "May we think it over?"

"We have a forty-eight-hour window."

"My mother will consider the offer. We'll talk it over and call you soon," Rija said.

Rija spent the next thirty minutes explaining to her mother what the lawyer had said. They both wondered how much the Flanagans would receive. Of course, it would be a much larger settlement for the death of her husband. Elena paced back and forth. "What should I do?"

Elena insisted they call Mr. Wysocki. "Maybe he knows about these thing." Happy to be asked, the storeowner thought Elena's pain and suffering was worth more than they offered. "You might be able to hold them up for a little more, given they want to get this thing out of the way. But is it worth it? If it isn't settled now, it could drag on for who knows how long."

Elena called Greenfield back an hour later and said yes, she would accept. The lawyers would take $56,000, and Elena would get $84,000.

Even before the check arrived, mother and daughter began a new weekly ritual. Most of Sunday morning was now spent poring over the newspaper's real estate section. Rija enjoyed pointing to an ad before reading it aloud. "Three bedroom, one and a half bath brick twin on a quiet street. Close to schools and transportation. One hundred ten thousand."

Elena shook her head. "Too much money."

Rija held up a photo of a rancher surrounded by trees at the end of a cul-de-sac. "How about New Jersey, Mama? This one is close, right over the bridge."

"What I do in New Jersey? I don't know nobody there."

"But, Mama, look at this. No stairs, everything on one floor, and Lili would have her own yard to play in. The therapist says the schools are good in New Jersey."

Elena frowned. "But where is the store? Where is the shopping street? We don't have no car."

"What if I get a car? Learn to drive it? You could too."

Unwilling to entertain the thought, Elena shook her head. "Cars cost money."

Car or no car, Rija knew suburban life was not for them. She knew they could buy a house but not the house she read about. Not the single-family house with a yard; the house all on one floor; a house that would be easy for Elena to navigate. That house would be in the suburbs, away from what they had grown accustomed to here. She knew her mother didn't want to go far from the hardware store on Kensington Avenue. And she wasn't sure that was what she wanted either.

September would soon arrive, and no matter where they landed, they would be moving. It would be best, the therapist said, for Lili to make a good start for the new school year. Rija was anxious to have Lili settled before school started. She agreed with the therapist, who told them it was important to avoid further disruption in her life.

Mr. Gracek assumed the role of the family's real estate advisor. "I'm always happy to share what I know about the real estate market," he had told Rija

Though he was losing his second-floor tenants, he was happy to drive mother, daughter, and sometimes his friend Mr. Wysocki around Port Richmond and Kensington. Driving up and down Port Richmond's streets, Rija noticed something new. "Why are we seeing so many "For Sale" signs on the old buildings?" she asked Gracek.

"If you notice, it's mostly the old factories and warehouses. Many of them have stood empty for as long as I can remember."

"Why are they up for sale now?"

"We've been rediscovered," Ted Wysocki chimed in. "The other day a real estate agent was snooping around the deli next door."

"Jimmy's Coca Cola?" Rija asked. "I worked there washing dishes. It was my first American job."

"Yeah, Jimmy's. He asked Jimmy if he wanted to sell. It seems that the government is offering special loans for redevelopment."

Despite Gracek's offer to act as their guide, Elena was slow to find the house of her dreams. They spent hours looking at houses, most of them two stories, with small rooms and a cement yard in the rear. After the third trip in four days, she was perplexed. "I don't see nothing I like."

Before Gracek pulled the car into a parking space, he asked, "What are you looking for, Elena?"

"I want light. My Lili, I want her to live in a house that is sunny."

Ted Wysocki, along for the ride, looked in her eyes. "I feel sunny when I'm around you."

Elena blushed with pleasure as she got out of the car. Ted held the door open.

"Wait, before you go in. I want to ask you something."

Elena blushed. "Go ask me."

"Do you want to go out to dinner Saturday night?"

Like a schoolgirl, Elena, blushing wildly, caught Rija around the waist as she washed dishes in their kitchen.

"Guess what? Ted invites me to dinner."

"Mama, you have a date!"

"No, not a date. Dinner."

"We'll go shopping! You must have a new dress, and then you should get your hair done."

Lili danced around the table, chanting in a singsong, "Baba has a date, Baba has a date."

"*Molim*, hush, hush."

Elena thought it over. "Yes, get my hair done."

Rija showed her mother a card. "Here's where I go to get my nails done."

She read out the address for Bella's Beauty Salon. "Let me call and make you an appointment."

Rija walked her mother to the beauty parlor, and when she returned an hour later, she was pleased to see Elena's hair was shampooed, cut, and curled in a style that curved softly below her ears. "Mama, you look ten years younger!"

Elena turned from side to side smiling at herself in the mirror. Out on the street, Rija caught her mother checking her new look in the shop's plate-glass window. "Mama, I'm so happy for you. Now I feel we are ready to make a new life for ourselves."

She tucked her arm into her mother's, and they marched down the street in step together. Their festive mood was matched by a cluster of balloons floating above a sign at the other end of Belgrade Street. The bright colors attracted their attention.

Rija suggested. "Let's go see what it is."

A sidewalk sign proclaimed, "Open House Today" and almost without having to ask, the real estate agent ushered them into a two-story three-bedroom brick house. The windows facing south filled the living room with sunlight. The dining room was small and a little dark, but the kitchen, with a fresh-looking coat of paint, featured sparkling appliances. Even the cabinets looked new. Behind the kitchen, a small den faced into a rear courtyard where flowers bloomed in pots near a rosebush in the small corner plot. Like the rest of the house, the courtyard was spotless.

"I love this house," Elena said.

Rija was surprised.

"I want it."

"But Mama, don't forget your leg. The stairs."

Undeterred, Elena told her daughter, "I can sleep first floor."

The agent hovering nearby moved in closer.

Elena asked, "What is price?"

"Sixty-nine, nine ninety."

Elena pulled a small pad from her handbag. "Write this for me?" She watched as the agent wrote out the string of numbers. With the scrap of paper in her hand, Elena walked through the house for a second time. "Good, I will take it. How do I pay?"

There was no arguing with her. Elena used the money from her settlement to buy the two-story row house with one bath and a tiny courtyard on Belgrade Street, two blocks from the school and the church. If she wanted, she could walk to mass every day without crossing dangerous streets. And now that Lili was going into second grade, she would even feel at ease, she said, if her grandchild needed to find her way home from school on her own.

Although Rija still thought of herself as Carlene's employee, she hadn't cleaned an office for weeks. She appreciated the offer when Carlene suggested that she and Rija set up an independent cleaning service and solicit bids for work. Even when she declined, Carlene still didn't give up. She offered to take Rija for an appointment with her small-business advisor.

"But the money's gone," Rija explained the afternoon Carlene stopped by to make her latest pitch. "My mother spent it on a house. Paid cash."

Rija decided not to mention the account she'd set up with Josef's money. She would keep that to herself.

"Oh," Carlene said, looking disappointed.

"I do have the key to Josef's locker. He told me I could have whatever was there. But I just didn't want to go."

"How about this? I could ask Rollie if there's a reward for information."

"If you want. But ..."

Despite a September date on the calendar, the Philadelphia streets held their heat, and the river breeze wafting through the window did little to cool the second-floor apartment on Mercer Street where Rija and Elena moved around each other packing and filling boxes. Lili bobbed across the room, tripping over family possessions.

With a sigh, Rija moved in front of the fan, taking a moment to brush wisps of hair off her forehead. "Lili, why don't you go upstairs and see if Timmy wants to play?"

"I don't want to play. I want to help."

"You can help by staying out of the way."

Lili's compromise was to sit in the middle of the floor, packing her Barbie clothes, as Rija worked around her. Her fears about the move and its effect on her seven-year-old had faded. Far from upset, Lili seemed excited. Not only would she have her own room, complete with brand-new bunk beds, but their house on Belgrade Street put her right around the corner from her school chum, Karen. Rija could imagine the two girls huddled together on their front steps whispering plans for their year in second grade.

After Rija persuaded Elena to recycle the used furniture accumulated from the Salvation Army and Goodwill, her mother directed Ted toward the kitchen table and chairs that were ready to go. Ted wrestled the table down the stairs, closely followed by Rija, who carried the chairs to the curb.

Out on the street, Mr. Gracek materialized. "I doubt this will last until trash pick-up tomorrow." He pawed through the leavings. "Someone will put it to good use."

"God bless them, they're welcome to it," Rija said with a laugh.

"Out with the old. I can see that this is a big change for your family," Gracek said.

"A sofa and chairs are already waiting for us in the new house, delivered yesterday. For the first time in my life, I bought brand new furniture. It never belonged to anyone else before."

"Could you ever imagine the way things worked out?"

Rija thought back to the previous September, a dark time when she was three months behind on the rent and afraid to answer the phone for fear it might be a bill collector. "So much happened. It went by in a flash."

Gracek waved his hand in a grand gesture as he warmed to his favorite subject. "Things are changing in the neighborhood, too. Have you noticed all the sale signs?"

Rija followed his gaze. "Yes, more signs every day."

Together, landlord and tenant craned their necks surveying developments on their block. Several recent "For Sale" signs near the corner were already covered over with the word "Sold".

"Tell your mother she bought at the right time. It looks like Port Richmond has been discovered, and the prices are starting to creep up. Some of the old-timers don't like it, what with the new people poking around, but what can you do?" Gracek shrugged. "That's progress."

Rija murmured agreement. It was hard to miss the groups of men arriving in shiny cars with out-of-state plates. Lately, they were almost a daily occurrence, wandering the streets in suits, scouting properties to buy.

"Damn!"

They turned just in time to see Ted slipping off the bottom step. Rija put out her hand to steady him and grabbed the old lamp, snatching it out of his hands just before it hit the pavement.

"That's it." Ted picked himself up and wiped his forehead with a blue bandana. I'm taking a break."

Gracek pulled a bottle of water from his backpack and handed it over. "What about you, Ted? Do you plan to sell like the rest of them?"

"This old-timer plans to stay put, but I can understand the ones who want to take the money and run. My assistant, Rick, just sold his house and bought a place in the suburbs. He said he did it for the schools."

Gracek cut in. "Why should the developers get all the good deals? If you hear of anyone else who wants to sell, let me know."

Ted broke into a sly grin. "How about this? If I help you find something, I get a finder's fee."

"Fair enough. I have the same deal with another friend of mine. He's the one that let me know about the old garment factory two blocks over on Westmoreland Street. You remember, I told you about that one?"

Ted nodded.

"After that deal closed, I gave him a nice piece of change," Gracek said. "The place needs a lot of work, but the structure is sound. I'm working on the first floor now, getting my office ready. The upper floors will be lofts and artist studios. Just the other day, the contractor and I were checking the wiring when a young architect wandered in asking about renting space."

"I'll keep an eye out," Ted said.

Rija listened closely. Gracek had a nose for opportunity, and she knew he'd been digging around the warehouses and factories that dotted the neighborhood. She wasn't shocked to find he'd actually bought one. Half-jokingly, she asked, "Are you looking for any investors?"

Gracek smiled his knowing smile. "What did you have in mind?"

"I have my paralegal certificate now, and I told you about my course in real estate law. I would be able to help you. Maybe answer the phones, show people around."

"The space is under construction. It won't be ready for a while, but let me think about what I might need. In the meantime, I think I have a new tenant for your apartment. They want to come by on Friday and have a look."

"We'll be sure to have it clean for you. But, until then, please think about taking me on."

"So long as you realize I don't have much to pay you."

"That's okay, I work for nothing and you teach me the business."

"Good deal!" Gracek's face lit up. "You're learning already. That's what we call sweat equity."

Mr. Gracek asked Rija if there was anyone she wanted to invite to the grand opening of Gracek Enterprises. She thought about asking Tony and then decided against it. She knew he would be fun to have at the party, but it would send him the wrong signal. She knew his feelings for her were genuine, but she couldn't seem to sort out her own. At a loss about what happened between them, she tried to avoid being alone with him ever since that night. She wasn't sure what she wanted from the relationship, if that's what it was. Best to keep things as they were.

It was quite a night. The ceremony lasted longer than expected. Two members of City Council surprised everyone by showing up to make speeches, patting themselves on the back for the success of the newly incorporated Port Richmond Business District. When the ribbon was cut, the photographs taken, and champagne toasts drunk, Ted surprised them all by treating everyone to dinner at the Hoffbrau House. As they were finishing dessert, he clinked his glass with a spoon and cleared his throat. With every eye turned in his direction, the soft-spoken locksmith lifted Elena's hand to reveal the ring on her finger.

"This is a night to celebrate for a lot of reasons. And for me the best reason is that Elena and I are engaged."

Rija burst into tears of joy. She'd known for days about the ring, but this was the first time she'd seen it. After all the loss and dislocation, to see her mother with a smile as bright and sparkling as her new ring was a miracle.

Rija ignored the headache from the previous night's wine, still excited about her new surroundings. She inhaled deeply, enjoying the clean fragrance of the freshly sanded oak floor. Two shades of creamy beige paint set off an exposed brick wall, a reminder of the building's earlier incarnation as a factory. From where she sat she could read the sign in the hall that read Gracek Enterprises.

Looking up, she saw Tony grinning at her through glass doors. He elbowed his way in with a pot of daisies in one hand and what looked like an equipment case in the other. With a bow, he set the flowers in front of her. "Office-warming present for your desk."

Rija smiled her thanks. "They're lovely."

"How's the first day on the job going?"

"Quiet, so far."

"I don't know if this is right for you. Don't you think you might get bored sitting in an office after everything that's happened?"

"It's a job, and in a way it's more than that. When I asked Mr. Gracek to hire me, I told him I didn't care how much he paid me."

Tony laughed. "Yes, I'm sure you were talking his language."

"But what I really want is to listen and learn. If he pays me a percentage for any new business that I bring in, that's fair. As soon as I get my license as a notary, like I plan to, that brings in more money too."

Tony agreed. "Sounds good. I've been thinking that maybe I should rent some space and set up shop here as an investigator. You know, part-time."

Rija wrinkled her nose. "Oh, I get it. So I can answer your phone for nothing too?"

"More than that. You can be Gracek's assistant but my silent partner. What do you think?"

Ignoring the question, Rija stood, pushing back her chair. "Let me show you a space that would be perfect."

She led him past the newly installed elevator toward a door tucked away in the corner. "Gracek didn't know whether he could rent this space. It's a little dark."

She unlocked the door to a small, freshly painted rectangular space. Tony moved past her toward the room's only window.

"Take a peek. If you look right between those two buildings there you can see the river, but don't tell your boss. He might raise the rent."

Rija stood on tiptoe and peered out. "I know. How's this for a name, Riverview Investigations?"

The phone rang in the other room and Rija wiggled away from the window, running to answer it. "Gracek Enterprises."

After a brief conversation, she told Tony, "That was my bank. I'm setting up a business account. I used to think I wasn't good with money. But maybe that was just because I never had any."

Tony laughed. "Now that you've got a bank account, that'll change. The next thing you know, you'll be looking for an accountant. So, let's get serious for a minute. I want to show you something."

Tony opened the case he'd left next to the desk and assembled a video unit on the table. "Voila, this is the start of my new venture."

"What is it?"

"The latest thing, video surveillance for the home and perfect for this neighborhood. We can sell these for $500 or less. You handle the telephones and I install them. It's the perfect sideline. I put up $2,500, you put up $2,500. Bingo! What do you think? Are you in?"

His arms reached to grab Rija's waist but she ducked. From a safe distance, she faced him behind a chair. Tony's eyes darkened. Perching on the windowsill, he selected a daisy from the bunch and held Rija's gaze while he plucked a white petal. "She loves me."

The petal fell to the floor.

"She loves me not."

She looked away before meeting his eyes. "I admire you, and I'm so thankful for all the help that you gave me, but I need a break. Right now, I am not ready for that kind of relationship. We can either have a romance or a business, and for now, I think the business is best."

Reluctantly Tony agreed to the new terms of their partnership. He rented the small office from Gracek, and Rija worked both as Gracek's real estate assistant and with Tony whenever they had a chance to do an investigation. As the calls and requests for information started to come in on their new line, Rija knew the spaces in the building would soon be filled. For now, there were just two other businesses in the newly renovated building, one of the first on Westmoreland Avenue in the Port Richmond Empowerment Zone, but it wouldn't stay that way for long.

From her desk, Rija could read the sign on the overpass, "Welcome to Port Richmond - Port Richmond Works." Cars pulled off I-95. Going left, she could see the piers along the Delaware River. On the right, the Number Fifteen trolley turned to make its way back down Richmond Street toward the Philadelphia skyline.

Historical Note

When, in the 1990s the former Yugoslavia began to unravel along ethnic lines independent countries emerged. Along with Croatia, Slovenia, and Macedonia, Bosnia-Herzegovina declared itself a sovereign state. But when ethnic Serbs boycotted Bosnia's claim of nationhood, violence erupted and Serbian paramilitary groups and militias eager to divide Bosnian territory fed the conflict. Bosnia's capital city, Sarajevo was soon blockaded and under a siege. By 1992, Serbian forces above the city bombarded residents with heavy artillery by night while by day snipers made routine comings and goings impossible. Inside city limits, poorly equipped Bosnian government forces failed to defend a population cut off from food and other necessities.

By the time NATO finally intervened on behalf of the city, nearly 10,000 people were killed or missing including over 1,500 children. An additional 56,000 people were wounded and thousands more fled Sarajevo, never to return. Before the siege, inhabitants numbered 435,000. Currently Sarajevo's population figures range from 300,000 to 380,000.

Source: World Factbook